EARTH TALES

T K Wallace

ARCHWAY
PUBLISHING

Archway Publishing books may be ordered
through booksellers or by contacting:

Archway Publishing
1663 Liberty Drive
Bloomington, IN 47403
www.archwaypublishing.com
1 (888) 242-5904

Because of the dynamic nature of the Internet, any web addresses or
links contained in this book may have changed since publication and
may no longer be valid. The views expressed in this work are solely those
of the author and do not necessarily reflect the views of the publisher,
and the publisher hereby disclaims any responsibility for them.

Any people depicted in stock imagery provided by Getty Images are
models, and such images are being used for illustrative purposes only.
Certain stock imagery © Getty Images.

Interior Image Credit: Bottle Tree constructed by Barbara Hurst.
Used by permission. Black and White image by T K Wallace.

ISBN: 978-1-4808-8311-6 (sc)
ISBN: 978-1-4808-8312-3 (e)

Library of Congress Control Number: 2019914496

Print information available on the last page.

Archway Publishing rev. date: 10/10/2019

Author's Introduction

The outer cover image is one of a bottle tree. Many cultures have forms of protection against negative energy or spirits. The bottle tree is believed to capture and contain spirits. You may feel at ease, safe, and protected while reading the following adventures.

This second collection contains a variety of stories. Each and every one is a solid product of my life and imagination. The project title Earth Tales gathers them together through form and function.

Herein are five script ready projects. These pieces are preceded by a cast list having been written with a film or stage presentation in mind. Also included are several suggestions of music and song lyrics. These are suggestions which support the scene, the scene change, or the plot.

My publisher has offered me editing services. But frankly, I cannot afford to pay someone else to distort my intentions at a nickel a word. Please understand that I respect the work editors do, but don't always agree with a predetermined style.

Most of the short stories are pure fiction. Four of the stories are of an auto-biographical nature, and three are created from both. You can probably figure out which is which.

So be it.

T K Wallace
Thunderbolt

Contents

1

San Fran Dayze 1
A Coney Afternoon.. 113
Crocker's... 143

2

Christmas Music to My Ears 177
Let's Blow Some Shit Up.. 187
Free Lance Writer... 205
Fred the Cop.. 243

3

Magnolia's 269
I Was In a Coma Once.. 291
A Baseball Story.. 305
Just An Idea.. 319
Rao's.. 383

1

Earth Tales

San Fran Dayze

A Coney Afternoon

Crocker's

San Fran Dayze

written by

T K Wallace

Cast

Scot Center	Rigger who sidelines as an undercover 'fixer'.
Iris	Station wagon driver.
Sheila	Reporter, lover, daughter of Magnolia and Rubin
Magnolia Thunderpussy	Bakery Owner, Media Diva, Joey Fucko's sister
Paco & Leon	Thug 1 and Thug 2
Dr. Evelyn	GP in the clinic, sometimes lover, and accomplice.
Rasta Ratso	Rubin's Henchman, Sheila's enemy
Rubin Thunderpussy	Entrepreneur, Media Mogul, Partner in Crime
Vinnie Stamatakos	Scoty's painting foreman
Uncle Joe Fukowee	Criminal soon to be at large
Zimmy	Hood at the window and painting contractor
Chartboy Bubba	Uncle Joe's go-fer
Aunty Kimbo	Scoty's Aunt, Ex FBI, Free Lance Investigator
Ninja Warrior Frogs	As Named
Gordon Clark	Explosives Expert
Agent Rhonda	Kimbo's gal friend, FBI
Agent Barny	Rhonda's partner, FBI
Bennie	Princess Captain
Chuck	Grumman Pilot
Wanda Gerber	Swan Captain

Scene 1

The hitchiker faces oncoming traffic. A car slows as it rolls by and a woman looks out at him. He smiles and wiggles his thumb but she continues without stopping.

Hitchhiking is a lot of things. One is standing and waiting. Another is an interesting way to pass the time while traveling. It is never boring, but quite often routine. And, it is sometimes quite challenging. Hitchhiking helps remind us of certain survival skills, the ones that shouldn't go missing.

Even though it's a cloudy day, he squints at the sky and thinks of Simon and Garfunkel at a music festival up the coast. A song plays in his mind as he extends his palm as if to check for rain. He whistles two notes softly to himself as a truck thunders by without stopping. He looks down and smiles as he changes to thumbs up.

Cloudy, the sky is gray and white and cloudy,

Trucks are the worst. The experience is like being assaulted by a passing weather squall. As the truck approaches at 60-70 miles an hour, the atmosphere is shoved aside. Then, as it passes, a strong following wind flaps and slaps everything with the massive roar of 18 huge wheels. But it's not over yet.

All of the air is drawn away by the passing behemoth creates a vacuum. As the pressure begins to equalize, a back draft of wind rushes through coating you with all the highway debris it carries. After the truck has passed, you are covered with road dirt and need a bath. Unless it's raining, in which case you get covered with road spray and all that it contains, and you really need a bath.

And it's a hitchhike a hundred miles,
like some rag-a-muffin child

The sun peeks through for a few seconds and he looks at his shadow on the pavement. The shadow then vanishes as he thinks of the music festival and recalls some snap shots in his memory. The most distinct is a Peter Pan banner which reads,

Never Grow Up !

They echo and they swell, from Tolstoy to Tinker Bell

- - - - - - - - - - -

Sc 2

Another truck approaches, but this one slows and then pulls over for a pick up. The hitch hiker turns and runs with his backpack flopping. He reaches the truck, mounts the running board, and pulls himself up by the door handle. He looks inside and sees a crazed looking, teeth grinding, sweaty driver, who licks his lips and says,

"Hop aboard!"

The hitchiker hopes his apprehension is not too obvious as he asks,

"Uh, Are you going to LA?"

The truck driver shakes his head and spits out,

"You're going the wrong way dip shit."

Our hitcher smiles and waves the driver away nodding thanks. He watches the truck roll away and says, "Yeah, I knew that. "

He continues walking the road with his back to the traffic. Nevertheless, he holds his thumb out in expectation of a ride as he listens to the song in his head.

Hey sunshine, I haven't seen you in a long time
Why don't you show your face and bend my mind?

He turns to face the traffic and improvises a dance step which ends with his arm outstretched and his thumb wiggling. Amusing himself, he tries it two or three more times before the move actually works. A large station wagon slows to look, and then pulls over to offer a ride.

He looks inside and asks, "Going into town?"

A gentle woman smiles and says, "I'm going up north to wine country."

He smiles and replies, "That'll do, thanks. Drop me downtown?"

He gets in as light rain begins to fall. The driver says, "Just in time." As they re-enter traffic, he looks at his destination, San Francisco in the misty afternoon sun. The radio plays a classic rock song by Melanie.

Lay down lay down, let it all down.

He taps to the beat as the rain drops are pushed aside by the wipers.

"Where you comin' from," asks the driver as she scans him with a glance.

"Out east, just finished a project, and I'm headed into town."

"You almost home ?"

"Maybe, You?"

"Yeah, Santa Rosa, I'm Iris," she offers a hand while looking at the road.

He shakes her hand while looking at her,

"I'm Scoty, thanks for the ride Iris, and the rescue from the rain."

He hears a clinking sound in the back. There are a few cases of bottles.

"This wagon is huge. I've never seen one this big."

"Biggest I could find. A Road Master, they say it's the largest wagon made."

He looks at the steering wheel, "Buick, eh, figures. What's in the bottles?"

"Wine. I have a vineyard. We needed some different bottles, and I know this woman in Fresno. We have this new wine, we offer special tastings, and all that."

He makes small talk as he watches the rain and the road. "A vineyard eh? That must be interesting."

She snorts, "Yeah, if you like watching grapes grow. What was your project ?"

"I'm a rigger. I hang things."

"Goin' to work?"

"Comin' from,"

"So, you hang things . . ."

"This last one was in San Quentin prison."

"Oh. " An awkward silence as the radio plays,

So raise the candles high, oh raise them high again.

"Did you hang, uh? No people I hope,"

He looks serious and says, "Don't ask." Her eyes go wide and he breaks up.

"Just kidding. I hang things, not people. This gig was a few painting platforms"

"Oh, those things they paint from that go up and down outside the buildings?"

"Yep, I hang them and then move them wherever, until we're done painting."

"Ah, so I suppose that means you like to climb," as they drive into the city.

"Yeah, yeah, I do. But, it's a job."

"I guess most jobs get to be routine."

"Like watching grapes grow?"

She laughs, "Probably, maybe like watching paint dry." They both laugh.

"May I ask, can you cut across Jackson and drop me in Chinatown ?"

"Okay, I guess. Tell me where to turn, I don't know downtown very well."

"Well, here comes a good short cut. You'll take Jackson to Van Ness, then you turn right. That takes you right over the Golden Gate. Turn left up here."

Iris trusts Scoty to know what he's talking about. A few blocks later he says,

"I'll get out here. Thanks for the ride Iris. Good luck with the new stock."

"Sure thing." She pulls over, "Here, take a bottle and try it out. Good luck."

"Thanks, now remember, go straight to Van Ness and

turn right. It takes you over the bridge. Safe travels," He tucks the bottle away.

- - - - - - - - - - -

Sc 3

As the station wagon pulls away Scoty hears a guitar and drums coming from across the street. He enters Chinatown to the music of the Ventures.

Walk Don't Run

At the corner of Jackson and Grant he stops at an outdoor cafe. He joins a guy sitting at the counter who is trying to order in sign language. He is dressed like Scoty, but speaks as an Aussie.

"No, this 'ere mate," he flashes the fingers of two hands, "But four pieces." He holds up four fingers and shakes them at the waiter.

The elder waiter smiles toothless and says "Two piece." Scoty smiles knowing the waiter speaks English better than the customer,

"No mate. No, four, see four fingers here? Four pieces, not two."

"Okay mister kangaroo, you want two order, right?"

Scoty turns as he hears the screech of tires turning too fast and Tina Turner,

Working for the man every night and day

The car draws close enough for Scoty to see two gun barrels in the rear window. He dives as the guns begin to fire. The waiter gets down fast, Scoty curses when he feels himself hit. He watches as the other customer gets taken out. The bottle of wine hits the street and shatters.

Big wheel keeps on turnin', Proud Mary keeps on burnin'

Proud Mary is playing loud inside the car as it speeds away.

And we're Rollin', Rollin' down the river.

- - - - - - - - - - -

Sc 4

Inside the car we see and hear the driver ask, "Did you get him?".

Thug 1 says, "Yeah I got him, him and another guy, they're both dead."

The driver says, "You sure you got him, the boss wanted him taken out."

Thug 1, "The boss should be happy. How many you hit Leo?"

Leo says, "I painted three or four people. Splat city in three colors."

Driver, "This will be on the TV news. "The Paint Ball Drive By."

Thug 1, "Yeah, I called it in 5 minutes ago. The press should be here any time."

Leo asks, "You think she'll be with 'em ?"

The driver says, "Yeah, she will if she knows what's good for her."

- - - - - - - - - -

Sc 5

The music behind the action takes on a faster beat.

Her cheeks are rosy, she looks a little nosy
Man, this little girl is fine

Emergency medical vehicles and other cars arrive as people jump out to aid the victims. Pandemonium really begins when the media trucks arrive and reporters with video crews start swarming. One reporter swarms faster than others.

Sweet little girl, that's my little Sheila
Man, this little girl is fine

Sheila leads a camera person and directs her,

"Get him, this guy. And get these two here and, the two over there, right?"

The camera op looks and says, "These two are wounded with paint."

"I can see that. Also, gimmee an outside wide shot and one in tight.. Okay?

"I gotcha, . . ." she turns to say,

"Oh, " they both say,

"And anything interesting you see along the way."

Camera op laughs and leaves. Sheila turns and says to herself.

"Okay, big breath. Focus but detach, and just do it."

Sheila starts to search the only bleeding victim. She rolls him over and looks. Then she blows out a breath, looks around and says,

"At least he's not here. Good."

The camera op comes back and says,

"I got what you wanted, but there were only five, not six."

Looking over his shoulder, Scoty shambles down an alley and around a corner.

- - - - - - - - - -

Sc 6

We look into an office with a handsome woman, Magnolia, standing at the window. Two men are there as well, Paco is standing, and Leon is seated.

She asks, "He wasn't there, Paco?"

Paco answers, "No, according to the news crew. Another guy kinda' dressed like him was there. He got dead"

Leon says, "Three people were painted with colors, like red, yellow, and blue."

Magnolia says, "Hey, fucking wonder bread! Holy Mary, what are the odds ?"

Leon offers, "Long odds. Shooter says he made an ID before he took the shot."

"What a mess. These are people who never had to clean after themselves."

Paco nods, "One dead, and four wounded with paint balls."

"They say four, but that's only those who stuck around after they'd been shot."

They pause and look at one another.

Leon asks, "Are you making a point? Or should I guess."

"Rubin's boys fucked up. The target was not supposed to be shot. Thank Mary he escaped."

"They don't miss." Paco shakes his head, "We don't borrow trouble here."

"Tru dat, we don't know. We don't even want to think about him being pissed."

Paco says, "Uh, boss? He's gonna be pissed either way, wouldn't you?."

- - - - - - - - - - -

Sc 7

There is hospital music playing as med people bustle by Scoty while he is being treated. We hear his swearing as a doctor inspects the stitches and pokes at his wound,

Dr. Ev smiles as she asks, "Does it hurt when I press here ?"

"YES!"

"Good, here?" she pokes again.

"YES."

"Good, here? " she pokes again, he grunts, and then again. "Here ?"

"Yes and yes, and stop that. I have feeling there, no severed nerves, okay?"

He tries to surround her with his arms but she pushes out of reach.

"You need to relax and heal." She folds her stethoscope

and says, "Ok, I guess you'll be fine. Get out of here, before somebody sees you."

She leaves. He looks after her and smiles, "See ya later." He lies back to rest as she leaves.

Out in the corridor, Sheila stops Ev, cutting her off with a wave.

"Yo Evelyn, you seen my Scoty?"

"Yo-YaSef, Sheila. Was that a lesbo dig, or did you get a dog ?"

Evelyn passes Sheila with a closed finger gesture to cut her off at the mouth.

"And no," Ev continues, "I haven't seen him."

- - - - - - - - - -

Sc 8

We see Sheila's report on a large overhead screen. The bar noise overrides the audio from the news cast but there are various shots of the crime scene under the banner that reads, "Chinatown" with Asian symbols along side.

- - - - - - - - - -

Sc 9

Through the mists of the mind comes a song, this time Richie Valens in Spanish.

Para bailar la bamba, se necesita una poca de gracia

Scoty wakes enough to wince, lay back, and enjoy the music for a moment. He nods in time. When he hears someone begin to open the door he rolls off the bed and drops behind it onto the floor. There is some pain involved.

The door opens. Sheila pokes her head in, looks about, and recedes. As the door closes, Scoty grunts and crawls to the surface. He listens to the music in his head, and softly sings along.

Yo no soy marinero

Sheila has opened all of the doors she can find, but hasn't found Scoty. As she returns along the hall, her footsteps make Scoty fall behind the bed again. The music takes over as she gets to the front door of the clinic. She opens it, looks, and leaves.

Bam- Ba, bamba
Bam- Ba- ba

- - - - - - - - - - -

Sc 10

Dr. Evelyn is changing the dressing on the wound as they sit beside a swimming pool. Scoty is trying not to wince at her touch. She notices his discomfort and says,

"Looks clean, what the cops call a T & T, Through and Through. Soft tissue only."

"Only ? Really? Soft tissue only ?"

"Easy cowboy, would you rather have a perforated lung,

or maybe a bone shattered? You wouldn't be bitching then, would you ?"

Scoty grimaces and internalizes. He brings up a forced smile and says,

"I do believe 'Thanks' are in order. 'Thanks. Ev', you take good care of me."

"Despite what you go through." She smiles and asks, "What was it this time?"

Scoty shrugs, "Drive by, wrong place, wrong time."

"Uh huh, and the paint ball victims?"

He pumps his shoulders. "Dunno."

"Would Shiela know?"

"Why would she know?"

She shrugs, "Dunno." She dismisses his question and stands apart.

"Evie? You wouldn't ask if you didn't-"

"She was on the snoop, asking for your skinny ass." She dives in the pool.

Scoty stands and looks at his ass. He shrugs, nods, and dives.

- - - - - - - - - - -

Sc 11

We see Sheila enter a night club. The singer on stage is ending a blues number,

It's 3 O'clock in the morning,
And I'm singing this song fo you.

Rebo nods to polite applause, and scans the audience. She gestures to the band, and, they all look at the house, and then to her as she twirls a finger. The band plays a hard riff. Sheila stops to listen as Rebo begins,

> **Now I don't hardly know her**
> **But I think I could love her**

Sheila stands transfixed at first and then begins to move with the music. The singer is singing to Sheila and inviting her up on stage, Sheila steps up to the microphone. The song turns into a duet as the two women sing face to face.

> **I want to do every-thing. What a beautiful feeling.**
> **Crimson and clover (da-da, da-da, da-da)**

The two kiss. The band all jumps and yells, "**WOO !**"

- - - - - - - - - - -

Sc 12

We see the two singers kiss on a big screen in an office suite. Watching the monitor is another pair. A fat cat, Rubin, who watches and listens to skinny Ratzo,

"Well at least she ain't suffering from 'failed mission syndrome'."

Rubin snorts, "Would you be? I mean, have you ever suffered from that retro psycho crap?"

"Naw, I'm not the type, don't carry it home at night. The wife wouldn't put up.-"

"You mean wouldn't put out,-" laughs Rubin.

"That either. Like, if I got fired or something, she'd have a right to be pissed."

Rubin asks, "But, for screwing the pooch as royally as this?" Ratzo winces.

Rubin yells, "Like shooting the wrong guy, and wounding several people from a moving car with Tina Turner blaring. Who were these cowboys?"

"Frankie's nephews", lamely utters Ratzo.

"You hired Frankie's nephews? Do they know who hired you ?"

"No way, they don't know no one or nothin' beyond me."

"You sure ?" pressures Rubin.

"Honest, code of the underworld. Nobody knows nuttin'. Nobody says nuttin'."

Rubin nods, "That's the best way, ain't it?"

Ratzo admits, "Yeah. Sorry."

"Somebody gotta pay, so the cops have somebody to blame."

"I took care of that. When the body is identified, the case goes nowhere."

The Cat man nods to the Rat. He looks at another screen and says,

"Sheila's here. Go bring her in."

As the Rat retrieves Sheila, the Cat checks and loads a gun.

- - - - - - - - - -

Sc 13

The Rat returns bantering with Sheila, he lets her sit without holding her chair.

The Cat says, "Now let's get started." He pulls the gun and shoots the Rat.

"Jesus Dad! " Sheila jumps and swears. As she watches Ratzo die Rubin says,

"Well, that's a good start. I always hated that guy. Ya know-"

"Me too, yeh, ya know? "

"Yeah, I know, he hired some idiots to take out your boy Scoty and they missed. Well they didn't exactly miss, they hit five other people in front of dozens of witnesses."

Sheila draws in breath and blows it out while checking the Rat again. She grimaces, swears, and kicks the dying gangster.

She says, "Yeah, I hate that too."

"Well, that's why you're sitting there, and not on the floor."

She smiles, "Thanks for the favor Pop. They weren't supposed to shoot him."

"I know right? And Oy, what a mess to clean up. Not your job, so never mind,"

They rise and he takes her arm to step around the body. Rubin orders,

"Gino, get rid of the rug in the office would you? I wanna new one."

Gino says, "A drop cloth would be cheaper."

"Hardee Har," to Shiela he says, "You got the story, right? I missed the news."

"Plenty of everything that sells, but Scoty went missing. What the fuck Dad?"

Rubin asks, "He wasn't there?"

"He was gone, possibly wounded, but gone. I think maybe he used a clinic in the mission, but I can't be sure where he is."

"They say he was seen taking pictures. Did you see a camera?"

"I didn't see much. The action took place before we arrived. I mostly saw the mayhem those stooges left behind."

"Stay on it please, and let me know when you find, ..whatever you find, okay?"

"I'm glad you appreciate my services, even better if you appreciated my worth."

The fat cat hands her a fat envelope. Sheila takes it and judges it by weight.

"Thanks Pop. At least with me, you get what you pay for." She exits into the club.

- - - - - - - - - - -

Sc 14

The band is playing and the lead is selling the song:

> *Here she come now, sayin' Mony, Mony*
> *Well, shoot 'em down, turn around, come on ho-ney.*

Sheila bops to the music and throws a kiss to the stage as she cruises through.

> *And I feel alright now.*

I say yeah (yeah), yeah (yeah),

Scoty and Evelyn watch her exit from the back of the room.

Dr. Evelyn watches Scoty more than he watches her. She smiles and sings,

Sweet little Shiela, her name drives me insane

She laughs at Scoty as he shakes her off but she continues, "You know why I brought you here? You know who owns the place right?"

"Yeah, Yeah, Rubin TeePee. He and his ol' lady own half the Haight now."

"Did you know they are also major shareholders in both KTST and KQSF ?"

Scoty looks at her, "Did not know that. I heard they were Shosone Indians."

"In case your anagrams are rusty, these are the Asian and Hispanic stations."

"Was it on the news ?"

"Yep. Looks like Sheila still works for them all doing the trilingual news."

"So I could have been shot in several languages last night."

The background music changes. **'Wipe Out'** plays as they walk from the club.

Ev asks, "Still don't want to tell me, or talk about why?"

"I still don't know much, so there's not much to talk about."

"Men. Such simple beings. So, you don't know? Or, you're not saying?"

Scoty turns and looks curiously as she smiles and shakes her head.

"Okay, I'll start, where were you all month?"

"San Quentin hanging paint truss."

"Did you piss anybody off? Spoil someone's parole? Hang the wrong guy?"

"Not that I know of. We worked too much. The place is old, older than the gold rush, needs a lot of work. We're only about half done."

"Half done? Why?"

"The contractor is only putting out the work as she gets paid. She wants her money in advance. I go when I get the call. So, it's taking a while. Big place."

Ev says, "So I've heard. How big ?"

"Big, maybe 4,000 inmates, It's over capacity by over 20%."

"Sounds ripe for trouble." The look at each other and Scoty speaks,

"Some say the crime lords already run the place."

Ev snorts, "Sounds like Club Fed."

"Others say the young criminals want to go there to get new contacts."

"So, doin' time in Quentin is like grad school for cons."

"Could be, I heard they run the hospital and recreation areas,"

Ev leads him, "And, when did your trouble start?"

"I didn't have any trouble. Well, I did get in this card game with some other workers. We were playing poker in the back of the truck stop that burned down, Did you hear about that down here on the coast?"

Music changes to '**Drift Away**' in the background,

Day after day I'm more confused
Yet I look for the light through the pouring rain
You know that's a game that I hate to lose

"You were there? Playing cards. And don't think it had anything to do with you?"

"Naw why should it? We were just playing cards when they made us all leave."

Ev exclaims, "To avoid a fire!"

We hear John Hartford's, **Bear Creek Hop**, playing throughout the next scene

- - - - - - - - - -

Sc 15

We see two FBI types in a surveillance van in the parking lot of the truck stop. They are watching the card game through scope hooked to a dash board display. One agent is smoking and the other is fussing with equipment, and complaining.

Agent 1, a female, says, "Look if you're gonna smoke, do it outside please."

Agent 2, a male, blows smoke and leaves the van by the side door.

Two hoods are standing watching the smoker as he leans against the van. One tips a can of liquid and watches it run under the van. The other turns the can sideways and let's it drain in another direction under the van.

The hoods both leave about the time the liquid surrounds the agent's feet. He takes one last drag in the butt and drops it. When flames cover his legs he dances frantically and calls to the other agent as the fire runs under the van toward the can. The van explodes but the two agents escape.

However, the fire ball ignites part of the truck stop as people flee the card game.

- - - - - - - - - - -

Sc 16

Ev asks, "Did you have your full kit with you? Did you take the bus?"

"Not exactly, I left the kit with Aunt Kim, decided to hitch and save the bus fare."

"Sounds like you got way from someone who wanted to see you."

Scoty plays dim, "Really? You mean I could 'a caught a ride from there?"

"No, but you missed a ride to the morgue."

"Why would I want to go to the, hey, you're not saying that, you mean?"

Ev will only look at him and smile as the music plays.

Oh, give me the beat boys and free my soul
I wanna get lost in your rock and roll and drift away

"And the moment you get back, the ambush happens in Chinatown?"

Scoty shakes his head, "Yeah, weird huh? I'm just glad she hadn't arrived yet."

"Who?"

"Sheila. We were supposed to meet there."

Evelyn tilts her head down and looks at him from under eyebrows.

"So she knew where you would be."

"Well, yeah, we had an appointment. You think that matters?"

> **Oh, give me the beat boys and free my soul**
> **I wanna get lost in your rock and roll and drift away**

"Maybe we should ask Shiela." She reaches over and smacks him in the head.

Scoty rubs his head and looks at her with curiosity as the thought dawns on him.

"OOOOO Ev, You don' think she- Naw, Ev You think she would-?"

Dr. Evelyn sings, "Her cheeks are Rosy, and she's a little nosey, Man that little girl is fine."

Scoty quietly admits, "And evidently a murdering little shit."

- - - - - - - - - -

Sc 17

We see a flashback of a prison building with painters on an elevated scaffold. Scoty is on the roof with a paint bucket on a line in hand. He snaps his harness onto a pipe and leans over to guide a paint bucket down the line. When it gets to the scaffold the painters hook an empty one on the line to be raised.

The other side of the building has a scaffold to be flown

which is still on the ground. Scoty hoists the hooks into the air and places each one over the superstructure. He goes back to the edge and flashes a thumbs up. The worker on the scaffolding pushes a button on the pendant and the scaffold rises about a foot off the ground. Scoty smiles and sits in a beach chair at a table on the roof, with an umbrella for shade.

When he sits, he begins to explore a new camera. It has so many bells and whistles there is a seventy five page manual in three languages. He moves his microphone on his headset down and speaks,

"You guys are set, Call me when you want to move."

The arm goes up and Scoty starts to play with his new toy.

- - - - - - - - - - -

Sc 18

Our point of view zooms into a window on the top floor of the building next door. We see several cons around a flip chart that has a picture of the Golden Gate bridge. In the next picture, one of the bridge towers seems to be exploding. A convict in medical garb stands at the chart with a pointer. Another stands at the window smoking a pipe.

"Zimmy, put down that shit and pay attention, this is serious."

"Yeah, sure,"

The chart flips the page to reveal both bridge towers exploding and says,

"We put the charges, here and here, on the top of each tower-"

An older con seated in a position of authority says, "Good, Nice and big, I like it."

Zimmy focuses on Scoty and his camera. The chart guy pauses and says,

"Thanks Uncle Joe. Yo', You so fuckin' smart you don't need to pay attention?"

"Yeah, I seen it when you turned the page. It's a fucking flip chart. If you computer generated that shit you could have emailed it, saved us a trip."

"Yeah, well, you can't hack a flip chart."

"You so smart, you don't know there is a guy on the next roof with a camera?"

The hoods in the room all crowd toward the windows and look out.

- - - - - - - - - - -

Sc 19

We hear a steam whistle blow. Scoty looks up from the new toy and begins to pack. A guy walks through the roof door carrying a stack of envelopes.

"You said you're good for two weeks from now right?" He hands Scoty a check.

"Sure thing Vinnie. But ah listen, I don't mind the schedule changes, but it's obvious we're not finishing any time soon. Right? I mean, you like my work right?"

"Sure Scoty, you rig good, Safety first right? What's up?"

"Well it's all of this gear I gotta haul around, Ropes and Hooks, and block and falls,- ya know, when we have to take it all home every few days, it gets old ya know?"

"You asking, can you leave it here? You know you can't."

"If we don't, some of us got to pay extra to store it, like, locally. Just so the inmates can't loot it, and use it for, whatever, ya know?"

"Scoty, I asked, it's against prison rules for contractors to-"

"I know, I've heard it Vin, It's just that I have to pay to store this stuff locally. Either that or I have to rent a vehicle to drive it back and forth, Will they pay for that?"

"Is a Rabbi Catholic? No! Duh? Here's your pay. Did you do the time sheets?"

Scoty hands them over. "Thanks anyway Vin."

"I hear ya." He looks at the sheets, "How much is the storage locker?"

"Uh, Let me look, Here hold my camera," he hands it to Vinnie.

"Nice, How big is the chip?"

"It's only 2 gig, It's loaded in the camera." Leafing through his wallet, "Here we go. I have it as, Great Bear self storage; $39 a month."

Vinnie takes a good look at the camera and then opens the one he has hanging from his neck. "I'll trade ya for this one. 5 gigs." He pops his camera open, ejects the chip, and inserts it in Scoty's camera. "There. Take your camera,"

He trades the camera for the time sheets.

"Huh, Look at that. Your time sheet is four hours short for this week. I'll make sure and change it before I sign it. That ought to cover storage. The other stuff can go on the truck for next time."

"Thanks Vin, that'll cover it. So, see ya in a few weeks."
They shake hands.

- - - - - - - - - - -

SC 20

Across the street the inmates shake their heads. The chart
cover is closed to reveal a Red Cross symbol. The speculations
begin to fly from everyone. There is a television distracts
Uncle Joe. A younger con asks,

"How much do you think he saw ?"

Zimmy says, "It don't matter. He's got a camera."

Chart boy Bubba asks, "I know! Did you think that was
a fuckin' blender he was holding?"

Uncle Joe, the older con says. "Look, here's baby Sheila
doing the news."

Chart boy says to Zimmy, "He showed it to the other guy."

Zimmy says to Uncle Joe, "They were fuckin' with the
camera, looks like they traded something."

Chart boy says, "I'll get on that, I'll find out who he is,"
and departs

"Have Rubin and his boys track the guy. Find the camera.
Hmmmmm."

- - - - - - - - - - -

Sc 21

We hear Eric Burden singing,

There's a light, ... A certain kind of light
That never shone on me, The way I want my life to be

We see Maggy sitting before a touch screen. She resembles her brother Uncle Joe, but most people are too polite to point it out.

"Hmmmm."

She reaches out with a stylus and swipes as she talks to Sheila,

"The spy-net caught sight of him the next day with Evelyn at the beach."

Sheila asks, "Where?"

"Up by Bolinas, some old hippie place, now it's a resort at the bottom of a cliff."

Sheila asks, "Marin county?"

"Yep, Point Reyes, right on the Pacific. Why do you want him so bad?"

Sheila admits, "Dad wants to talk to him. I kinda' like him."

"Why?"

"I've known him a while, just casually ok? He's funny, he makes me laugh."

"Hmmmm."

"No. No Hmmmm. Why does Dad want him dead?"

"Rubin doesn't want him dead. He wants to know what the kid knows, some job-"

"Scoty was out of town rigging for the past month."

"Yeah, up in San Quentin" Shiela looks at her mother who says, "And yeah, that's who wants to know."

"Uncle Joey?"

"My dear saintly brother."

To love somebody, To love somebody, The way I love you.

- - - - - - - - - -

Sc 22

Uncle Joe says, "Hmmmm."

We now see the resemblance as he reclines in a barber chair.

Bubba says, "We found out the guy is a rigger and he works for Norma Paints. We think the rigger keeps his work kit in a self storage cube. There's only one, so I checked with the manager."

"Good. Did we get the fuckin' camera?"

"His gear wasn't there and they don't admit they ever heard of him."

Joe thinks, "Hmmmm. Maggy says he's healing up from a gunshot wound."

Chart boy Bubba says, "Whaaa?"

Joe swears, "Rubin's stooges. Those idiots give violence a bad reputation."

"So, what happened?"

"They were supposed to 'take him in'. Instead, they tried to 'take him out'

"Hey, no limit on stupid, eh? Rubin must be pissed."

Joe nods, "Yeah, he's down a few guys right now. He did the Rasta Rat for it?"

Bubba chokes down, "About time."

Joe says, "I heard he made baby Sheila watch."

"She probably enjoyed it. They hated each other."

Joe is surprised, "Why?"

"Something old, Ratso been around a while. And he hates Lesbos."

"I heard my niece was Bi-"

Bubba says, "Nobody cares, but Ratso, he was always making cracks and shit."

"Not the best thing to do in a - ", Joe quotes, "Sexually Transparent Family."

"Yeah, well, when he went down, the average IQ went up."

Joe wonders, "Was Sheila there at the restaurant ?"

Bub answers, "She was too late to see it. If he was hit, he split quick, no camera."

"Hmmm,. . . ."

"I found out Alvin was on the gate."

Joe nods as he lights up, "Good, somebody saw him leave."

"He said the guy was rolling a large work case."

"We know he took the bus into town. But, we think he hitch hiked to Frisco."

Joe is preoccupied, "Why ?"

"The bus driver from the Frisco route said he didn't ride with him. I showed him a picture and he thinks he saw Scoty hitching a ride on the highway."

"Did the driver notice a tool kit?"

Bubba negates, "Nope just a backpack."

"Hmmmm. Go back and find where he was spending his nights. Search there first. Then find the other guy we saw on the roof and ask him."

- - - - - - - - - -

Sc 23

Music foreground is,

> *Bo Diddley bought her a diamond ring*
> *If that diamond ring don't shine*
> *He gonna take it to a private eye*

The music fades into the house as we see a man approach the cottage. A woman is watering her plants beside the front door. The music fades into the house.

"Pardon me. Do you know a Mr. Scott Center?"

"Yes, I know him, Why do you ask? What's your business?"

"We are interested in speaking to him about work, Mam, what is your name?"

"Kimberly Canter, I'm Scoty's Aunt. He's my brother's boy."

> *Bo Diddley caught a nanny goat*
> *To make his pretty baby a Sunday coat.*

"Well how nice, We've seen what a fine job he's doing out at the prison and wanted to know if he would work with us, uh, doing rigging for our painters."

He hands her a card. She reads the card and looks under his left arm.

"So, uh Mr. Zim? You're a painting contractor?"

"Yes Mam."

"Do all of you wear guns?"

She gestures to the gun with the garden hose and soaks the contractor.

"Oh my, I am so sorry, did I get you-"

She gestures again only this time spraying him thoroughly.

"Oh gee, sorry, that kind of got away from me."

Sputtering, he says, "May I ask, does he live with you?"

She sprays him again,

"No, but he's kin, so I feed him when he drops around. Why do you ask?"

"I don't' suppose –" But he cannot finish for she has spayed him again.

Ugly ask Mojo, where has he been?
Up your house, and gone again

"No, I don't suppose you do." She points the hose down, "I'm sorry, mister,"

"If you could tell us where to find-" And he gets wet again.

"No, I couldn't do that. Do I have to answer you? Or, should I call the Sheriff ?"

She holds her line of defense with a garden hose. The contractor backs away.

"Thank you Ms Center. Please give Scoty my card. Good Day."

He tips his hat, turns, and walks away, only to have the hat sprayed off his head.

- - - - - - - - - -

Sc 24

Scoty decides he needed to speak with Rubin. He places a call to KXSF and leaves a message for Sheila. He fakes his voice to sound nasal.

"Miss Shiela, oh, I'm sorry I don't know your last name, Shiela, you a reporter right? Well, there's some suspicious activity going on at the restaurant across the street..... there were people with guns and people being dragged and carried... ... it's the place down on Jackson..."

- - - - - - - - - - -

Sc 25

Scoty waits out of the rain as the news van sprays water to a halt and Sheila bounds out. She is moving quickly and almost doesn't see him, but stops when she does.

"Wo, there, oh, uh, Scoty."

He says, "I think you owe me an apology."

"You're right, but it was a mistake, and listen, I gotta' go for a minute -"

Scoty admits, "I faked the call. I need to speak with you."

"You? Oh. Uh, No suspicious restaurant, uh, terrorists?"

"Nope," He pinches his nose and says in a nasal voice, *'I called you'.*"

Sheila squints and turns and waves to the crew,

"False alarm folks, I'm gonna stay, find out why. See you back there later."

As they grumble and depart Sheila turns a commanding squint into a smile.

"I think you're more than a painter."

"Right. I'm a rigger. You owe me an apology." He opens the door. They enter.

"I think -" she says and is stopped by Scoty who repeats,

"I said, You owe me an apology,"

"For what exactly." The server approaches and asks,

"Juice? Tea? Coffee?"

"I'll have a Tinker bell." Scoty raises two fingers. The server nods and departs.

He asks, "What are we having?"

She says, "You don't get out much do you?"

"Do you even hear me when I speak? And, you owe me an apology,"

"Lemonade and Pink Grapefruit ice cold... and, okay,... I'm sorry,.. happy?"

They stare at each other until she says,

"You have nice eyes."

"That's the first thing you ever said to me."

"The color changes in different light. They're almost always blue green, except-"

He waits and stares at her with a smile. She squirms as she thinks, and says,

"You're right of course. I apologize for being late. But I'm glad I was."

"What's the deal here?"

"It was a mistake. They were supposed to bring you in, not take you out."

"Sheila, people died. "

She reflects on the shooting of the Rasta Rat and admits,

"Quite a few now. It was a huge screw up and people have been punished."

Scoty marvels, "Really . . . and that's just that."

"Anyway, Mom said Dad called, he still wants me to get a hold of you."

"Yeh, I got that impression."

"Good, did you call him? Do you have his number?"

"No, Not yet..I don't have his number." The drinks arrive and they share.

"Pretty good, yeah? Now, come clean with me. You're not a painter, right?"

Scotty's phone rings. He looks at the display, takes the call, and says,

"I'm a rigger. 'scuse please, Mama Kimbo, how are you?"

We see Aunt Kim through her front window gesturing and barking at Scoty,

"Are you in trouble? I know you are. You're in more now buddy boy, for not warning me."

"Trouble, me? You know me, -"

She goes off and Scoty listens as he holds the phone from his ear.

Sheila plays with her own phone and watches him listen and mumble responses.

"Yes mam, No Mam. I won't Mam, I swear Mam.." And he disconnects.

Sheila looks up from her phone. She hands him her phone.

"If you wanna talk to Daddy, just push send."

Scoty waves the phone away,

"No more talking, I need to See Rubin. He crossed the line."

Sheila must ask, "What did your Aunt have to say?"

Scoty says, "That someone sent a painting contractor around to see me."

Shiela asks, "Yeh, So ?"
"This one carried a gun."

- - - - - - - - - -

Sc 26

Scoty and Shiela drive across town as we hear the music
background instrumental music by the Ventures,

Telstar

As Shiela drives Scoty asks, "Did you notice we were
being followed?"
Scoty looks behind them.
She says, "What model ?"
"Looks like a Lincoln."
"Shitty tail car. It's not Dad's. Maybe they're Mom's.
Lemme call."
A high speed dare devil car chase through San Francisco
excites and terrifies many innocent pedestrians and drivers.
We see a few fender benders of personal vehicles dodging
Scoty, Sheila, and the tail car damaging dozens of other cars
to entertain us with destruction.
Scoty asks, "Did you get yer Mom?"
Sheila replies, "Yeah, there'll be a couple of guys waiting
outside -"
They pull around a corner, stop and get out. Two suits,

one dressed as Scoty and one wearing a bad Sheila wig get in and drive away.

- - - - - - - - - - -

Sc 27

The music coming from the lobby follows them into the elevator.

> *Well be-bop-a-lula she's my baby,*
> *Be-bop-a-lula I don't mean maybe.*

"Daddy loves the oldies, He 'specially likes this song, when he's with family."

> *Well be-bop-a-lula she's my baby,*
> *Be-bop-a-lula I don't mean maybe.*

When the elevator opens we see Rubin dancing free style with Magnolia. Their fingertips are linked and they dance with one hand free.

> **"She's the one that I know. She's**
> **the one that loves me so."**

"Here we are, Mr. and Mrs. Tee Pee, how charming. Family is nice, eh?"

The music plays out as they walk to him and exchange handshakes and hugs.

"Mr. Scoty, You don't know how embarrassed I am for all of this foolishness."

"Rubin, this 'foolishness' isn't over yet. Somebody crossed the line."

Maggy speaks, "Oh dear, they didn't shoot at you again did they? They were only supposed to make sure you got here without harm."

Sheila adds, "I thought they were yours."

"Not that, somebody visited my Aunt, someone with a gun."

A collective gasp goes up from Rubin and Maggy.

"Fortunately Aunt Kimbo, was watering her flowers at the time. Said she turned the hose on the hoodlum and soaked him several times."

Rubin and Magnolia stifle a laugh as Sheila nods,

"That was good."

"Not Good ! Somebody involved an innocent relative of mine. Not Good !"

Sheila asks, "Your aunt is innocent? I thought she was a retired Feeb?"

"She is retired. Got it? And she is no part of this, whatever this Is."

Maggy nods in agreement, "Hmmmmm," greatly resembling her brother.

"What's this all about ? Enough is enough, and this is more than enough."

Maggy says, "The armed contractor was from Joey."

Sheila says, "He's supposed to be dead."

"That's what he wants the courts to think. Everybody knows he's just in prison."

Scoty asks, "Why ?"

Rubin answers, "Why else? Money. The answer to 'Why', is almost always 'Money.' They never found the bundle he stole and he wants to keep it."

"I don't blame him, it was almost, what, 250 mill? And what does this have-"

"He's doin' easy time in Quentin. He goes by the name Sylvester Wilson."

- - - - - - - - - -

Sc 28

We see Uncle Joey in his barber chair with a quartet of convicts playing music.

We hear strains of. **A Train.**

- - - - - - - - - -

Sc 29

The juke box starts to play Jerry Lee,

Come along my baby, whole lotta shakin' goin' on

Maggy shrugs and leans across the table into Scoty's face and says,

"He couldn't know what you knew, who you are, or what you saw. So he wanted me to talk to you, and find out."

"About what?"

"About who you really are, and what you saw."

"Saw what?"

Maggy says, "I'm tired, you wanna play?" Rubin nods.
"What you saw while you were out at Quentin."

Woo-huh, come along my baby, really
got the bull by the horn

Scoty stops and thinks and then walks to think some
more.

Well, I said shake, baby, shake
I said shake, baby, shake

He gestures briefly as he sits and faces Rubin,
Scoty asks, "Okay, then. How bad does he want to know?"
"What are you suggesting?"
"I saw a lot of things, and I heard a lot of things up there."
Rubin asks, "Anything about Over the Bridge?"
"Yep, saw that, 'Over the Bridge'. You bet. What does he
want to know?"
Maggy asks, "What do you know?"
Scoty states, "Everything I know is for sale."
Maggy and Rubin sit back and say, "Hmmmmmm."
Scoty attacks, "I thought we were here to get some shit
straightened out."
Maggy says, "We are but –"
"No 'Butts', straight business. I thought you were natives;
Shosone, right?"
Rubin owns up. "I am a native Shosone. She's a 'Fukowee'."
"Fukowee?"
"Yeah, her people got off the boat and said, 'Where 'da
Fuck are We'?"

"Funny, Let's get back to it. If Uncle Joe wants to know what I know, he could come to me and ask. Where I come from, that's the way it's done."

Maggy says, "Yeah, 'xcept he's in jail. Where are you from ?"

"Jersey. For him to send an armed man to question my frail retiring Aunt -"

Loud snorts as we see the drenched hoodlum standing in front of Uncle Joe.

"That crosses the line, and he knows it. Now he has to pay for what he wants."

Rubin asks, "To Atone?"

Scoty confirms, "To Atone."

Rubin swears, "Shit."

Maggy considers, "How much ? "

Scoty flashes an open hand and says, "5K."

Rubin swears, "Shit ."

Maggy asks privately, "Should we find out from Joey if he wants to pay?"

Rubin decides, "I don't think so. I'll cover it, just to find out if he's bluffing."

He takes out a hand full of gold coins.

"Kugerands, One ounce each." He counts five down onto the table and says,

"To Atone ! Now what do you know?"

Scoty gathers the gold coins and says.

"They've got plans for 'Over the Bridge'."

Rubin slams a hand on the table.

"Damn. You got pictures?"

"I've got pictures?" Scoty thinks quickly. "Have I got pictures!"

Rubin slams the other hand.

"Double Dog Damn. Okay. I need the pictures."

"Me too -"

And then shake, baby, shake
Come on over, whole lotta shakin' goin' on

Maggie snaps, "What? What's the stall? You want more -?"

Scoty notices that Sheila and her parents turn to him and harden their eyes.

Scoty holds his hands up, "No, Magnolia, Rubin, No disrespect. There's already been enough of that behavior."

Maggy says, "Too true. You got photos? We've been told to get the photos."

Scoty deals, "You wanted information. I gave you information. That was the deal. Now you want the photos?"

Rubin says, "Yep. You gots, I wants."

Scoty laughs, "I got photos, but to tell the truth I don't know what I got."

Maggy snorts, "How can you not know, what you have?'

Scoty says, "I dunno."

Rubin asks, "Don't talk stupid. How can you, not know, what you don't know?"

Everyone shakes their heads and blinks at that one. Scoty says,

"Because I haven't looked at them yet. I just back got to town and people started shooting at me. Or was that my imagination?"

He bares his shoulder bandages and looks at them. Maggy and Shiela look at each other, grimace, and grin.

Scoty points at the stained bandage. "Nope, look, that's my blood."

Rubin swears, "By the spirits of my ancestors, that was a mistake."

"Hmmm. You're Shosone right? That's you tribal name; TeePee? Like the tent?"

"No, they're initials, TP. The name is Thunder Pussy."

"Wo! Is it true that Indian names, … – maybe I don't want to know."

Maggy is mortified. Sheila smiles, nods, and says with family pride,

"We're the only Thunderpussy in the bay area. Let's get that cleaned up."

- - - - - - - - - -

Sc 30

'Here's a little song I wrote
You might want to sing it note for note'

Uncle Joe is not a happy man. He storms about his hospital suite with bars on the windows. He leads a comfortable existence. He does not like change, and he certainly does not like surprises. He reads from a pad to as he paces.

"Oh great, just fucking great."

Watching, Zimmy listens and asks, "Now what?"

"The fuckin' paint rigger knows somethin's in the fuckin' works."

"Says who ?"

"Maggy. She and the family had a sit down with this guy, Scott; somebody."

Zimmy asks, "What could he know. Did he get pictures."

"Yeah, they think so."

In every life we have some trouble
But when you worry, you make it double

"What did she do?"

"She says Rubin paid him 5K to get the truth. She says he's got pictures"

Zimmy swears, "Shit,"

Joe paces as he adds, "Yeah, apparently a fuckin' shit storm went down. People dead, wounded."

"Whaaa?"

Joe says, "Shit. I hope Sheila got good air time out of that."

"Hey, We found the supervisor and we're going to meet with him today."

"No shit?"

"No fuckin' shit."

'Don't worry. Be happy'

- - - - - - - - - -

Sc 31

We see Zimmy at another front door. He knocks and Vinnie opens,

"Hello. Listen, No Salesmen, okay? I don't accept

business calls at home, and I expect you don't either, so why don't you go-"

The hood asks, "Are you Vincent Stamatakos?"

"Yes, how do you know - ?" The visitor quickly flashes a badge, too quickly.

"I know as much as I could find out from your company, Norma Paints. The young lady there was not very helpful."

"Not much to find out. Obviously my name and address. Is there some problem?'

"Do you work with a Mr," he pretends to consult his notes, "Scott Center?"

"Scoty,? Sure, Is he okay?"

"As far as we know he's fine, but he does happen to be a person of interest in a case I am working on. May I come in ?"

Vinnie opens the door, "Yeah, sure,"

They enter and the hood steps inside as he says,

"We think Mr. Center was shot two days ago in San Francisco. We are trying to locate him to ascertain his, uh, well being, and his health, and all."

"Shot? Two days ago? And he's missing? And you are, who?"

The hood says, "We are concerned that he may need assistance."

"Okay, I didn't really see your badge. Who are you, and who do you work for?"

The hood grabs Vinnie by the shirt and forces him backwards.

"We are the people trying to locate him. You're a little slow aren't you? I seem to be repeating myself,"

"Hey, no need for any of that." He pushes himself loose from the man's grasp.

"Look pal, the easy way or the hard way, I don't care, in fact I would enjoy the hard way cause I'm a little pissed at my results so far. So, spill it, have you seen him?"

"Not since work the other day. We finished, he got paid, and split."

The hood asks, "Where did he stay while you was working at Quentin?" He pulls out a gun.

"With his Aunt, somebody, over in town somewhere. Now look, okay?"

"No, you look pal. You see who's got the gun? Me, not you, so I ask the questions and you answer them, okay? You get it?"

"Yeah, No, wait, I mean, Sure, okay, fine, what do you need from me?"

"That's better. I need a contact number and the names and numbers of any known associates."

"Sure buddy, there's his Aunt-"

"I spoke to her already."

Vinnie pauses and then asks, "Is she still alive?"

"Very much so. I don't shoot people unless I have to, so don't tempt me."

Vinnie shrugs, "She's the only person I know of, he don't hang with the painters."

"You and him were using a camera on the roof the other day. Why?"

"It was new, he just bought it, and he was trying it out."

"Did he shoot any pictures that day?"

"I imagine so, I mean it's a camera, right? So maybe, from up there? Uh, birds? Uh the buildings, the job we were -"

"Save it. You changed the chip on his camera. Where's the old one?"

"How can you know that?" Vinnie looks at Zimmy and continues, "I traded him the chip that came with the camera for one from mine with more memory."

The hood inquires, "Do you have this chip?"

"Sure, maybe in my camera, I put it there"

"Please get the camera and let's take a look."

Vinnie does so and they scroll through the memory of photos.

"These are all pictures of birds and buildings. Where are the others?"

"What others? This is the chip we traded for. What's there, is there, no others."

The hood pops the chip from the camera and wraps it carefully.

"I'm gonna take this to my boss and he may have more questions for you. In the meantime, you never saw me and we never had this meeting. Got it?"

"Ok, but what about my chip?" Vinnie follows him out the front door. "I can't take any pictures without that chip. Or, would you prefer I report it stolen?"

The hood reaches into his coat. Vinnie stops as if thinking a gun, but Zimmy takes out a wallet instead. He draws and throws some cash at Vinnie,

"Ain't no stealin' if I pay for it, is there? Take a ton and forget me."

Vinnie gasps as he grasps the money. The hood departs holding on to his hat.

- - - - - - - - - - -

Sc 32

We hear the background music of **Drummers Drummin'**.

Scoty, Sheila, and Evelyn look at the chip contents and see the flip chart with title 'Over the Bridge' hand drawn across the top. The next one looks like something on top of the bridge towers, but again it is hand drawn like cartoons.

The next panel shows something on top of the tower exploding. The next panel shows a star burst above the bridge with the words. " ***Get Out'a Jail Free*** " written in the sky in fireworks. The three of them look at each other and then shake their heads,

Dr Eva asks, "Do those look like explosives or fireworks to you?"

Shiela answers, "Both, maybe either, kinda. What's the next one show?"

The next photo shows paint rigging and the next shows hook attachment points.

Scoty says, "That's it. Looks like I got these four, like, drawings of the bridge"

Ev says, "So what's the big deal?"

Sheila says, "Dunno. Can we blow up the flip chart pages?"

Ev asks, "Let me get this straight. You pealed Rubin 5K for these 4 cartoons?"

"Yeah, well, I guess so."

Sheila says, "He's gonna be pissed. So is Mom."

"Let me enhance these." Scoty moves to the keyboard.

Ev laughs, "You got 'em for 5 large on a chance there would be something?"

We hear the background music change.

Well gonna write a little letter
Gonna mail it to my local D.J

"Yeah; so? I saw an opportunity and I took it, alright? " admits Scoty.

Ev says, "Sounds like you took Rubin. He's not going to be a happy camper."

"Hey. Let us not forget, he owed me for those goons shooting me…..."

"That's true, that's on him, well, on him and mom."

It's a rocking little record
I want my jockey to play

"And for the hoods coming to Aunt Kim's home."

"Those are on Uncle Joe."

Ev asks, "We still don't have an idea what he wants to do. Why is he so pissed?"

"Naw, you haven't seen pissed. He was curious, the rest was a mistake."

Roll over Beethoven
Gotta hear it again today

Scoty muses, "It is also highly frowned upon for anyone to climb the Golden Gate with or without explosives. Therefore, the plans must be top secret, right?"

Ev says, "That's true, even if it's a prank, people would get arrested for trespassing, possession, etc."

"Maybe it's a prank, but maybe not. So, he's got reason to

be paranoid, right? There's a legal risk at the federal level in what they're doing."

Sheila says, "All too true, but what do we tell my parents?"

Scoty says, "Nothing for now, not yet."

"Must I point out that you've been paid? Therefore you owe them."

"Okay, I can honor that. Show them the photos, all except the last one."

Ev muses, "And we leave it open as a mystery for Rubin and Magnolia?"

We hear the musical background of the James Gang's,

Ya Dig ?

Sheila asks, "You think they'll buy it?"

Ev Says, "Depends on who's selling it."

Scoty says, "Tru-dat, You? Me ? Evelyn?"

Sheila says, "No, I think we get Mom and Dad to sell it to Uncle Joe. They put out good money for the photos in his behalf. They should show him what they found."

Scoty adds, "I love it."

Ev says, "You know that's not the end, right?"

Sheila muses, "Let's play the cards we were dealt, and see what they got. Uncle Joe might not be too anxious to let Mama know some of the plans."

Scoty says, "But, everything he holds out, could work against him."

Sheila says, "How can we know what he plans?"

"We can't. We have to go with the flow. Besides we need a little extra help on this one. Your kind of help Ev,"

Ev asks, "What can I do?"

"Be what you ready are; a Doctor."

- - - - - - - - - - -

Sc 33

The scene is people on a public beach in San Fran facing the Golden Gate bridge. Some people are stacking kindling and fire wood around a roughly carved standing figurine. Another person is unloading a trash bag of clothes, and another is dumping boxes of stuff to spread around the base of the bonfire. The fire builder kneels beside and strikes a match. The kindling catches and starts to build. The effigy at the apex begins to take flame as one onlooker says,

"Great burning, man-."

- - - - - - - - - - -

Sc 34

In the hospital room of Uncle Joe, Rubin, Magnolia, and Ev observe a doctor writing in the patient chart as he speaks,

"Well, You have a marvelous metabolism for recovery, almost like it never happened. Now, uh, Sylvester, you say these chest pains, they come and go?

Uncle Joe sits unaware he has been asked a question. So the Doctor repeats,

"Uh, Mr. Wilson,?"

Magnolia bumps Joe's arm. "Sly honey? The doctor asked you a question."

Uncle Joe shakes his head, "Uh, yeh, you tell 'em Sis."

Maggy says, "Sometimes his hearing comes and goes too, uh, right after the chest pains. Maybe we should have that checked too."

The doctor looks and blinks. He looks at the doors of the room and sees two uniformed orderlies who appear to be standing guard. He writes in the medical chart.

"Mr. Wilson, it seems nothing has changed . So, I recommend you remain here, under observation, for another 15 days." He writes as he moves to the foot of the bed.

Dr Ev. moves to his side and confers, he erases 15 and corrects to 60 days.

Maggy moves in, takes his arm, and walks him to the door, She discreetly places an envelope into his coat pocket as he leaves.

"Thank you Doctor, thank you so much for taking such good care of my brother."

Uncle Joe hops out of bed and stretches. "How much did you give him?"

Maggy says, "2K, nothing's too good for my big brother."

"You can add it to the 5K I gave the rigger for the pictures," says Rubin.

"You got 'em?"

Rubin throws the photos on the bed. Uncle Joe paws through them.

"Shit, he got the flip chart. Where's the rest?"

"These are all he had. Right?"

Uncle Joe is adamant, " 'dese ain't worth jack shit. Where's 'de 'udders?"

Ev steps forward. "Scoty sent me along as insurance. These are what he shot. "

"Wrong !" Uncle Joe throws down another set. "We got these from the supervisor, Vinnie. They changed chips!"

Maggy looks at Vinnie's photos compared to Scoty's photos. Then she asks,

"He shot these too?"

Dr. Ev looks at the two sets and interjects, "Maybe the supervisor shot these?."

Joe blinks, then says to Rubin, "And you paid 5k for these?"

"Yep, sure did. Better safe than sorry. I knew you wanted to know, what he knew. How much did you pay for those?"

Uncle Joe fumes, rifles the photos, and storms about.

"Yah, yer right, of course. I needed to know what he knows. I owe ya."

He gestures to one of the orderlies who hands over a briefcase. Uncle Joe opens it, counts out 7 packets, and shuts the case. He hands a few to Rubin and a couple to Maggy with a kiss on the cheek.

"You two looking out for my welfare don't go unnoticed. But, as for you," Uncle Joe turns on Ev, "You know too much. They shouldn'a brought you here-"

With hands in the air Ev says, "Gosh Mr. Wilson, right, I don't know nothing. Scoty doesn't know anything. He and Shiela sent me as guarantee. I'm a real doctor. Under my recommendation your doctor extended your observation to 60 days."

"The rigger and Sheila sent her?" asks Joe, Rubin and Maggy both nod. Joe continues to ask, "And why ain't my lovely niece here herself, tellin' me this?"

Maggy offers, "She doesn't like hospitals or prisons. This is both, right?"

Joe laughs, "Yeah, I forgot, would be nice to see her though-"

Ev says, "Plus, Sheila thought Scoty's help might come in handy."

Uncle Joe and Maggy face off in a double, "Hmmmmm."

Rubin throws him a tablet, "She asked that you give her a call. Just push 5."

- - - - - - - - - -

Sc 35

We see a team of four ninja clad covert operatives prepping gear in a boat. The captain and his mate pass around the boat re-arranging fishing poles.

Two of the coverts study a map. The map holds a picture that repeats itself in the background of the bay. We see a double vision of Alcatraz island.

- - - - - - - - - -

Sc 38

Background music changes to the **Peter Gunn Theme**

Joe pushes 5 and holds up the tablet to see Shiela say,

"Uncle Joey, Hey, glad you're not dead. Everything okay with Mom and Dad?"

"Hey baby girl, who's this hoodlum you hanging out with?"

"Scoty ain't no hood. He's a good friend to me, and no threat to you."

"You say so, they say so, ok, but her. Who is she, and what does she know ?"

"Ev is a doctor. We felt a second opinion of your disability could come in handy. So what's all this Over the Bridge stuff you've got going ?'

Uncle Joe tries to shush the tablet, "Shhh Shhh shhh. No more of 'dat talk."

Sheila laughs, "Oh right? Like who doesn't know at this point? It's kind of like being a little bit pregnant if you ask me." Maggy and Rubin look at the ceiling as if they are deaf. Uncle Joe finger punches the tablet.

"Alright, alright, you made your point."

"No, not quite. Ok listen, I don't want to know. But, whatever it is, you have not been careful enough. Others know, so you need to CYA, ok ?"

Joe asks, "CYA, Catholic Youth Association? That was a long time ago -"

"No. Uncle Joe, CYA; Cover Your Ass."

Uncle Joe grumbles and Sheila repeats, "OK? . . . ."

Joey crumbles, "Ok. Ok alright, I will, ok baby ?"

"OK. Be safe. Love ya, lemmee talk to Mom,"

Joe grumbles as he gives up the pad to Maggy. She walks away talking.

Uncle Joe says, "She's right. That stuff in the pictures was all canceled yesterday. Too many people knew. I wanna meet this guy Scoty"

Rubin chimes in, "Loose Lips, eh?"

Joe asks, "You know how many people it takes to keep a secret?"

Ev says, "One! Anymore and it's not a secret, right ? ".

They all nod and Maggy rejoins the group.

"Yoo. listen up kids,"

- - - - - - - - - - -

Sc 39

We see the night sky over the prison, It is clear with a slight breeze. Joey says,

"The hospital stands 4 stories tall. From the roof we can see over 20 miles away."

Off in the distance we see a small flare go up. It is followed by two streaks from rockets. The third streak goes even higher. The first two explode into sparkles and spell out.

'**Go Indians**'

A guard walking the top of the wall stops to look.

The third rocket flies higher and when it explodes we read,

'**Shosone**'

On the roof of the hospital we see a team of people watching equipment. Inside the top floor we see Uncle Joe watching and talking with several people taking notes.

"The letters were too small. How far away is that ?"

"Two miles from here sir."

"Can the letters be twice as big ? Can we see that ?"

The tech speaks into his headset and nods to Uncle Joe,

"Yes sir, We should be able to see it from here in a few seconds, Manny? Yeah, You were right, please show us the 'other' one, Okay ? ."

On the monitor, we see the small rocket trail, in the sky the large letters spell,

'SHOSONE'

Uncle Joe smiles and offers high fives all around.

- - - - - - - - - -

Sc 40

Up on the roof, one of the technicians also enables a transmission of the test to an unknown source. People on the receiving end watch their screen in approval and chatter in approval.

- - - - - - - - - -

Sc 41

The instrumental music of '**Watermelon Man**' comes from the speakers.

We see an outdoor restaurant. Scoty and Shiela are looking over the seating area. She puts down the pad and says,

"Whatever it was on the bridge, it ain't no more. You managed to fuck it up."

"I didn't' do anything. If he changes plans, it means he's up to something else."

"Wo wait, Uncle Joe ? Sound the alarm, he's a criminal, but he's family."

Scoty nods, and ruminates, "Right? Is this your parent's place ?"

"Nope, this was Madam Sally's place. Mom asked to meet us here."

"Really? Sally Stamford. The Madam Mayor of Sausalito?"

Sheila says, "Yeah. She said she got elected because sex was the only thing she could get all of the politicians to agree on."

"Where was she when I was coming up?"

Shiela scans the menu, "That was a rhetorical question yeh?

As they are seated, he says, "So let's order while we wait. How many are we?"

"Ummm, make it for 6. They're coming down from Quentin."

Scoty pauses, "I heard that Evelyn is still alive."

"Yep. Turns out she was useful. Mom got Uncle Joe to chill about her."

"I keep thinking about that last slide, you know, the thing from Monopoly."

"Sure, the Get Outa Jail Free card."

"Ya think that was part of the plan?"

Shiela shrugs, "Probably, now we'll never know."

"Ya think Uncle Joe was planning a jail break?"

"Hard to tell with my Uncle Joey. He's very creative, but rather unpredictable."

Scoty asks, "Are you ready to order? Hand me the menu. Why the bridge?"

"Hey remember, the fireworks we saw were up over the bridge?"

"Yeah, I'm having the salmon. Why? Is that important ?"

"Let's order for everybody; drinks too. And maybe a dance while we wait?"

- - - - - - - - - -

Sc 42

A server takes the order as the juke box begins to play "Since I Fell for You'. Scoty stands and offers a hand to dance with him. She accepts and they step together.

You made me leave my happy home
You took my love and now you're gone.

"Can business wait? It's going to be a nice sunset." Sheila dances close.

"Yeah, well maybe. Your family is connected right? Who do you know that makes fireworks big enough for the whole city to see?"

Rubin, Maggy, and Ev enter the restaurant. The maitre de escorts new comers to a large center table laden with dinner. Ev looks daggers at the dancing couple, steps up to grab the cocktail shaker and pours a tall one. The dancers join the party and everybody gets comfortable. Maggy's face is partially obscured until she sits and we discover that she is really Uncle Joe in drag.

"So 'dis is da guy ?"

Ev smirks as Scoty re-focuses. Rubin says,

"Yep, this is him. Scoty, meet my brother in law, Joey Fukouwee."

"Wow," Scoty is amazed, "You busted out just to meet me?"

"Don't get flattered kid, I needed some stuff I can't get through channels. Is that Salmon fresh?" Scoty offers the plate for Uncle Joey to sniff.

Rubin says, "He and Maggy switch for shopping trips a couple times a month."

Joey says, "And I wanted to look you in the eye, and tell you, to stay the hell out of my business."

"Aren't you taking a big chance? Dressing up like her and appearing in public?"

Ev scans the other patrons and most look like cross dressers.

Sheila says, "Naw, no worries. Nobody looks twice anymore."

Two hoods walk in carrying several bags of stuff which Rubin receives, checks, and accepts delivery. Another goomba takes the purchases away.

Joe says, "Good, at least that worked. I hate going into town if I don't have to."

Scoty says, "As long as you're here, you'll answer to me. What's the idea of sending an armed moron to my Aunt Kimberly's place?"

Joe remains quiet, but he frowns into his drink.

Nobody says anything but Scoty. "Has he dried out yet?"

Uncle Joe replies, "Ask him, he's standing behind you."

Scoty looks, turns, and throws a pitcher of water at Zimmy, soaking him.

"Guess not eh? Next time you bother my Aunt you'll get the opposite."

The hood sputters and begins to draw on Scoty. Uncle Joe stops him,

"No. Stand down," the hood stops, Joe asks, "What's the opposite ?"

"The opposite means this time my Aunt will soak him with gasoline. Then she'll throw a match on him. Then, MAYBE she'll use the hose again, Maybe not."

Ev breaks the silence, "I can think of better ways to go. Don't piss her off, okay?"

Uncle Joe looks at them both and then at Sheila. She speaks,

"Just to clear the air, we should admit that we drew first blood."

Joey stands and points, "He started it by taking those fucking pictures."

"And you've seen 'em. What did they show? Cartoons of the bridge right ?"

Joey sits again, "I'm just not sure I've seen all of them."

Rubin says, "Why? Do you think there's more?"

"I paid for the other chip. Yours are prints, they're not the chip, are there more?"

Scoty looks at Sheila, then at Rubin. Ev is rolling her eyes as Scoty says,

"God hates a liar. Yes sir, there is one more. As I took your money, here it is."

He throws down the last photo of the bridge towers. Above the towers are sparkling words floating in the air.

Get Out of Jail Free

Uncle Joe only glances at the last photo before he speaks.

"And God loves an honest man. There's hope for you, If you stay out of my way."

Rubin holds up the photo, "What does this mean? Do I get my money back ?"

Sheila nips it in the bud, "Dad, you've already been repaid from Uncle Joey."

Rubin back pedals, "Oh, right, but Scoty held out on me to begin with."

"That's not true Rubin. I could have charged you more, but I didn't, right?"

Ev laughs at the confusion Scoty has attempted and she says,

"Yes, Yes, all that and more are possible. The plans have been changed right?"

Uncle Joe is nodding, "We'll have to see what happens after you'se butt out."

They all watch him as he gathers the photos, rises, and replaces the veil.

"How do you get free passage to and from the hospital ?"

"They think I'm Maggy, and I paid for the place."

Scoty asks, "Wait, you what ?"

Ev nods, "That would probably do it."

Joey says "Rubin, if you please," and he allows himself to be led away.

- - - - - - - - - - -

Sc 43

We see a group of ninja like characters crawling ashore. They drag lines with them as they crawl up the side of a small outcropping. The lines are attached to reels which begin to turn and drag three bundles out of the water and onto Alcatraz island.

At the same time we see another two ninja types crawling from the water. They are laden with loaded wet packs and start the slow climb up both legs of the Golden Gate bridge.

At the same time we see two more ninja types climb onto a pier in the Presidio.

- - - - - - - - - - -

Sc 44

Through the morning mists of the San Quentin prison yards we see a group of convicts working as grounds keepers. Soft music is emitted from the prison speakers. Cat Stevens can be heard singing, '**Morning Has Broken**'.

Sweet the first rain all, Sunlit from Heaven,
Like the first dew fall, on the first grass.

The cons are under the supervision of several lazy guards who are enjoying coffee and breakfast pastries. The delivery boxes hold donuts, crullers, and croissants. An older con watches as one by one, the guards seem to be drowsy on their feet.

One guard asks, "Hey convict. What's that you're planting today?"

"These? These just so happen to be the warden's favorites, Gladiola bulbs."

"Lemme see the paperwork." He inspects the carton and looks at the permit.

"We thought the warden would like to see them when he came to work."

"Well, okay, but what that stuff you're spreading all over the top?"

"Just fertilizer boss."

Another guard offers, "Hey Jimmy, can't fertilizer be made into bombs?"

"Yeah, Yo convict, where'd you get this stuff? Lemme see the package."

"No package boss. When we asked for the money to buy some, the ol Cap'n told us to go to the stable. This is horse shit."

The other guard nods, "That's what my kid uses on the roses. He says it's the best, so I get some there too. It's okay."

"Okay then. Hand me another cruller."

"Sure is nice of the bakery to send these out every week. Good thing we have to inspect them to make sure they're safe."

From a window on the top floor of the hospital we see Uncle Joe watching. He smiles as he takes a donut from a similar box labeled Magnolias.

- - - - - - - - - -

SC 45

At the Peek-A-Boo porn shop in downtown Frisco we see a private workspace behind the dance areas. This room looks technically proficient. There are several people at a table apart from the screens and computers surrounding them. They all look at a device on the table that looks like a can of prefab potato chips.

The leader place several lanterns on the table with a box of matches. He raises the hood of one and looks at the others. As he lights his lantern, the others follow suit.

Terrorist # 1 says, "Now gentlemen, for the purpose of this demonstration I would ask that you turn over a cell phones and com pads to my assistant. You will get them back, we just want to make sure they still work."

Terrorist 2 "Can't we just turn them off?"

T 1, "Certainly. But, if you ignore this warning, I won't be responsible for the consequences."

The group stands and shuffles all sorts of personal equipment into the bags offered for protection. The leader does the same.

"I believe in being prepared. Good, I'm glad you take the possibilities seriously." The people around the table all nod.

"That harmless looking can of, whatever they are, is where the device will activate. The 'pulse' that is created will, of course, be of limited range, say as big as this room. And it will be shielded to outsiders by the walls around you."

One asks, "If it's going to explode, why would we want to be in the same room?"

"Because you won't feel a thing, unless you are driven by

a computer. It fries computer chips. Secure the doors please. Good, now is everybody ready ?"

They all nod in some version of acknowledgement or another. The scientist picks up a remote and holds it over his head before saying,

"As our Italian friends would say, Andiamo."

As he pushes the button all of the screens around the room flash and fry. The lights go out but the emergency lights all flash on and off and begin emitting smoke. One man grabs his smoking breast pocket to remove his com unit and keep from being burned. One man grabs his heart and falls to the floor.

As he stands in the dim lantern light, the terrorist watches the man twitch a few times and expire. He shakes his head and says,

"All kinds of things are driven by computer chips these days."

- - - - - - - - - - -

Sc 46

A man and a woman covered with transparent rain gear approach the front door of Aunt Kimbo's cottage. She opens the door holding a flame thrower behind her back. The weapon is lit and her finger is on the trigger. She says,

"Looks like word gets around."

One says, "Thought you'd laugh" She disrobes "These won't do us any good."

Aunt Kimbo laughs, "Not against this baby. " She pats the flame thrower.

The man is getting out of his wet suit and says,, " Take it easy okay? I saw a guy cooked by one of those, it wasn't pretty."

Aunt Kimbo relaxes the weapon, "Yeah, you never forget that smell. It lingers."

The female agent gives Kimbo a hug, "Nice to see you girl, how's retirement?"

"It has its moments. Almost got to cook a couple of Feebs this morning."

The male says, "Funny. I'm Barny Solomon." He shakes her hand. "Looks like you two know each other," he turns and says, "Rhonda didn't mention that."

"I wanted you to get your own impression." They laugh and go inside.

- - - - - - - - - - -

Sc 47

In the kitchen, Aunt Kim assembles tea, "Rhonda, you be mother ?"

"Posolutely. Let me have that. So tell us about it. Barny will record."

Barny withdraws a recorder and places it on the table between them.

"This hood came looking for my nephew Scoty. I didn't have anything to say, but he was packing, so I soaked him with the hose."

Barny laughs, "With the hose? We know you got better protection around here."

"Yeah, sure, inside the house, but I was watering the flowers."

Barny smirks, "So he got wet ?"

"Head to toe, with me acting like a little old lady, 'Oh So Sorry' and 'Oh Dear'."

Rhonda asks, "You get him on camera ?"

"Yeah from the front door cam. I'll post it to you ."

Barny says, "He musta left mad."

"Spittin' mad. Ha! Or at least spittin water."

Rhonda sits smiling and shaking her head as she says,

"Well, you're still at the front, Kimbo. You know he was the Fucko's boy, right ?"

"Wait, who ?" Rhonda pulls out a pad and shows a photo to Kimbo.

"Joey Fuckowee, Uncle Joe, At least that's what the Bureau calls him."

Kim pauses and asks, "What else do we know ?"

"Well, somebody spotted Scoty taking pictures on the roof across the way, Uncle Joe asked around, and sent a hood to see you, and to see Scoty's paint boss, Vinnie."

Kimbo says, "Better luck there?"

Rhonda reports, "Vincent says he had another chip. Claims the thug took it and gave him a ton."

"Not bad for a guy so sick he has to stay in the hospital, " smirks Kimbo.

Barny says, "We know that Uncle Joey runs the hospital like he owns it."

Kimbo answers off hand, "Well, that's probably because he does."

Rhonda, sits up, "That's not in his file. How do you mean ?"

Barny is interested, "How could he own the prison hospital?"

"He put up the money to have it rebuilt.

Barney says, "Wow."

"It's a good job too, right? So he kind of lives there for now."

Rhonda admires, "Seeing you is always such an interesting visit. Say again?"

"See, a few years back, when 'de Schwartz' was Gov'ner. the prisons were outsourced to be run by corporations. The operators needed contractors to do maintenance and upkeep. Uncle Joey's dummy, T. T. M. & R., got the job of renovating the prison men's and women's hospital by offering the best bid."

Barny marvels, "No, shit. I heard the hospitals cost like 2 million each."

"He had already been arrested, this was before he was convicted. He knew a prison term was coming. So, he figured what the fuck? The top floor renovation was finished just before he was sentenced. So, when he got there, he had a place to stay."

Barny scans his pad and laughs, "That floor is listed as research."

Kimbo says, "Figures, what do they know about Scoty?"

Rhonda says, "Maybe nothin', as far as we know, but lookit, I have to ask."

"Go ahead."

"Your nephew, is he honest?"

"Good question –"

- - - - - - - - - - -

Sc 48

Scoty and Evelyn are watching the sun go down beyond the GG bridge.

He says, "So, Aunt Kimbo called and said the Feebs were by to see her."

Ev asks, "Is she in trouble ?"

"No, she used to be one. She said they knew about the soaking incident."

"Really, the Bureau cares about what happened to Uncle Joe's minion ?"

"Apparently. She said they were amused."

"So she keeps in touch ?"

"Yeah, we talk every few days." He smiles at her.

"No. I meant," She takes a swing at him, "She keeps in touch with the agency ?"

"Yeah, I suppose so, how else ?"

Ev only says, "Hmmmmmm."

"Hmmmm what ?"

"Hmmmm, just thinking is what. Anyway, what do you know ?"

"Me ? I din't know nuttin'"

Ev throws her drink on him, stands and starts away. "I am so done with this."

Scoty, amazed and wet, says, "What ? What did I do now ?"

Ev spins, "You're such a jerk. You are playing me- I am way done with you boyo."

"Playing you? What do you think- How can you - What's got into to you ?"

She takes a breath, collects herself and says, "Probably

you and Shiela slow dancin 'got into me'. Am I a fool for – for believing that we - or what ?"

Scoty can't quite grasp what is happening, "No Ev, You're not a fool, I'm, uh, sorry ."

She wipes her face and says, "You're sorry, I'm not a fool ?"

"No, I'm not- I mean Yes I'm sorry- Oh shit, ya know, why do women do this ?"

Ev smiles, "Because we can, ... and because men are so simple."

"We are? I'm sorry, we are simple."

"So you gonna tell me the truth ?" She opens her hand toward him. "It's a test. Or do I walk away for good?" She waves goodbye and turns to leave.

"No please don't. So, you want, why do you want the truth ?"

"Please,-"

"The whole truth ?"

"And nothing but the truth, so help you God. " She stands with hands on hips.

"Okay, but there's a lot to tell. How about you ask, and I'll tell as much as I can."

"No! I fucking knew it !" She walks away. "You've been lying to me all along"

"No, come on now, you've never wanted to know until now."

She shakes a finger at him. "Well, I know, what I know, ya know ? "

"How can I know what you know, or what you don't know, maybe."

"First just tell me, cause this is actually the most important. Do you Love her ?"

"Who, Sheila? Are you kidding? She's a sociopath, a wealthy, well connected, potentially homicidal, sociopath. I try not to get involved with those."

He looks hard at her and yells, "NO !"

She blows out a breath she didn't know she was holding.

"Good." She nods, "Okay." And then smiles, "We'll go from there."

He is playful. "I hope we can go from there. Will you come home with me?"

"Yes, now Second, why were you shooting photos of Uncle Joey ?"

"He was under observation. Someone, wanted to know what he's planning."

She pokes at him, "So, you were up to something?"

"Glad you used past tense, I was, but now I'm not. After Uncle Joe told me to buzz off, I turned over my information and was paid for services rendered."

"And now, you're done with them?"

"Not quite. I saw a couple of 'tunitys along the way. They could be profitable."

- - - - - - - - - - -

SC 49

The Ninjas have landed on Alcatraz and are scaling the side facing the city. They are quiet and convert. And they are practically invisible against the rock face.

The Ninjas crawling along the top of the Golden Gate are working silhouetted against the night sky.

The Ninjas at the pier on the Presidio are diving back into

the water. They leave behind a box with dim lights against the interior.

- - - - - - - - - - -

Sc 50

Back at Kimbo cottage, Rhonda asks,

"So, do We know who Scoty was shooting pictures for ?"

Kimbo replies, "We, don't know."

"Do 'We' have any guesses ?"

"Sure, all the normal ones."

"So, you're not saying."

"If ya can't say it fer sure, maybe it ain't worth sayin ?"

"We got wind of a meet with Scoty and Joey Fucko at madam Sally's."

Kimbo confirms, "In Sausalito, sure."

Rhonda pushes, "You don't seem surprised that the Fucko was out on the town."

"As far as we knew, he goes out every couple of weeks, but never on the town."

Rhonda says, "You've tipped your hand. Who is 'We' and what is going on ?"

"Yeah, school yard rules, I'll share with you if you share with me. OK ?"

"Natch. Spill ."

Kim looks at Barny and asks Rhonda, "Is he housebroken ?"

"Not yet but we're working on it, Barny, be absent please."

Barny says, "Joseph is a person of interest from an ongoing investigation,"

Kimbo pleads, "May I know why ?"

Rhonda answers, "He seems to be involved with known terrorists."

- - - - - - - - - -

Sc 51

On the end of the dock at Fort Mason is a new box marked, 'Ecological Water Survey Station. Property of the US Government.' There are hoses running in and out of the box with a water meter in a position to be easily read.

The pump that is processing the water passing through the box has a water filter that is cleared every day as the meter is read. A nice young woman in a park ranger's outfit takes the numbers on a chart. It all looks very neat and official.

The very same box has been deposited on the utility dock of Angel Island.

'No Sugar' is playing as we watch a switch board operator testing the circuits.

No sugar tonight for coffee,
No sugar tonight for my tea,

- - - - - - - - - -

Sc 52

Maggy is having a cuppa with Rubin at the counter of the bake shop. He asks,

"So how was the food ?"

She shrugs, "Not bad, it was cold,"

"Why cold?"

"Because I don't look anyone directly in the face when I'm being Joseph. I always sit with my back to the door, and ask them to leave the food on a cart."

"Couldn'a been that bad. What did you have?"

"Borscht and shrimp scampi. They were both cold."

Rubin admits, "Sounds better than we had at Sally's."

"Joey has an arrangement with the kitchen in the hospital."

"Joey has quite a few arrangements."

"R.H.I.P."

"True dat. It's good to be king. Or at least let other people think you're king."

Maggy nods and asks, "So, how did it go with Scoty."

"Joey told him he didn't trust him and demanded the other chip."

"Hmmmm. What did Scoty say?"

Rubin answers, "Played it straight. He gave over the chip and one last picture."

"Really. What was it ?'

"A shot of the flip chart. It said, 'Get Out of Jail Free' spelled out in fireworks."

"So he was shooting pictures for information."

"Yeh, Scoty gave Joe the chip. They shook hands and Joey told him to butt out."

"Hmmmmmm."

The musical back ground is **Ain't Too Proud to Beg.**

I know you're gonna leave me, But I refuse to let you go.
I will beg and plead for your sympathy,

cause you mean that much to me

- - - - - - - - - - -

Sc 53

A video technician / repairman is walking and talking to his partner on headset. There is a lot of traffic noise around him. Another person is with him also on headset.

"Hey, how do I know? They say the camera is out. They say go fix it, so I go. I'll get back to you when we get there, okay."

The other man has a cowl but pushes up his headset . He says, "I appreciate the opportunity to shoot from up here. Thanks for calling."

He holds up a hand to slap five, As they do so, a few bills change hands. Our view backs out and we see them walking up a safety lane atop a large cable up the side the Golden Gate bridge.

We see the inside of a control room and watch a monitor labeled South Tower, Two images of men walk steadily up the ramp way between the cables. One Tech says to another,

"These two are cleared by central. Camera 9 is out again."

Another says, "I hope they find the cause, number 9 has been intermittent."

The music of Credence Clearwater streams across the bay,

I feel earthquakes and lightnin'
Looks like bad times are on th' way.

The photographer shoots photos as they climb. The repairman has a backpack which holds the replacement camera for the bridge position. When they are in place up top, the two men make good time in their tasks.

The repair technician does his job in one place, but the photographer is all over the place. As connections are completed, the tech asks and receives the word that the new camera is working. The photographer notices two boxes, both are blinking. He gathers them and replaces them with two new two boxes. The bridge video tech whistles and the shooter complies by turning his camera toward the tech for one more.

The photographer loosens his cowl to reveal Scoty. He helps the technician pack up. The dead camera is in the back pack and secured to the tech's back. He says,

"Thanks, shit don't fall up."

As they descend we get another unique view of the bridge and the bay. But up on top the photographer has left two blinking radio control boxes with antennas.

- - - - - - - - - - -

Sc 54

The blinking light times to the opening instrumental strains of **Jingo.**

Out in the bay aboard a yacht a technician is watching screens. On one we see the same overhead shot of the bridge and the bay. The bottom of the screen has two red boxes that read, 'Receive', and 'Send'.

We see another screen showing a side shot of a Pier which is labeled 'Presidio'. We see a third screen of an island labeled 'Alcatraz'. We see yet another screen with another view of the bridge labeled 'Angel Island'.

We see the screen labeled Presidio where a technician stands in front of the water testing station on the pier in Fort Mason. He has the box open and watches a series of lights blink on a panel affixed to a device. He smiles and closes the lid to the box and uses a portable tool to screw it firmly shut.

Jingo continues to play.

- - - - - - - - - - -

Sc 55

Uncle Joe and the terrorist from the fireworks test, and the pulse test are standing on the roof of the hospital. They watch a technician install a camera on the water tower which faces the prison yard. The tech plugs the camera and asks,

"You got a picture?"

The response comes back, "Yeah, lemmee test and adjust it."

We watch another technician in the security station operate the camera's pan, tilt, and zoom by a remote control joystick. The water tower technician places another black box with indicator lights lit and blinking beside the first one.

The technician beside Uncle Joe is sharing the screen with Joe. The tech says,

"That's number five. Looks like we're ready when you 're ready sir."

Jingo plays into the next scene and finishes.

- - - - - - - - - - -

Sc 56

Evelyn watches as Scoty stands, holds, and kisses a woman before she leaves. From behind Ev we hear yet another woman say,

"Well Shit." Ev turns to Sheila who says,

"Yo Doc, I think we've been had."

Ev returns, "In more ways than one."

The two of them attempt to follow the woman but loose her at the first turn. They bicker as they differ as to which direction the woman went. They turn and walk back to the restaurant. Scoty spots the two and walks toward them,

"Isn't this delightful ? A lovely night and two beautiful women to entertain. Who's the lucky guy?" He waggles two thumbs up.

Sheila says, "We could have been a foursome. Who was your friend?"

Scoty looks at her and Sheila continues, "Evelyn would like to know."

Ev looks and begins to laugh, "Why you-, don't put words in my mouth bitch ."

Scoty quickly says, "Okay; If you don't want to know, good, I won't answer."

Ev says, "Well, I mean who could she be? Probably no one, right? Some, No One, you needed to hug and kiss before she left, right?"

She finishes and stands beside Shiela with their arms folded and feet tapping.

Scoty is amused to say, "I was having a drink with Aunt Kimbo. Too bad you were skulking about or you could have met one faboo lady."

Sheila attempts, "She looked pretty young for an aunt."

"How old do you have to be? She's a bit older than me, always has been."

Ev admits, "I'm sorry I missed meeting her."

"She's worth knowing."

"I would enjoy that, just to compare notes on you ."

Scoty can only smile and say, "Next time perhaps."

Dr Ev says, "Sheila wants to know, what did she want ?" They exchange glances.

"To meet with me while she was in town. She doesn't come down much. She heard I'd been shot."

Sheila asks, "Did you tell her the goon attack was a mistake?"

"Yeah," to Ev, "She inspected your work. You passed."

Ev admits, "Usually do."

To Sheila he says, "Are we gonna see your Dad?"

"Yeah, he's at the studio, I'm on in an hour and done after that. Can you wait?"

"Sure, are you in Ev, can you join us ?"

Dr Ev smiles, "Wouldn't miss it."

The instrumental background is provided by Ethan Miller, **Last Night**.

- - - - - - - - - -

Sc 57

Aunt Kimbo watches the girls fail their attempt to follow. She window shops her way along and then stops to examine herself in a mirror. She covers the black dress with a black hooded sweater. From her handbag she draws a black veil, affixes it, and stands waiting at the curb .

When the limousine arrives she gets in and sits across from two other woman who are similarly attired. Kimbo removes the veil and says,

"Am I addressing Joseph or Magnolia ?"

A woman removes the veil and speaks, "I'm Maggy. You can speak with me."

"Okay, I guess she can just listen."

"It's okay, she doesn't speak English. She wouldn't understand anyway."

"Oh, really, where is she from ?"

"Jersey"

"Hmmmmm. Sounds like a good story."

"Usually is with my family."

"I've come to speak about your brother."

"My brother's dead."

"Not yet, but he might be killed soon."

The other veiled woman; Joey, says, "What makes you say that?"

Last Night continues to play.

- - - - - - - - - - -

Sc 58

A black clad figure crawls along the girders toward the camera position atop of the Golden Gate. Down below traffic has been stopped with search lights pointed toward the sky.

A technician watching the camera feed begins to jump and yell,

"I've got something, south tower, right by the camera. It keeps blocking the shot and then moving, Oh, there it is again." The shapes on the monitor are way out of focus.

The figure inspects and photographs the two blinking boxes without touching them. He moves out of camera range and then positions himself. Shouts from below,

"There he is, on top of the south tower!"

Search lights barely illuminate the bandit jumping from the tower and falling gracefully while deploying a para-wing, which unfurls, catches the wind, and he glides away into the darkness.

- - - - - - - - - - -

Sc 59

Sheila is behind the studio glass giving a report on camera. Scoty, Ev, and Rubin are seated in a posh suite. Scoty is filling his drink glass as he asks,

"Do you really watch the news? Do you read the newspapers too? How about periodicals? How many subscriptions do you have?"

Rubin is distracted and annoyed at his viewing being interrupted.

"Yo, would you shut the fuck up ? I want to watch the show."

Ev says, "He hates watching the news so he creates an argument or discussion instead, thereby distracting us from watching or reading the news."

Scoty merely says, "True. Guilty as charged, but with good reason."

Rubin explodes, "What, why, what do you mean? Why can't you just be quiet?"

Scoty says, "No chance fancy pants. I need to talk to Uncle Joe. Mano y Mano."

"He was in just yesterday, you saw him then. He's back, you know, back in-"

"Yeh, I know; 'Upstate'. But I need to ask him some questions, have a talk."

"What kind of questions?"

"Information kind of questions. I have Info' to trade, and I'm after some too."

Rubin snorts, "Shit, What's it going to cost me this time?"

"Are you offering to pay what I'm going to charge Uncle Joe?"

"I don't know, maybe, depends on -"

Scoty flashes both hands.

Rubin says soto voce, "Ten K?" He scoffs,

Scoty only nods yes.

Rubin shrugs, "I don't know, maybe not. This one may be Joe's bidness."

"You tell me when and where, and I'll be there."

We hear the theme from **Dragnet.**

- - - - - - - - - - -

Sc 60

Kimbo is sitting with Rhonda and another Feeb at a conference table.

"So the Fucko and his sister Magnolia were in the limo,

we were all dressed for a funeral and the old guy lifts his veil. I almost had to laugh."

Barney asks, "Does he knows who's playing him ?"

Kimbo answers, "I don't think so, Uncle Joe doesn't work for anybody but himself and family, in that order."

Rhonda asks, "What do you think? Does he know or not?"

"I don't think so. If he does, he's not saying."

"Did you find out what he's planning for his release party ?"

"Nope, He wouldn't say. I asked three times. He just smiled, didn't say shit."

"So, that's all you got ?"

"It wasn't a waste of time, but he didn't give us what we want."

"How was it not a waste of time ?"

"Because he reacted to the info of a possible death threat. And, once I revealed our info about his accomplices being terrorists he clammed up tight."

"So you think he didn't know ?"

"It was more like, maybe he suspected, and started thinking about what needed to be done. No more conversation or discussion. They got out at Forrest Lawn and the driver brought me back. Thank god, those Nun shoes were killing me."

Last Night resumes

- - - - - - - - - -

Sc 61

Scoty and Uncle Joe meet in the top floor clinic of the prison hospital. Scoty is dressed like a nurse and Uncle Joe is dressed like the semi-retired wealthy crook he is.

Scoty says, "Thanks for seeing me. Why did I have to wear this costume?"

Uncle Joe says, "I just wanted to see if you would do whatever I asked."

Scoty removes the wig, "Huh, you really like messing with people don't you, like in the Magic Christian?"

"Love it, Especially when you flash some cash, and wait for them to play the fool. People can be funny without even knowing it."

"Well, I happen to be here for cash. I have some info' I think you should hear."

Uncle Joe smirks, "So this ain't no, I've missed you, visit?"

"After you telling me to buzz off?"

"I told you to Butt Out, and you didn't."

"Which means your luck is holding."

Joey is taken aback, "How's dat?"

"Because I have a thing for you?"

"This ain't no gay thing is it?"

Scoty gets serious, "Nope it's a 10 K thing."

"That's a pretty big thing."

"That's what she said."

"Ha, funny."

"Just kidding, wanted to make you laugh. Here's what I have for you."

Scoty opens a doctor's valise which holds two black boxes. The two boxes are still blinking as active electronic devices.

"I found three boxes. Let's just say, I knew where to look, of course, on top of the south tower."

"So who says they're mine ?"

"These two are yours as far as I can tell. You interested yet ?"

"Kiddo, so far these ain't ten cents worth of interesting, let alone 10 K."

Scoty pushes on, "These were made by Lung Sing inc. These others were made by them too. But, they sold me all the info I asked for, you interested ?"

"Nope."

"They say it was paid for by Lung Chun law firm. This, number two lawyer, sold them to T T M & R, one of your companies."

"Okay, okay, It's just a, uh, a birthday gag. Like a party favor. What's it to you ?"

"Ten K to me, do you agree?"

"It's just gonna be fireworks."

"The ones I left? Yes, nice big fireworks, These two, No fireworks. Something else."

"So those are not mine."

"Ten K says they are."

"I don't even know what they are, I don't even know they was there."

"Do we have an accord? Ten K for my help in this matter ?"

"Oh alright, Ten K, whad-do ya think, whad-do ya know, whad-do ya say?"

"I think you're being set up."

"Set up for what ?"

"As the fall guy for a terrorist event."

"Through this thing ?"

"This thing triggers a SEMPE device. That anagram stands for a Stratospheric Electro Magnetic Pulse Emitter. These devices left up there would shut down most computers within range." He snaps his fingers.

"Who did it ? Who put 'em up there ?"

"Aunt Kimbo tells me that the Feeb's best guess, is they are yours."

"That's bullshit,"

"I know, right ? Think about it. Maybe whoever put your receivers in place, put these in place too. They would have to customize to eliminate frequency conflicts."

Handling the box Joey says, "Damn. These take out electronics?"

"These are short range. Everything driven by computer chips, like all transportation. buses, trucks, cars, motorcycles. These are relatively small, bigger ones do banking, power, industry, the list goes on and on."

"They're so small. You saw these devices up top ?"

"I couldn't leave them there."

"What's the range?

"Not quite sure, I'm guessing they only take out a location, like the Bridge traffic."

Joey looks at one the SEMPE devices. "Fuckin' techno shit."

"Please notice that I haven't shut them down, Someone else is controlling this, as soon as we shut down, they will know. We lose the hand and maybe the game."

"You're smarter than you look." He takes out a fat envelope and pulls 10 stacks. Joe looks into the envelope, tosses the extras to Scoty, and says,

"Good job. "

Scoty is surprised and says, "Thanks, hey-"

"Sorry kid, just trying to lighten the load. Too much catastrophe for a sunny day."

"So where else do you have fireworks going off?""

"Hmmmmm."

We hear **I Can See Clearly Now**

> *It's Gonna Be a Bright,*
> *Bright, Sun Shiny Day*

- - - - - - - - - - -

Sc 62

Mama Maggy and daughter Sheila seem to be unconcerned with being watched by agents Rhonda and Barny. They window shop along Ghirardelli Square and walk the tourist paths along the wharf. Finding a park bench with a view of the water front, they sit and watch the bay.

They have a tourist map of significant sites of interest. The map is elementary for two natives but they are using it as cover. Certain sites have been circled. Shiela hands her mom an ipad.

"You, don't need to know how I know, but here ya go." She shares the pad.

We see the waterfront with X's and O's. Sheila points to an O over Alcatraz.

Maggy says, "I think even the Feebs know about that one."

Sheila pulls out a palm sized radar dish and sweeps the area in front of them. At one direction the pad beeps and the dish points and we see an operator in a van. Sheila presses a button on her device, and the van operator rips off his headset.

"That's probably the closest one. Bet he won't be working for a while."

Maggy says, "I like that, can I have one of those ?"

"Well they're not quite legal yet. Scoty got together with one of tech kids at the station. She's a veteran and she built some design. It detects and then scrambles directional microphones."

"What's this one?"

"This one detects the fireworks locations."

"I'm sorry Uncle Joe wouldn't tell you what he's up to." She puts another finger on the pad and says, "Here too." She is pointing to an O on Angel Island.

"Wo, oh yeh? Aren't those immigration halls and stalls a national landmark ?"

"Especially if you were Chinese and came here looking for work."

She moves her finger to another site marked Alcatraz. "Here." and then moves it to another marked Presidio, "And here".

She sweeps her detector again and picks up two beeps. She pans back and presses a button. We see a puff of smoke coming from a building top. She pans again and discovering another signal, takes it out. They watch another puff of smoke come from the top of the museum.

Maggy packs the pad, refolds the map, and says, "I know we can't be too cautious about what we say, but I believe there is another one up here. " She points to the map and her finger circles a dot that says, San Quentin.

Sheila whistles and then says, "You want to have some fun?"

"Born ready."

Sheila stands, takes a lighter and sets fire to the map. Maggy and she turn the map until the whole thing is smoldering embers. They drop the map and walk across the street and up the hill. The two ladies circle and then stop and watch a team of people rescuing and examining the burned and useless piece of tourist memorabilia.

We hear the **Get Smart** theme

- - - - - - - - - - -

Sc 63

Rubin is tailing the techno-terrorist through downtown. The tech leads him to the St Francis yacht club at the foot of the Golden Gate bridge. However, the tech does not enter the club. Instead the suspect walks along the shore front where he meets a guy who has beached his jet ski. The two of them exchange a few words, some money, and a wind breaker. The suspect pushes off and rides out into the bay.

The **Get Smart** theme continues.

- - - - - - - - - - -

Sc 64

Kimbo and Rhonda are having sunset drinks at Madam Sally's in Sausalito. They are kicked back and wearing shades. Rhonda is saying,

"Whatever they have, it does damage, we're trying to identify the trigger device."

Kimbo is snide, "Reverse engineering is pretzel logic."

"All the Internet chatter has gone weird. At first it was like OTB, then went dead."

"Or maybe it's the calm before the storm. According to Lung Sing, the un-sub hasn't been there since he picked up the last of the five displays."

"Yeah, yeah, and that was a week ago. . . . . where have they gone ?"

Kimbo says, "Patience is like a virgin waiting for the right time and place. I think they're out there waiting for the 'Go'"

"So you think it's all is set, and now they wait?"

"Hey, you think the date of 9 / 11 was a coincidence? No, it's the number Americans call when the shit hits the fan."

"Okay assuming you're correct, you can buy the next round, Waiter?"

"Let's look at potential dates coming up. April has several, The international film festival, the cherry blossom festival, what else ?"

"The international beer festival, Caesar Chavez day, Earth Day."

"None of those ring, how about May?"

Rhonda stands and brandishes her chest, "This is a job for the internet."

Kimbo does so as Barny joins them. He carries a paper bag and says,

"Ladies, boat drinks at sunset? I'm proud of you."

"Okay looks like, during May we have a wine festival, a food festival, and a carnival on the waterfront."

Barny says, "While you two are scanning dates I've been meeting with Scoty."

Kimbo smiles and asks, "And how is the fair haired lad ?"

"Concerned to find out I knew some stuff which you, and you only, knew."

"What did you say ?"

"Very little, He accosted me when he saw me watching Rubin. But then he asked me what I knew about Uncle Joe?"

"And you held out on him I hope?' says Rhonda.

"Well kinda, I wanted to know what he knew, so I played him, ya know?"

Kimbo says, "This is starting to go full circle."

"Right? So spill Barny, what did you tell him?"

"Not as much as I, uh he said to tell you, he gave me this."

Barny opens the bag and takes out a remote SEMPE trigger; still blinking.

Kimbo and Rhonda are startled upright. "Christ. Where did he get this ?"

He replies, "Didn't say, I'm not sure what 'this' is. He said Kimbo would know."

"It's a fry all your circuits device. And it's still active, waiting for a signal."

"He didn't give a clue as to where he got it, but he said there were three more."

Rhonda says, "Damn,"

"Uh, he also said that the three locations were for sale, 50 K each."

Rhonda says, "He should know that the policy of the current administration is that we don't negotiate with terrorists."

Kimbo laughs, "He's no terrorist, Scoty is a rabid capitalist, a whore for hire. Is that redundant?"

Barny says, "That's a relief. Maybe we can find out something from the receiver."

Rhonda says, "Just don't turn it off. In the meantime, I'll get the money, If you'll be the courier."

- - - - - - - - - - -

Sc 65

Rubin and Uncle Joe are meeting in the hospital wing. Dinner is being served by lesser inmates in proper attire. Joe eats sparingly while Rubin talks as he eats,

"I'm just saying is all. The boat will be at the dock waiting for you to get there."

"That day is soon coming. My last day will also the longest day of the year, the summer solstice. I think that's going to be it."

"Sounds like a long day, that's for sure."

Joey says, "You should give Sheila an anonymous tip for news coverage."

"You want to tell Maggy?"

"Sure, on the way to the boat; not before."

"Are there any loose ends? Scoty maybe?"

"Actually Scoty needs to meet with Gordon, you know, the techno specialist guy. Can you arrange it? Anonymously, of course. Just leave him a note or something."

- - - - - - - - - - -

Sc 66

Scoty and Evelyn are dancing under the stars to soft music coming from her apartment. **'I Can't Get Started'** is the dance tune.

> *Although the north pole I have charted,*
> *I can't get started with you.*

The whoosh of an arrow distracts the two of them as it embeds itself into the roof ledge of the balcony. Scoty says, "Missed by a mile," and snuggles her cheek.

Ev says, "Piss anybody off today?"

Even though he shrugs, she rolls her eyes, and pulls over a chair to get the arrow. Scoty says, "Humph, These look like tribal markings. Let's see the message."

They both look at the message untied from the arrow. He reads,

'80 foot Swan, Dark Blue hull, at 37.82, -122.45.'

"What's that?" asks Ev

"Opportunity," says Scoty.

- - - - - - - - - -

Sc 67

The jet ski leaves the public beach again as a fire rages behind. The burning man thing is really taking off and people from the north side of the city are showing up to get rid of all kinds of leftover shit. The terrorist, Akbar, knows little and cares less about the frivolous causes which San Franciscans support, but this 'cause' is starting to get in his way.

He churns the water machine through the night toward the dark shape on the bay. The sail vessel is anchored with the dive platform deployed. Akbar secures the jet ski and hops aboard the stern. A voice surprises him,

"I'd stop right there, you might not like what you see down below."

He spins toward the voice and out comes a knife. "You are trespassing and I have every right to kill you."

"Alright, go ahead, but I told you not to go there."

Akbar goes below only to find his people slumped over, some with arrows through their heads. There is blood running down their faces. He returns topside.

"Who are you and what do you want?"

"My name is not important and I want 100 K or the entire operation is blown."

Akbar has emerged with a gun. He points it at Scoty.

"I think you get nothing." He raises his gun hand. But so does Scoty. At that instant a small harpoon pierces the terrorist's gun hand.

"Oh too bad, I hope you can shoot with the other hand."

Scoty picks up the gun by the butt as if it is a soiled diaper. He flings it overboard while saying,

"Nasty things are often used by nasty people. Now, I won't ask you again,100 K.

"Look in the food locker under the galley sink."

"Okay. Then go get it and bring it up." Akbar makes his way painfully and bloody handed.

During his absence Scoty slips a waterproof bag under the seat in a storage compartment. Akbar brings the cooler with one hand sets it on the deck. Scoty opens it and counts out his share, then shuts the cooler. As he loads a waterproof backpack, he says,

"I always try to leave things better than I found them. So I'll give you something for this. I hope you know that your total patsy, Uncle Joe, is breaking out tonight. You should look for his signal."

Scoty dives over the side and disappears into the night.

Akbar is confused but cradles the cooler and goes below. He pushes bodies out of the way and notices that one victim has an arrow falling askew. She is wearing a fake headband and the blood is ketchup. Others start to moan and move as well.

"Get up you fools! Why have you been taken so easily? Up now, the game has begun." Akbar runs about removing fake arrows and restoring the operators to their seats. "We must be ready, the signal is coming."

- - - - - - - - - - -

Sc 68

Uncle Joe is being processed as a prisoner being released into civilian life. He stands looking at convict garb and throws them to Rubin who throws them out the window. Instead, he chooses a double breasted suit, a pale shirt and a colorful tie.

As he dresses Rubin takes a picture and says, "For Maggie's surprise."

The door opens after a knock. A guard says, "Excuse me sir, but the warden is here with your effects, Shall I show him in?"

Uncle Joe says, "By all means, please do." The warden enters with an assistant.

"Mr. Wilson, we are so sorry to see you go"

"You're too kind, my friend, too kind." He passes a gratuity into the warden's hands during the handshake.

"I must leave of you now. Could I have a late checkout. Say about 5?" Uncle Joe Fuckowee laughs. The warden grins.

"Of course, I imagine you will have a car waiting."

"Too true, too true. My oh my, how time does fly. Rubin, please have the porter pack my things, I'm sure it's all there. Thank you warden."

"Its been a pleasure having you in residence, but I won't say come back soon."

They both have a laugh. Joe stops first and looks at the warden who says,

"Well, then thanks again. Bon Voyage and all that. uh good luck, sir." He exits.

We hear the music of Leon Russell singing **Stranger in a Strange Land**

How many years has it been since I was born?
How many years 'til I die ?

- - - - - - - - - -

Sc 69

At precisely 5pm, Uncle Joe takes the elevator to the ground floor and walks out of the prison a free man. He is smartly dressed with a fresh flower adorning his lapel. As he approaches the car Maggy steps out as if waiting on him. She is dressed just as he is dressed down to the flower. He puts out his hand and says,

"What the hell?"

"I thought it would make you laugh," she takes his hand and kisses his ring.

The ride to the marina is short and playful. Maggy provides two scantily clad ladies in the back of the limo who serve drinks and fawn over brother Joey. A few minutes away the private dock is occupied by the Princess, a party boat outfitted for luxury. Scoty and Ev are waiting on the bridge with champagne.

As the captain moves the boat away from the dock, the party and gets underway. Entering the upper harbor, Uncle Joe sends a message on his smart phone to Akbar. On the other end of reception Akbar reads, 'The game starts in 15 minutes'.

Akbar goes below and warns his crew that they have 15 minutes. Each operator clicks a ready switch. The SEMPE box on San Quinton's water tower blinks and awaits further commands. The SEMPE box aboard the Swan go active in the bag under the seat and awaits further command. The SEMPE boxes in possession of the Feebs are still blinking but closed into a bomb box.

The good ship Princess cruises a bit and then docks again. Moored along the other side of the dock is one of world's most reliable seaplanes; a Grumman Goose, warming up. Uncle Joe disembarks the Princess and climbs aboard the Goose. The engines are warm and he waves as the sea plane glides away from the dock and turns into the wind, revs the engines, races forward, and takes off. The crew aboard the Princess resume the harbor cruise as clock registers 10 minutes.

Scoty is on the bow with a set of binoculars. He spots and points out a boat.

"Kimbo and the Feebs are over there. I hope she listened to my instructions."

Rubin and Magnolia are comfortably lounging inside watching a shot of the harbor on a large screen.

- - - - - - - - - -

Sc 70

Uncle Joe is flying over the bay in the goose looking at the lights and skyline. He is all smiles for a change, and checks his watch. Through his headset he says to the pilot,

"5 minutes til show time. Loop us back to where we can see San Quentin." The pilot does so. Uncle Joe warns the pilot,

"In a couple of minutes you should stay at least a half mile from the prison."

The pilot looks at him and asks, "Do I wanna know why?"

"Your navigation equipment won't like it."

"The, uh, equipment won't like it?"

"Not even a little. Seriously, we had a guy with a pacemaker, and he . . . Oh, there's the alarm. Two minutes, just keep your distance and give me a good view."

We hear Eddie Cochran's **Somethin' Else**

Here comes that girl again,
She's shore fine looking man, She's somethin' else.

- - - - - - - - - -

Sc 71

On board the swan, Akbar is timing down with his smart phone.

"Ready to activate the devices and the fireworks in 30 seconds. Standby."

The scene shifts through quick looks all of the players in all their positions while the clock counts down. At 0:01, Akbar yells

"NOW !" and the button is pushed. All of the boat systems shut down.

We hear **Can't Ya Hear Me Knockin'** playing between and behind the next few scenes.

- - - - - - - - - - -

Sc 72

The San Quentin water tower receiver goes green and a speaker on top issues a loud and resounding 'Ca-Lang'. The lights all over the prison go out. Inside, all of the cell doors slide open. The prisoners run about and exit to the amazement of the guards. A few protests are quickly solved. The population is outside when the sky is lit with a laser written message, '**Get Out of Jail Free**'.

Within an instant, the flowers around the main gate which are surrounded by explosives ignite and blow the iron work, the gate, and bars of away from the portcullis. The entrance is open for people to come and go as they wish. Outside, there is a small gathering of people waiting for the exodus.

The music continues.

- - - - - - - - - - -

Sc 73

Aboard the Princess Scoty hurries everyone to the stern to watch the direction of San Quentin. Maggy and Rubin are amazed at the distant site. Maggie can only admire,

"Nice Jo Jo."

Dr. Ev asks, "Are we here for the Joey Fucko show?"

Scoty says, "Watch the sky."

The music continues.

- - - - - - - - - - -

Sc 74

The swan is under surveillance at the very second its power it goes down. Inside the Feeb boat all systems go dead. Kimbo swears,

"Fuckin 'A', is Scoty good or what? Captain, what is our status?"

"Working on that. All systems seem to be dead at the control level."

Rhonda shows up in assault gear,

"Ready when you are boss."

They look over the side to a row boat with two sailors waiting at the paddles. The two women look at each other and Rhonda says,

"The Navy still does low tech, okay? It's about as low tech as we have."

- - - - - - - - - -

SC 75

Akbar is yelling in a foreign language until he stops himself. Flashlights and lantern lights go on, and he begins to yell in English.

"What the fuck happened ? Where are the fireworks. Why have we no power here?"

One technician is swearing as he opens a mother board to release smoke.

- - - - - - - - - -

Sc 76

Uncle Joe is laughing a clapping his hands in delight, "That bunch will scatter so far and wide it'll take major work just to find half of them."

The pilot is checking and rechecking in wonder,

"You called it safe. You're okay Uncle Joe. Where to now?"

"Fly us out over the bay so I can play with my remotes. Angel Island first."

- - - - - - - - - -

Sc 77

The sky is aglow as Scoty switches the monitor to show the shattered gates of San Quentin and prisoners streaming forward. The cut in is Shiela saying,

"This video is a live feed from San Quentin."

Maggy dances and claps pointing at the screen, Rubin beams with pride.

Scoty asks the Captain, "Do you have the Goose in sight ?"

"No Sir, but I am in contact with her pilot, She'll be here shortly."

"Are we to the west of Angel Island?"

"That's a copy, just as ordered, may I ask why ?" He is distracted, " Oh there's the Goose now."

Scoty runs outside yelling, " Show Time."

- - - - - - - - - -

Sc 78

While flying over the San Francisco's Angel Island, Uncle Joe presses a button on the remote wand. An explosion on land sends a skyrocket into flight. At the apex of flight an explosion happens and the words once again, ignite hope.

Welcome to All

The pin points of light hang in the air.

- - - - - - - - - -

Sc 79

Evelyn holds a camera pointed at the words over Angel Island. Within seconds the image is transmitted on the 'Special News Broadcast' on screen. Sheila is on camera telling everybody to look outside, and to keep watching over the bay.

- - - - - - - - - -

Sc 80

Aunt Kimbo and her Feeb powered assault craft are nearing the swan. Akbar is seen through the side ports of the sail craft as he rages about in partial light.

Team Feeb consisting of Kimbo, Rhonda, and Barny board the swan at the stern swim ladder. The two sailors secure the little boat and follow the team armed.

Akbar cannot get any answers about the meltdown so he grabs a pair of binoculars and heads up the companionway. He is greeted by the muzzle of a short powerful looking automatic weapon.

- - - - - - - - - -

Sc 81

The Captain of the Princess says to a public address microphone,

"Our next way point is Alcatraz island on your left folks."
He speaks to the pilot of the Goose,

"Okay Goosey, Tell Uncle Joe we're in place."

Up above we see Joe push another button labeled Alcatraz.

The rocks that support the prison begin to glow and flash in a rainbow of colors. The prison itself is dark but the massive rock base shines one very large word above the waterline;

FREEDOM

In white light and rainbow colors pulse behind.

The nightclubs along the wharf downtown empty out onto the street to cheer the fireworks. The Grumman Goose flies low and drops hundreds of packets labeled 'Birth Control'. One bar labeled BOYZ and another labeled GIRLZ starts to cheer as this segment of the news comes on screen, with Sheila reporting on mysterious mischief.

- - - - - - - - - - -

Sc 82

Scoty and friends are having a good time cruising the bay and watching the light displays. As they near the end of the Presidio a beam splitter from a laser show creates a words and a symbol which illuminte the end of three piers in Ft Mason.

The big bright flickering words say,

WAY OUT

There is a large arrow pointing toward the Golden Gate.

Maggy exclaims, "Oh look Rubin, it's just like the subway signs in London. They all say 'Way Out' too."

- - - - - - - - - - -

Sc 83

Akbar is being loaded from the Swan onto a homeland safety vessel. He and his terrorist sympathizers are all wearing wrist and ankle restraints and under heavy guard. Barny is taking care of the transfer while Aunt Kimbo and Rhonda are looking around and admiring the ship.

A Naval officer approaches agent Rhonda with a handful of charred electronics,

"We traced the signal from San Quentin's explosions as originating here. There are other SEMPE devices aboard that were activated as well."

Kimbo can only smile and say, "His mama would have been proud."

Rhonda ruminates, "I sailed one of these in the Golden Rock Regatta once. We raced the windward islands from St. Martin down the islands to St Kits and back."

Rhonda asks, "How did you do in the race?"

"We won the week. Finished with three firsts, two seconds, and a third."

"She is a sweetheart, what are we gonna do with her, impound?"

"No, the boat is leased, we'll release her to the owners after the arraignment. For now we lock her up tight and leave her at anchor. She'll be safe."

Akbar is screaming about the fucking convict that

masterminded the entire thing, but no one is paying any attention. After a moment Aunt Kimbo takes a gun and shoots Akbar in the chest with a knockout dart. Rhonda watches and begins to count,

"4,... 3,... 2,..."

We see Akbar start to speak but passes out in between number 2 and,

"1."

- - - - - - - - - - -

Sc 84

The pilot of the Goose is amused enough that he asks, "So, What's Next ?"

Uncle Joe says "I want you to circle the Princess, will ya? Get as low as possible so we can bomb them good."

The Princess is cruising slowly toward the bridge as the Goose commences her run. The pilot has her nose directly on the nose of the ship as she pulls up and dozens of two winged twirly birds are released and twirl their way down to the deck of the boat.

When Scoty and Ev catch some of the twirly birds they realize they have candy. Each confection is a wrapped fortune cookie. The paper which reads

"Come to Cozumel for Christmas."

The Goose then heads west toward the bridge when the cable swag between the towers lights up forming a big smile. Rockets streak up from the bridge and explode in the place of eyes which twinkle above the smile. The Goose flies straight over the top and does a wing waggle as she flies away.

Ev is nodding and smiling as she admits, "Not bad for an old crook."

Maggy laughs and says, "Hell, that's not bad for a young one either." She takes Scoty's arm and asked privately, "So, how much did you gross from playing all sides?"

Scoty smiles and says, "A bit, but somehow It never seems like enough."

Ev says, "Really ?"

He asks, Maggy, "How much did your brother get to keep?"

She smiles, "A little over of 225."

- - - - - - - - - - -

Sc 85

Later that same night a stealth boat approaches the Swan. Several ninjas board the vessel. They work quietly on headsets and directional illumination in preparation to sail. The most noise is made by the anchor being raised by elbow grease.

The fore sail is unfurled as the boat begins to move slowly. A Ninja raises his hood to reveal Uncle Joe's face. He is all smiles and calls,

"Captain!"

Another Ninja raises her hood and answers, "Aye."

"Raise the main by half." The Captain repeats to the crew. "Raise the main by half. "The main sail begins to rise. Uncle Joe is standing at the helm with the Captain, when his phone tingles.

Scoty's face appears and asks, "Hey, there you are. Where are you?"

"Singing the swan song m'boy."

"She is a beauty Joseph, too bad she had to be sacrificed."

Several cover plates are being removed by the crew as Uncle Joe palms the remote control he has been playing with all evening. He flips a switch and the boat becomes alive at several electrical and mechanical read outs.

"Looks can be deceiving. We're gonna get out of here."

To the Captain he says,

"Let's go south, but run without lights for a while, straight out at first and then stay well off the coast. Scoty?"

"Yeh Uncle Joe ?"

"Dos Vedonya."

"Don't get none on ya."

end

A Coney Afternoon

written by

T K Wallace

You ever feel the need to go to the beach? To feel the sand around your toes is an honor as you walk with bare feet? Ever feel the need to wade in the surf of some friendly coast line? I feel this need all the time.

I was not alone in the desire to feel my toes in the sand and see the ocean from the boardwalk of Coney Island. There were dozens of us, not quite hundreds. Those numbers will start in a couple of days on the holiday weekend. Memorial Day starts sometime Thursday afternoon and lasts until early Tuesday. It's a four day weekend that some manage to expand and lengthen into five or six.

When traveling to the beach by train from Manhattan you must ride longer than most commuters, because you are bound for the ocean front in Brooklyn. But today was just Wednesday, so the D train was not crowded. Everything seemed abnormal as usual, with the exception of several students boarding the train being chased by a witch. The teen reaction ranged from amused to spooked.

Three boys were laughing and taunting the spooky one who hissed and cast a spell in some unknown language. Two other kids who were afraid told them to stop. The witch glared and drew air, she breathed in and out as her arms went up and down. Her fingers were contorted at strange angles.

She was quite distracting. So I closed the book I was trying to read and asked the kid next to me if they were going to take her with them. He and his friends looked at me like I had grown an extra head. One asked,

"What?"

So I explained and asked again, "She got on the train with you. And you guys are having fun making her, crazy, or whatever. When you get off, are you taking her with you?"

That got me noticed by the witch. She began to move toward me and denigrate in some unknown tongue. Well, I don't do that to others, and I won't have it done to me. So I called her out and put a stop to all that noise.

"Hold on there! Don't you hiss at me. Yo' slingin' spit all over the place. Behave yourself in public and leave these children alone or I'll have somebody bounce a pineapple off the side of yo' head. Now git!"

Several other patrons began to applaud as the evil one hobbled away hissing and spitting as she went. She left a sort of trail in the train car, kind of like a slug.

I sat down again and tried to read when two Asian alien tourists asked me directions to the Statue of Liberty. So, I got up again and showed them a map mounted on the wall of the car.

"Okay, you are here. See? The statue is down here See?"

"Yes Yes, are we green train?"

"No you are on the D train; the orange line. But, you can go back into Manhattan, or get out here and walk over to the harbor to catch the statue tour boats."

What I didn't bother to say was they should take a shorter ride on the Staten Island Ferry. It passes in front of the statue as it goes across the harbor and back. There is usually no line to get on the boat. And it's free, courtesy of the city.

♦ ♦ ♦ ♦ ♦ ♦ ♦

I spent the rest of the trip re-reading some interesting history I pulled up on the net about Donald Trump's father, Fred, and some real estate shenanigans he had pulled to get control of park land back in the 1960's.

Fredrick Trump thought he could build up scale residential housing on the boardwalk with private beach access. He bought the attraction named Steeplechase Park and had the buildings torn down without permission. The local leader of the democratic political machine was in favor of the project. All Fred needed was the right mayor to reclassify public beach land.

Fred's man, Mr. Beam, was defeated by Mayor John Lindsey who hired Robert Moses to define public park land. 'Public Beach Area' was defined as, "All of the sand between the boardwalk and low tide". The boardwalk was expanded and extended to five miles, the entire beach declared as public land, and the Trump project collapsed.

20 years later Fred sold all of the land on the other side of the boardwalk, the land under the old Parachute Jump, and under the Cyclones baseball stadium, back to NYC for 2.8 million, or 1.5 million in profit. There was a news photo of young Donald hanging out with fashion models ant the demolition team. His hair was perfect.

◆ ◆ ◆ ◆ ◆ ◆ ◆

The subway rose above ground and became a train, and got us there in due time with no further incidents. The main exit allowed me to exit onto Stillwell Ave which leads straight to the beach. The station is diagonally across the street from Nathan's. Supposedly re-known for their Hot Dogs, I've always found them to run second for that particular fare. The truth is the Hot Dogs are for the tourists and the seafood is why locals by the hundreds still go there. They hold their annual hot dog eating contest on July 4th. Dogs will be on sale for a dime. There is a sales limit of 20 per dog eater.

I had some clams with tartar sauce and a tall, cold lemonade while sitting outside watching the tourist choreography. The outdoor soundtrack was largely Motown with some bad boy and bad girl music mixed in. I shared an umbrella table with a dentist and her husband from Jersey. They were just thrilled to be there. They had figured out that the amusement park was behind them. But they hadn't figured out where the beach was and wanted directions. Let's hear it for the NYC tourist industry, right? Yay.

♦   ♦   ♦   ♦   ♦   ♦   ♦

I walked toward the amusement park entrance and stopped at a place I recognized, The Eldorado Arcade. It has been there separating visitors from their money for at least 40 years They have hand operated cranes which can snatch prizes for you. They have 10 Ski Ball ramps for rolling the ball to a fortune of tickets. They have dozens of pinball machines. There are a few motion simulation rides that you play while riding inside.

And they have an air hockey table. I was taken by this and stood to watch for a moment. The final amusement at the back was a bumper car rink which made me smile. It had come full circle, for this was the first motion simulation ride we played from within.

I saw a maintenance guy park a bumper car and exit the rink to talk with the ticket seller. At the same time I noticed that I was standing beside a video game which had Pac Man on the screen. As I gaped the screen changed to Galaxians, then as I watched it changed to Space Invaders. I said something like " Wo. Space invaders." The maintenance guy walked by so I asked him,

"Do all of these games come in one box?"

"Yes Sir, there are ten different games. Which one do you want?"

"I don't know. Do you work here?"

"Yep, sure do."

"This is a great arcade, my name is Ted, what's yours?"

"Hiya Ted." We shook hands, "I'm Thomas, you like the old school games? Not many places you can play Pac Man anymore."

"Too true, Thomas. Did you know that Pac Man was based on a free computer game that was given away with early Texas Instruments computers?"

"Nope, I did not know that."

"The game was called Munch Man and it was in black and white."

"Is that so, We get a lot of older gamers showing their kids where it all came from. We've been a location for film and TV shoots."

"The place is a classic. This machine doesn't look like it takes tickets. Are those quarter slots?"

"Yep 'cept it's a dollar a game. We got change, you wanna play?"

"I do, but not today, today is for the sun."

"We're open later, come back by. Try your luck." click "Try your Luck."

"Thanks maybe I will." We shook, "How long have you been here?"

"Well, I've worked here the entire time I've been on

earth." He looks up. "They said they'd be right back." He smiled as I arched my eyebrows.

♦   ♦   ♦   ♦   ♦   ♦   ♦

I felt the draw of a time machine as I passed the air hockey table. It was as if an invitation was calling to me to come play. I shook my head and resisted the impulse to dump huge amounts of change on pinball machines.

When I reached the front entrance three kids were making a scene by chasing each other. The lead kid did not look where he was going, he ran into me and fell down. The other two were brandishing water guns and quickly overtaking us.

The first kid was dodging back and forth behind me using me as a shield as he squirted them with his own weapon. His friends ran him around shooting and shouting as I got most of the water. I waved my arms and yelled,

"Enough!" They all stopped, looked at each other, and then ran away.

There I stood as Thomas came out and looked me over. I smiled as I looked at him and shrugged. He took off his cap and scratched his head as he asked,

"You still got your wallet?"

My eyes widened as I felt my empty back pockets with both hands.

"Oh No," then I pulled my wallet from a front pocket and said,

"Here it is. They must have got the fake one." Thomas laughed as I pulled out another fake to put in my back pocket. I made the three fingered sign of the Boy Scouts and said,

"Be Prepared. Troop 99."

◆ ◆ ◆ ◆ ◆ ◆ ◆

I began to walk into Luna Park and found the major entrances half chained off, but with lots of people inside. I stopped at a Balloon Dart stand and asked why the gates were closed. An unusual looking lady working the runway said,

"They're painting everything in sight. Which is okay, but they're painting everything blue and orange."

"Blue and Orange?"

"Yeah, it's the new colors of Luna Park."

"But not you guys?"

"Nope. They don't own us yet. They got the Cyclone now."

"Will it be Blue and Orange too?"

"God, I hope not."

"They got the Wonder Wheel," indicating the Ferris wheel.

"Yep, I don't think they got enough paint for that big sucker."

"Wasn't this Wonder Wheel park?"

"Yeah, 'Dino's', long ago . . . . . You ever come here as a kid?"

"Never did. I moved here as an adult."

She asked, "Ya ever ride the Cyclone?"

"I wanted to ride, but I don't fit in the little wooden roller coaster cars."

"You're lucky, the last time I rode it I couldn't walk right for a week, It was too cramped, and we were bounced around on cheap padding from the 60's.

"Wanna try your luck?" She holds up some darts.

I drew myself up to bullshit height,

"Sorry Sister. I could cheat ya. I'm a Pro. You could lose your shorts."

"Say what, a Pro? What kind of Pro ?"

"Yep, Balloon Dart Champion; Pro circuit." .

I looked at her as she shook her head.

"How about 'I have no money for darts", she looked at me again and snorts,

"Then you best keep movin'."

"May I walk through?"

"No, they're painting. I told ya b'foe. You got ta walk around."

She pointed, and I did as she said. I walked around and came up to the street that led to the Cyclone ticket entrance and to the beach. When I got to the end of the street it looked as if the beach now had a grand staircase for an entrance. It looked like something from Emerald City in the Wizard of Oz. The staircase formed a huge half round with three tiers of very easy steps before you reached the top.

I found it enhanced the view. Seeing the beach and breathing the ocean breeze is therapeutic to me. And to be standing at a stairway worthy of Coney Island Beach made it all, 'mo'betta'.

I walked along the boards and parked at a bench to disrobe. The sun felt so good I took my time shedding my excess gear. While I was removing my shoes for a walk in the sand, a small alien looking child ran up from the beach, looking about franticly and crying. She mounted the boardwalk and ran across into a section of picnic tables.

Two mature black women stepped up to the boardwalk and asked,

"Did you see a little girl come through here?" asked one.

The other said, "She looks about four or five and she was upset."

I asked, "Where are her parents? Do they know she's lost?"

"What kind of a parent doesn't know, that their child is not there?"

I add, "Yeah I saw her. I think she was scared, running, she ran across the boardwalk to the other side. She ran in around those picnic tables."

"Oh my goodness, you don't think she'd leave the beach."

"I think she was way lost too, the way she moved and she was cryin'"

We watched the girl run back across the boardwalk toward the beach

"Oh look, there she goes back to the beach."

A man walking a Labrador stopped for her. He allowed her to hug the dog and asked what was wrong. A young Latino couple stopped as well.

I said, "Looks like she's in good hands."

"Yeah that kid has his phone out. I hope he's callin' the Police."

"They'll take care of her."

I turned and looked, "You know what I'd think we gonna see?"

"What?"

"I think we should watch for a frantic parent or a young couple in a panic. They should come running up from the beach any minute,"

"I hope they checked the water first. That'd scare them right."

"Sho' would scare 'em right, There was another drowning yesterday, out off-a Rockaway Beach. Undertow has been a lot worse since hurricane Sandy."

One of the ladies spots a young oddly colored woman yelling and running up from the beach. As she makes it to the boardwalk, one lady yelled,

"Yo ! Here she is ! Miss? Over here." She points to the crowd that is pointing the little girl toward her mother.

"You called it, He called it; didn't he Merle?"

She offers me a high five. I take it. And offer one to her partner. She takes and gives.

"You sho' called it right, Look at them they both scared each other."

We see the mother and child in the dubious bliss of fear and relief. They hug as the mother reaches out to thank people who helped. Her skin color had returned to normal for the beach.

"If she were your child, this is what you would want to happen. I figured the Mom couldn't be far behind."

A woman standing near said, "I'm just glad she wasn't found by some pervert."

We looked at each other and I said,

"I don't know where they are from, but we would never have allowed that to happen, would we?"

"No way, ooh look how happy they are," The mother gurgles her thanks as she passes with her child in arms, headed back toward the beach.

"Now, You keep an eye on her!" called the other as they left me to the sun.

◆　◆　◆　◆　◆　◆　◆

I sat there on the bench catching the afternoon sun from the west as the wind shifted around to the south, blowing on shore from directly over the water. I sat there alone and enjoyed the afternoon.

After a while my feet started twitching and flexing on their own. As if being summoned to duty, my feet needed to be in the ocean. And so, I did wade. I stayed and waded until my feet went numb from the cold salt water of the North Atlantic at Coney Island.

I watched others get in and out quickly yelling about the temperature. I continued to move but not fast, just enough to keep some blood moving. A pair of well tanned brothers ran past playing catch with a Frisbee. They were fearless as they ran to dive in the cold surf for the disk.

I waded until the warm dry sand on the beach looked inviting, warm, and toasty to my imagination. I scooted from water to the sand and stood there warming up when my eye caught the sight of flight. High up over the amusement park were several kites riding the constant breeze flapping their edges and tails.

I scanned up and down the beach until I traced kite lines down to locate the flyers. They were on the beach and further away from the water. There were four kite boys tending these beautiful colorful kites flying over the island. The high flyers were stake rigged in the sand with visual warning flags until the lines were at least ten feet above the beach.

The elder kite tender was Little Jorge. He is a slightly built mixed Latino with brilliant golden eyes and a shy smile. Big George was totally different. This guy must have weighed 300 pounds and was a tan as the inner hull of the coconut. I'd say 200 pounds of his weight was above the waist. Below the waist he was tiny.

Carlos was a skittish tan man who looked Italian to me. He was the first to ask my name, shake my hand, and ask where I was from.

"Where am I from? I am from here. I live uptown and I have these days off to heal from open heart surgery." I showed them the scar on my chest.

They all stopped to look, and then nodded and said I was looking good and ask how long since my surgery. I was proud to say 12 weeks. I was out and about with my doctor's blessing.

They all wanted to drink a toast to that and their cooler had what we needed. Out came a frozen bottle of Bacardi Gold and some small cups. We all drank a toast to my scars. I informed them that one drink was my limit.

I understood my surgery was not the first reason they needed for a slash of ice cold rum. They agreed that we didn't need any more, for the moment, and the bottle and cups went back into the cooler. But, In the corner of the cooler I saw an old style bong, a particular type of a water pipe made from bamboo.

I asked if that were a real bong. The cooler guy, Manny, looked at me to size me up before answering. He asked "Que?" as he closed the cooler. I looked him over and decided we were about the same age; 50-ish, and replied,

"Well, the best Bongs I ever saw came from folks I know who served in Nam. Two pieces of bamboo One big and one little, both cut off just below the divider. The small short stem is inserted into the face of the big stem just above the water line."

They looked at each other and laughed as Manny said,

"And boom, you got a pipe." He opened the cooler again and hauled out the bong and offered it to me.

"Aw, come on now, this is not right, the first time I meet some pot heads on the beach, nice beautiful day, ice cold rum, the kites are as high as I want to be, and my chest and I, have to be healing?"

They all laugh with me as I looked the bong over. "That's a nice one, was it handmade?"

Manuel spoke, "I did it up from the bamboo my brother has in his yard."

"Where'd you learn that way?"

"Serving time, Nam-time, that's an up-country style bong. You?"

"Boy Scouts of America, coastal Georgia."

"You had bamboo?"

"It's semi tropical so the Army had a growing and testing area for bamboo. The tropical aspects are like Vietnam. We were allowed to take away any bamboo that had already fallen down."

Carlos says, "Sweet."

"I had a friend who showed me the simplest way. We made Bongs like yours."

Lil George asks, "Really?"

"Been a while, maybe 30 years or so . ."

Manuel asks, "Then you don't mind me asking, how did you make the bowl?"

He smiled at me with a glint of curiosity. I could only smile back as I thought, and then I thought out loud.

"Bamboo is really just very large grass. And it takes in water like crazy. No native bong lasts more than a few months unless the inside is treated not to absorb the water. Something like bees wax is good but you still have to clean it."

"All true, he knows things boys, Please Master Jedi, elucidate …."

"As to the bowl: The small stem is inserted into the face of the large stem so it slips underwater inside. We cut the top of the small stem just above the partition. Then inside we inset a cone shaped pipe screen in common plaster. When it dries hard, we bore a hole through the bottom of both and you have a fireproof bowl."

"The boy has been there and done that. He's right on."

Little Jorge has been standing by listening and saying nothing. He laughs and it is an unusual sound. I realize that he has an artificial voice box. He sees me look at him. He shrugs and says in his mechanical voice,

"Smoking is bad for you, I tell everybody, and sometimes they listen."

He opens the cooler to take out a plastic tub. He cracks the top open,

"Have a brownie."

"A brownie, like an electric brownie?"

"I just wanna' fly kites." He offers, I look and they smelled great.

"May I have a couple? Thanks, I have friends. I'll just take these for safe keeping, You know, so, uh so you, don't have to worry about where they went, okay?"

"Take whatever you want, but don't smoke, ok?"

"Good advice. May I come back another day?"

Lil Jorge says, "Sure we're always here,"

Big George says, "This is our real estate, just down from the Aquarium."

"I'll be back."

Carlos shouts, "We'll be here!"

I sauntered off toward the boardwalk in search of a cold drink.

♦   ♦   ♦   ♦   ♦   ♦   ♦

Coney Island beach faces south toward the shores of New Jersey on the right, and the shores of Rockaway Beach on the left. Straight ahead is the Atlantic Ocean.

I walked along the boards until I came to the pier. I heard it had taken some damage during the hurricane, but to my great surprise the pier had been totally rebuilt. It was long, strong, and healthy standing in the sunshine being trod by tourists and fishermen alike.

The Coney Island pier is a T shaped structure with northern and southern spires about three quarters along the length. There is one slight bump to the western side. A tanning area extends over the surf rather than the beach.

The tanning area is currently my favorite spot on the pier. For starters, it is shaped like four small rolling hills. The surface is Epay wooden slats closely spaced for the rolling effect. Epay wood is dense and therefore slower to heat than many other types. So, it is comfortable to lie upon without any covering.

Nonetheless, the area was the place where the unusual occurred. So naturally, I ran into someone I knew. It is kind of unusual, accidentally seeing one person you know out of how many other New Yorkers?

'Silky", Silverman was a damn good framing carpenter

and put most men to shame. She and her two sister / friends, Jane and Linie, were two top shelf, off Broadway carps. Silky would knock out the big stuff and Linie would finish the fine work. Jane could out do them both.

As I found out, Jane was no more. She had been lost at sea after a head wound. She was knocked over board during a storm and never found.

Silky was damaged by the loss as well, She was dealing with grief in her own way. Her self prescribed medication was liberal doses of baby dykes and porn studio work; no booze or pot. She claimed it was doing her good and helping her heal, so who am I to say otherwise. If you think it helps; it helps.

Besides, Silky's new babe, Linie, was also a massage queen. We ate the brownies and settled into the wind and light. She worked me so well, I fell asleep during the act. All I remembered was hearing Silky talk about the costumes she and the Linie were wearing for the Mermaid Parade. If my imagination was correct, the crowd will get excited over these girls.

When I woke up they were gone but the fragrance of coconut oil and aloe remained. I yawned, stretched, and rose into the light of a beautiful early afternoon. The beach beckoned and I was soon bare foot in the sand. I walked back toward the amusement park thinking of munchies.

◆   ◆   ◆   ◆   ◆   ◆   ◆

Up by the boardwalk was the commotion of a school outing. There were maybe a dozen kids playing in the sand being overseen by a half dozen teachers, all of whom were perched on a boardwalk bench. They were shouting orders at the Hebrew school kids down in the sand.

I perched on the next bench away, rubbed the sand from my toes and thought once again that a bare foot beach walk would always be a great pedicure. The sun felt good so I stretched open toward it and arched backward. I wanted the full effect of the sun upon my chest and stomach. My solar battery must have been way down. This felt like something my body needed. Hey, a soft breeze, some light, and we're styling.

The sun and wind made me drowsy while doing as little as possible. I was there for maybe half an hour. Still a little stoned as I drifted in and out with the boardwalk cacophony. It is amusing to close your eyes and only listen to the active world around you.

One voice, a younger voice was getting through, fading in, saying,

"Yo Mister. Are you alive in there?"

I was coming to when the sunlight was shaded by someone standing in front of me. I opened my eyes to see three other same agers.

"Yo Mister, you be hot and thirsty, we gots water, you wants?"

I turned and blinked. I saw a young fem, maybe Latina?

"I'm sorry, you woke me up. What you want, Water? I don't have any water."

"No poppy, we got de water, you wants?"

"No, I got. Would you mind moving out of my light? I just had surgery and I am trying to tan myself."

They all lean in to inspect.

"Nice scar."

Two yuppies with halos in walking shorts stop to look. One looks more closely than the other and asks,

"Clean work, NYPH?"

It took a second to consider my reply.

"No, I think they used a saw."

"Ha, good one, my bad", and the Yuppies glided away.

The salesman did not, "Yo, I was selling water, you wants?"

"How much?"

"Dollar a bottle."

"Well good for you. You should make money."

`"How many you want?"

"None, I just had some lemonade."

"Yeah, from where?"

"Nathan's."

"hhmmmm, let's go. Sorry we woke you up." And the light was restored as the pack moved on.

I watched long enough to see them approached by a street soldier. He told them they could not sell water here. This was the beat of another person. Or something like that, because the first pack left.

The beat owner eventually strolled by with a small megaphone hanging around his neck. Without using said device he asked,

"Water Mister?"

"How much."

"Two dollars."

Without moving I said, "Nope, too much. The kids you run off only wanted a dollar. You're too greedy, no deal."

"No huhu skinflint." And he left pulling his cooler back onto the beach.

I watched him walk away and realized that the day was getting late, and I had to get back into town. It took me a while to put on my shoes and longer to put on some of my clothes. I did put on the shirt but could not yet close or button. I didn't want to leave the beach, but it was almost time, and I need to piss.

♦ ♦ ♦ ♦ ♦ ♦ ♦

Ruby's is the last bastion of the older Coney Island heart and spirit. Mind you, there have been several.. She faces front on the boardwalk. The bar runs the whole left side. The other side of the entrance has four walk up lines for ordering seafood, burgers, and pizza. The portable dining area is expandable.

The bar side outdoor dining area is mostly drinkers. There are three long tables which are occupied in rotation by floating parties of locals, semi locals, tourists, etc. They come at different times of day and night.

The restrooms at Ruby's are always blocked with 'For Customers Only' signs.

I was standing and looking into the bar as a middle aged man spied me watching that circus in motion. He waved and invited me for a beer. As I stepped across the line of acceptance he asked,

"Don't I owe you Twenty dollars?"

When I said, "No," he said,

"Oh, Good, Can I have it now?"

I replied, "No", but I admired the talent to devise such a plan.

The long bar inside Ruby's runs along the western wall

from front entrance to the back wall. Behind the bar from
bottle height up to the ceiling are pictures. Hundreds of
framed pictures, from back when they were taken, hanging
there for people to enjoy.

As I walked the perimeter of the room I found a unique
photograph of Babe Ruth. He's sitting on a bench among
a bunch of kids. He is speaking to their serious attention. I
could only smile as I continued toward the Clam Bar.

◆ ◆ ◆ ◆ ◆ ◆ ◆

There was a supervisor inspecting the serving area. He
had two clam and oyster opening knives in hand. He was
saying,

"These look dull, all worn out. Let's replace these."

I interrupted with, "Sorry, Sir? May I speak with you?"

He turns toward me pointing two knives. I look, smile,
and ask,

"Two knives, Yo', you live uptown?"

"What?" but the cooks snicker.

"Sorry, bad joke. I wanted to ask permission to use your
Men's room."

"Would you like to buy some water?"

"No, and I read the sign. That's why I asked permission."

"If you bought some water, you wouldn't have to ask."

"How much?"

"Two dollars."

"Nope too much. But I will make you a deal."

"Oh yeah?"

"Those old knives you're throwing out? I'll give you a
dollar for 'em."

"Done.", I gave him the dollar bill, and he offered me both knives.

I took them and tucked them away. He folded the dollar and almost slipped it into his shirt pocket. Almost, he missed. The folded bill fell to the floor as he moved away. I stopped and stooped and picked it up.

"Merci.", and so I peed for free. It was a little smelly, but it was free.

♦   ♦   ♦   ♦   ♦   ♦   ♦

As I walked the boardwalk I looked off to the surface and saw a free attraction that had tremendous possibilities, the Coney Island Historical Project was now occupying a lower store front under the boardwalk. They did require a modest donation. I had to go in and see what they had. My reward was finding a piece of my own past, for there sat Skully.

The large fabricated skull I saw before me came from an off Broadway show called 'Spook House,' by Harvey Fierstein. The giant white dome gleamed just as it had as the bowsprit of the set. We did the show at Playhouse 91 on the east side. The plot was about a dysfunctional family that ran a Spook House, Anne Meara and James Gammon starred.

One afternoon I remember working on Skully in the lobby when Harvey walked through. I was installing CO_2 vents for the nostrils to blow smoke as the eyes rolled. When I saw Harvey watching I asked him what the show was about.

In his unique voice he responded, "It's about a quarter of a million dollar tax shelter for the money we all made offa La Cage,". He laughed and kept going. I laughed and kept working.

Sometime after the show closed, Skully was donated to the Coney Island history project as a memento. Skully was one among many such mementos on display there in the mini-museum just off the boardwalk. It made me smile as I strolled.

♦　♦　♦　♦　♦　♦　♦

While walking down the boardwalk, I felt a shadow, or the feeling of someone following me. I did a quick dodge to see who dodged with me and saw them. The Latina water fem and one of her gang were not far behind.

Their cover being blown she approached and offered a hand which I shook.

"Gabriella,"

"Kenny."

"This is James." We shook.

"Kenny. What's up, no water I hope."

"Naw, but thanks for telling Alfonso off. There's no 'turf' on the walk."

Gab says, "Yeah, only on the beach, but they do it their way."

I ask, "You know what I don't like? On the beach, the vendors who use Mega phones. Now other people are using Bull horns to out-do the mega phones."

"Right? And the old men with the mega phone don't even walk, he just stand there making noise."

"Yeah, I don't buy from them either."

We pause, so I ask, "So what's up Ms Latina Lady?"

"Well, it's kind of personal, and I'm sorry to ask, but do you mind, would you mind, if I ask you about your scar?"

She was actually embarrassed. It amazes me to this day.

"Not at all. Which Scar?" I pulled my shirt back. "This new one is from open heart surgery."

"That is so amazing that you can talk about it like, Out loud and shit"

"It's just life, well in this case it was life or death, but still,-"

"Me Too! I got stabbed from behind."

James said, "She's got this scar and it freaks her out that it's too ugly to show."

"Oooh, I'm sorry. That musta hurt. So, how big is your scar?"

"Not too big in the back. But the knife cut through a lot of stuff they had to repair from the front so, they did it and it left a huge scar down the middle."

"Like, what was cut? What did they have to repair?"

"My liver, stomach, kidney, intestines; I was stabbed several times ."

"And why aren't you dead?"

"Friends. They got me in time."

"So, you lived. Right? You're here, so you lived right? That's the good part."

James agreed, "Right, she lived."

"Well," I spread my hands, "That's Life. You lived. How long now?"

"About eight weeks." We are all silently digesting.

"Well, shit,... ... .what can I tell you. I can tell you that the skin color will never match again. I can't get my scar tissue to tan the same. But –"

She shifted uncomfortably. "But, what?"

"I can only tell you that healing Is easy. It's watching your friends change that hurts. Having people turn away because you've been damaged."

"Yeah?"

"Yeah, cost me a girlfriend once, too bad, sweet girl, except for that."

She agreed, "Wow, yeah, some people can't look at it can they?"

"No, some can't bear to look. But you will always have a story to tell. Every scar has a story."

"Really?"

"Each and every one."

"How many scars do you have?"

I have to smile, "Several more now, fresh from the Operating Room."

"But, how do you take it? I mean, I feel people looking at me."

"To tell the truth? I don't have time or room in my life for what other people think about some things. Like a scar? Hell, I got so many scars I can't be bothered." I stepped back and spread my arms.

"I've been shot," turning my ass, "I've been sliced open with a straight razor." I raise one pant leg, "I've been hit with a car, I've been knocked unconscious, stabbed, had three bloody fights, two of which I won,"

Raising my left hand, "And I managed to live through a friend helping me remove and finger and a half off this hand. And I lived and managed -.",

During this explanation, I strip off my shirt and the kids get a look at the two knives I have stuck down the belt line of my pants. I put them there for convenience without a thought of what may or may not be legal.

"And I managed to heal. Each and every time, I lived and healed. But, I've never made time for what others might think."

"YES!, that is So what I needed to hear. My thanks to you."

"And you are embarrassed yeah? Is it big? Can I see you scar?"

She looks at James and he nods no, "Sorry, James doesn't like me showing."

I grimaced, "Well, then honey, I'm sorry to say it, but if he can't get over that, you could do better than him," I turned to James,

"Sorry dude. Just keeping it simple." He barely smiles back.

"No, no he's great, he just, it's just that out in public, he's-"

"Baby, you are who you are. Cain't be no one else. Why even try?"

And with that bit of preaching I turned and walked away. I walked slowly down the ramp and onto Stillwell Avenue.

Gabriella came running down the ramp yelling "Hey, uh, don't go."

I turned to her and as she pulled up short she raised her shirt to show her fat scarred tummy.

"James is wrong, I'm not ashamed, but listen, you wanted to see right?"

"Sure, I showed you mine."

"Well, I got to ask, would you pay to see mine?"

"No, would you pay to see mine?"

"No, you know what I mean, what I am, I mean professionally, right?"

"Not exactly following here."

"Do you think guys would pay to see me, me even with my scars?"

"Do you have more than the one you told me-?"

'I've had three cesareans, you know, from kids."

"You've really got three kids?

"Yeah, really."

"Well, you're gonna love this, wait til I tell ya."

'What?"

"They found out what causes that?"

"What causes what?"

"KIDS."

We all laughed but I cut it short.

"Ya got to use a condom. Wait, you're only like 25 right?"

"Yeah, 23, So what?"

"So nothin'. I cannot judge nor condemn what a young man may want to do with a beautiful young girl like you. Just be careful, and stop caring too much about what other people think."

"I'm glad I met you."

"I'm glad I was here for you to meet."

"Thanks."

"I am sometimes convinced, that I am here to help."

We smiled at one another, then turned and walked in different directions.

♦   ♦   ♦   ♦   ♦   ♦   ♦

As I stood in line at Nathans waiting for another lemonade, i thought about boarding the subway while armed with two clam knives. Luckily I thought of it before I was a victim. I decided to stop by the police booth on my way into the station and turn in a couple of possible weapons I found in the street.

Behind Nathan's a small group of small adults walked down the back street toward an unusual transport landing in the alley. The outer shell of the lower half opened as a ramp. The passengers began to board. In the distance I saw Thomas the arcade mechanic running toward us.

I yelled, "Hey Wait." to the leader of the expedition. The entity looked up and motioned for Thomas to hurry. When Thomas arrived they embraced one another. Thomas looked at me, smiled, and gave me a thumbs up. I returned the same as the ramp withdrew and the transport began to ascend. I could only smile as I walked toward the train terminal thinking of Thomas's ride home.

I unpacked my writing pad to use on the train platform. I wanted to put down an outline for the days' events. The lemonade cup was braced between my feet as I wrote. After two pages full of notes and some diluted lemonade I was able to board the D train for Manhattan. I three pointed the empty drink cup and wrote my way home.

New York City day trips can be such fun.

end

Crocker's

pilot

written by

T K Wallace

Pilot Cast

Maybelle, or 'Ma' Crocker

Jacob, or 'Paw Paw' Crocker

Percy Crocker, Ma & Pa's adopted son

Aunt Sister Crocker, Maybelle's next oldest Sister

Uncle Mister Crocker, Sister's husband

Pepper Crocker, Mister and Sister's daughter

Aunt Baby Crocker, Maybelle's thirds oldest sister

Uncle Junior Crocker, Baby's Lover

Salty Crocker, Baby and Junior's son

Them Others, Delmer Barfer, Cosmo and Gizmo Barfer

Tall Agent, Gordon

Short Agent, Rick

Elmo Jackson, 'hood 'shiner

Author's Note:

Welcome

Crocker's guest house, restaurant, bar, gift and bait shop is situated along a state road in Carolina. Their property bridges the border from north to south, but to the Crockers, it's all Carolina.

Come on down and have a taste of low country livin'.

Scene 1

This morning, Mister Crocker is playing a guitar and Junior Crocker is playing a banjo. They are sittin' and pickin' workin' their way through ol' John Hatrford's, 'Bear Creek Hop'. An official looking black car, pulls up, stops, and two suits emerge. The music fades as they enter.

Maybelle, or 'Ma Crocker', is wiping the counter as two customers, hopefully, cash customers, enter. The taller one says,

"Hello, top of the morning to ya."

Ma doesn't really look up, just a glance,

"Well, you top it off with some business and it'll be a damn fine morning. What can I do for you?"

The tall one says, "We're looking for Crocker's. Is this it?"

Ma answers by waving a fly swatter at a fly and asks,

"Can you read ?"

The taller answers, "Read?"

Maybelle studies him as if seeing him for the first time, and ignores the other guy altogether.

"Yeah, Read, R.E.A.D., as in, 'read the sign over the front door?"

"Well, yes Mam, I can, "

He withstands the stare from Ma Crocker and quickly exits, pauses, and then returns. Ma is polishing the cash register as the agent begins again,

"I see by the sign that this is Crocker's."

She stops and stares again.

"Uh huh."

"I'll take that for a Yes. We are looking for Mr. Jacob Crocker, is he here?"

"Nope."

The shorter one interjects, "Well, that's too bad, we were hoping we would find him here."

"Why's that?" Ma places a shot gun on the bar.

The tall suit lifts a brief case onto the counter and starts to open it. Ma stops him by placing the barrel on the case top.

"What you got in there sonny ?"

"Why, this? This is a brief case."

"Oh, yeah ? You keep your briefs in there?"

The shorter agent snorts and receives a look from his partner, so he says,

"None of your lip lady. You got a license for that firearm?"

"Yep, you got one for being ugly?"

"Say what?"

"Well, I could change guns and still have a license, you and ugly got no such choice. It's hard to get away from a face like that."

The tall agent says, "We are looking for Jacob Crocker in accordance with an incident which occurred in the Wacamaw state park on May 30th of last year."

"A State Park, huh, that sounds official. What kind of an incident ?"

The shorter one answers, "It says on this warrant, he is wanted for not appearing in court on the date and at the time he was ordered to do so."

"Well, interesting and important as that may be, why was he 'sposed to be in court?"

"The warrant reads, Improper Hand Gesture."

"Which one?"

The tall agent asks, "I'm sorry ?"

Shorty sees his chance, "Which word don't you understand ?"

Ma turns toward the taller, "Did you hear something ?"

The taller one asks, "Like what ?"

"Like some annoying little noise, sounded like it come from far way ."

"Would you be referring to my partner?"

Ma leans over the counter top, "Well looky here, Was that you ?"

"Mam, if you tease him, he'll just get worse."

"It'd be a short tantrum though wouldn't it?" They both snort as Shorty bristles,

"Look here you old B-" Shorty stops as he looks down a shotgun barrel.

The tall suit shakes his head and quickly exits the front door.

Ma says, "So, an improper hand gesture." She withdraws the gun and points her index finger at the agent. "Like this ?"

Shorty speaks, "You better believe it." He opens the case. "We also have bench warrants of suspected aliases for him which extend over several years."

"You have not!"

"Yes we do!"

Ma Crocker rebuts, "No, you do not."

"We do so!"

"Lemmee see 'em." She lays down the shotgun, holds out her hand and receives a sheaf of papers from Shorty. Ma Crocker wanders as she reads.

"Hmmm,"

She walks about and shifts through the papers, then she asks, "I'm gonna get a cup of coffee, you want one?"

"No Mam. Please produce Mr. Crocker."

"All in good time boy, all in good time. That other fella, he want a cuppa?"

"I hope he went to get a gun, seeing as you drew one on me."

"Ha. Sorry about that, " She picks up the shotgun "I'll be right back." She goes through a door as the tall one enters armed with weapons in both hands.

Shorty says, "You won't need those. I've got her under control."

"You do huh?" He holsters his service revolver, but keeps the other one handy.

Maybelle comes out of the kitchen with a cup of coffee reading a paper

"It says here, there's a good sale at the Gator Hole shoppin' center."

The taller of the two asks, "Which store ?"

Shorty asks, "Where are the warrants I gave you ?"

Maybelle answers, "What warrants ? I went into the kitchen to get coffee, I asked you if you wanted any, and you said No."

"You gave her the warrants for Jacob Crocker?"

Shorty tries for confidential, "She wanted to read them."

"And you just gave them to her?"

Ma protests, "He didn't give me nothin' I never seen no warrants."

"Mam, the reason we came here today was to find Jacob Crocker who did not appear for his court date this past week. I showed you the paperwork when we arrived."

"Maybe, you never allowed me to read anything, or let me hold anything to read. So I don't know what you had, do I?"

The three of them stand and look at one another until Ma asks,

"You sure you don't want any coffee before you go ?"

Shorty asks, "But I, she asked me, -"

"Come on, you've done enough damage for today. Mam? We'll be back with the proper paperwork soon enough. Tell Jacob not to go anywhere."

As they leave, they are being watched from a tree stand. The watcher remains until the car is out of sight, and then climbs down.

The instrumental version of 'Will The Circle Be Unbroken' covers the scene change and the open of the next scene.

Scene 2

Two country folk are out in the woods walking slowly with guns cocked in readiness. The older woman's eyes sweep right to left, the younger woman's eyes sweep from the tree tops to the ground. The elder stops, and holds up a hand to stop the other.

"Shhhh," The younger stops and looks where the elder is looking. She squints and waits sharpening her focus into some bushes and trees.

Sister, the elder, sniffs the air wrinkles her nose and asks, "You smell that ?"

The bushes part to reveal a man holding an old double barrel on them. He declares,

"Ya'll ought to know better, sneakin' up on a man while he's working."

The younger says, "Sounded more like snoring. We could hear ye' from out by the road."

"Out by – you couldn't hear me that far, could ya Sister?"

Sister goes to him, hugs him, and says,

"Nobody but us coulda' told, right Pepper ?"

"I thought it was a chain saw," seeing she has said the wrong thing, "But from a long way off, uh, maybe even further."

"Uh huh. You funnin' me girl?"

"No sir Paw Paw. Your snoring sounded way far away, didn't it Sister ?"

Sister can only frown and shake her head, "I swear, children have got more careless than we ever were. Pepper, he was working, but he was resting too."

Paw Paw says, "Ain't much else to do while you're waiting. Come on back."

He leads them through some woods into a clearing. There sits a magnificent still at least 6 feet tall with a large copper coil coming out of the top and being held in place over a large mason jar. The golden corn liquor drips out several drops at a time.

"Maybelle said to tell ya that some State suits came by this morning."

He smiles at her and pulls out a small tasting cup. He puts it under to collect a few drops and offers it up.

"Sister?"

She looks at the cup and then answers, "Nope, too early for me. I still got shit ta' do today."

Jake asks, "Where's Mister ? What's he up to ?"

"Yo brother is working on stuff back at the gift shop."

Pepper offers, "He's trying to get the 'lectronics goin'."

Jake is still holding the cup so he offers it to the younger.

"Pepper? You Pepper right ? Thought so. Do me a favor, taste this, no don't think about it, just taste and if it don't agree with ya, spit it out."

Pepper takes the cup and tastes. She twitches and spits,

"Yoww. That is nasty. I think it burnt my tongue."

"Hmmm, not ready yet, okay," looking at his pocket watch, "Let's go see what's cooking 'round here."

He walks the two toward a clearing. We see paw Paw Paw's location as a plume of smoke coming out of the trees. As they look out over the valley they see a few other plumes coming from the woods.

"So, Staties, huh?"

"Yep, they had warrants. You were supposed to go to court for that one said 'Improper Hand Gesture'."

"Haw. I 'memeber getting that one. Officious little bastard wanted to see my identification, so I said sure, got it right here."

He reaches into a front pocket and pulls out the finger, straight up.

"It was meant to be funny, but he didn't laugh. You believe it? That feller wrote me up."

Pepper says, "Hard to believe."

"I know, right? They's lots more offensive ways-"

Sister says, "I know, like, " She holds out three fingers vertically, " Scout's Honor !", or sideways like," Read between the lines."

Pepper holds up one long finger and says, "I always liked, Sit and Spin!"

Sister leans forward and pulls down her eye lid with her middle finger,

"Look into my Eye."

Paw Paw laughs and holds up three fingers, "Or even, The Great Speckled Bird."

"How do you do that? You half bend the fingers outside of the middle, hmmm, that's cool."

"It's a Southern thing. But, ain't nothing to get bent about." All three all laugh.

Sister asks, "Paw Paw, Why did you do that?"

"As I remember, it was about questioning his authority."

Sister says to Pepper, "Here comes a lesson, of what Not to Say, listen."

Sister continues, "In what way Paw Paw?"

"I believe I implied that his I.Q. rendered him unable to understand the situation."

The ladies wait while looking at him. He repeated himself, and waited for a response.

"Okay, I asked him, Are you Stupid or Somethin?" They all have a chuckle.

"Anyways, he demanded my ID."

"And we know how that turned out. Anyway you missed your court date."

"For the finger?"

"Maybe, Maw said there was more, but she kind of 'lost' the warrants."

"God Bless her big bottom. How'd she do that ?"

The three of them return to the camp. "Dunno, Pepper told me. Hon?"

"Well, she said she might have lost 'em over the stove in the kitchen, but she also said that she doubts she ever laid eyes on 'em."

"Good on her, and good for me."

Sister asks, "What you wanna do?"

"Me? Nothin', just wait. If I have to go in, I will."

"OK so we wait. Then what?"

"Whatever judge gets the case will probably laugh it out of court."

Pepper speaks, "Maw says they had other warrants outstanding."

"Could be, hard to prove 'less I confess. So, for now we wait. First we have some lunch, and then we sample that Shine again."

Both Sister and Pepper decline the experience.

Jake asks, "Who's mindin' the bait shop?"

"Baby and Salty boy."

Scene 3

The Live Bait shop is not crowded but it is busy. Proving her ability to multi-task, Ma's youngest sister, Baby, is on the phone and dipping minnows. Her nephew, Salty, is helping by holding the jar.

"No sir, we are not in Juniper Beach. We are in North Juniper Beach." She pauses and says to Salty,

"Bring it up here, Salty, hold it up here!", then to the phone,

"No, not you Sir, Yes Sir, North Juniper, okay, good."

"Aunt Baby, You want the little jars or the bigger ones?"

"Two tall ones and two short ones sweetheart, Not you, no sir. Well, good, we'll see ya soon. What? Where are we ? I just told ya, North Juniper beach. .okay, well, where you comin' from ?"

"You want two and two, or more than two?"

"Two each is fine for now. . . .okay . . .we're up 17 on the south end of north beach. We're on the left just past the Righteous Church. . . . . . that's okay, I'll go slow, We're on south end of North Juniper Beach, yes, Juniper, . . if you get up to north beach, you've gone too far, we're on the south side."

"You want me to dip 'em for ya ?"

"Sure honey, go ahead. . . Sir? Sir? Oh good, just look for the sign on the left what reads, 'Crocker's', it's the first one on the left just after the Righteous Assembly . . . . . that's fine, that's okay, good luck then, bye." She punches off the mobile.

Salty asks, "How full you want 'em ?"

"About halfway. Why do you think people have such a hard time with directions ?"

"Aunt Sister says some people are just 'natural' stupid."

"She ought to know,"

"Why, what's that mean, Natural' stupid?"

"Well, I guess it means, they have a talent for being stupid, it comes to 'em naturally."

We see and hear movement outside the front door. Salty looks at a face squashed against the glass of the window and says, "Like Them Others?"

Aunt Baby looks out front and says, "Oh Lord. Is the front door locked?"

"Yes Mam, You didn't say we were open yet."

"Good, then duck down."

The two of them do so as the first person at the door finds it locked. Two other people crowd to the window to look inside. Seeing no one, they move along to the next entrance.

Scene 4

Maybelle comes through and unlocks the door as she says,

"Baby, if you just wait on Them Others, they won't hang around asking for you."

She keeps moving as Baby says to Salty.

"Well shit Salty, set your cap for a bumpy ride, cause here we go."

The 'Live Bait' doors swing open for three brothers to enter.

The older says, "Hey Salty boy. Hey Baby, how you?"

"Hey Delmer, see ya got the younguns wit cha. Ya'll going fishing? Need some bait?"

"That we are, that we are, ain't we fellers ?" The others just nod.

Baby is relieved, "So what cha got in mind?", but none speaks.

Delmer blushes and says, "Grouper I guess."

"So you want blood worms or what. Salty baby, serve the man."

She walks away but notices the other brothers watching her.

"Can I help you two fellers with something else?"

They both grin hideously at Baby and then one another. Baby is alarmed.

A connecting door opens, as an effeminate man enters, Baby says,

"And here is 'Mr. Percival' to help you two."

She drags Percy into place in front of them. He frowns,

primps at the displacement, and then offers to help. The smiles of the other brothers fade fast as Baby exits saying,

"Thank you Spice boy,"

She checks on Delmer and Salty as he takes payment and gives change.

Delmer says, "Thankee Salty boy, Say Baby, ya wanna go fishin' wit us ?

"No thanks Delmer, I gotta work."

"Too bad. Uh, say, you hear that yer Pa was wanted?"

She frowns and then says, "Yep, for this and that over the years." She moves him aside,

"If this a new wanted situation, we should take it outside. I don't believe in discussin' the elders business in front of the young ones."

"Okay, jeez, I just heard was all. Hey you others! I'll be outside."

Delmer exits and Baby turns to Salty.

"Delmer prefer a jar over a bucket ?"

"Yes Mam, he brought in his own jar to use again."

"Oh Salty, you didn't re-fill-"

"Heck no Aunt Baby, not after last time. I'm still smartin'."

"Where's his old jar?"

"Rinsed and already dryin' in the sink."

She kisses him on the head, "Smart kids are the best reward. Listen, go help Percy with them other brothers will ya? I'm going out."

Baby exits through the lobby waving at Maybelle as she proceeds.

Scene 5

Delmer is waiting for Baby out by his truck He is parked beside the fruit and vegetable stand known as the Gift Shop. She walks over as he examines a squash.

"Thank you for taking that gossip about Jake outside."

"Sure, I know what you mean, my family does all that on the back porch."

"As it should be, now what's all this about Jacob?"

"Don't know much really, heard the Staties had a warrant for him."

Baby yells, "Maybelle! Can you come out here ?"

Delmer says, "Uh, I should be goin'."

"You ain't still afraid of her? After all this time?"

"Baby, you know I ain't afraid of much, but your older sister is one of 'em."

Maybelle comes out with a long handled wooden spoon.

"Is this one still bothering you? Lord Delmer, Ain't I taught you better?"

Delmer is intimidated, "Yes mam, No Mam. I mean, I-"

Baby interjects, "May, stop scaring him like that, Delmer has some news."

Ma Crocker waits, "Really, well Delmer, go ahead, let's hear it, spit it out."

Delmer is shaken, "Well, it's just that, we heard, they heard mind you, -"

Ma says, "Lord, the boy ain't got the common sense God gave a hop toad."

She whacks Delmer with the wooden spoon.

"Damn it Delmer, spit it out-" and she threatens him with the spoon again.

Delmer sputters, "Okay, don't hit me again, Pa Crocker has a warrant out with the Staties."

Maybelle, says, "Hell, boy, everybody knows that."

Baby asks, "We do?"

"Everybody does by now. Delmer, you best to keep Crocker business out of your mouth before you rile somebody."

Delmer is taken aback," I didn't, I wouldn't, sorry, I-" Ma Crocker whacks him again.

"Sorry is as Sorry does, young man. I thought I taught you better when I had you in grade school. You keep gossiping other people's bidness, somebody gonna to shoot you. And Delmer ?"

"Yes Mam?"

"You're looking at a woman who keeps a gun handy. You got me?"

"Yes Mam."

"Good. Now Git, and take those two cretins in the bait shop with you."

"Yes Mam." Delmer scurries toward the bait shop and yells,

"Cosmo, Gizmo, come on, you croûtons. Ma Crocker don' want the likes of you around."

"Hold up there, Salty, Percy, did them others pay for their order ?"

Them others, Cosmo and Gizmo, emerge from the shop each holding jars of bait. Salty follows them out the door carrying an old wooden box that had originally contained long neck beer bottles.

"Here now, Salty what else do they have there? You boys need to make a phone call?"

Baby says, "I got a mobile right here."

Gizmo starts to speak, but he begins to stammer and is replaced by his brother Cosmo,

"Ms Crocker, we axed Salty boy if'n we could, could,-"

Gizmo speaks, "–If'n we could borree a telephone set-"

"–we goin' fo some cat fish-"

"–an they won't take yer bait-"

Aunt Baby asks, "Salty, did you rent them that poachin' rig?"

Salty hands the rig to Delmer who puts it in the back of the truck.

"Nope, Ma says we don't have one, so how could I rent it?"

Ma Crocker weighs in, "Smart children are such a blessing."

Baby chimes in, "De Ja Vu. Didn't I just say that?"

Ma continues, "You boys remember the penalty for telling anyone where you got that poaching rig?"

"Yes mam, nothing on credit, Forever."

Ma confirms, " Tha's right, cause how can I do bidness from behind bars ?"

Gizmo stammers, "–that ain't never-"

Cosmo finishes, "–never stopped ya befoe' now."

Delmer punches him, "No Mam, uh, Yes Mam, come on boys, let's go fishing. Don't' worry, we'll be back with the rig and stuff."

Baby, Maybelle, and Salty watch them load in and drive off.

Scene 6

A roadside billboard has a fish and game warden pointing a finger.

"NO POACHING ! This means YOU !"

The inside of the truck shows the three of them laughing. As they pass we see a hand out each window and the top brandishing the finger.

We see the three of them in the boat. They take a short piece of pipe from each side of the crank set and drop the pipes over the side. Delmer takes the set from the box and cranks the handle. The water around them lights up briefly and fish begin to float to the surface. The fish are collected by dip net into the boat.

Scene 7

Our point of view pans up away from the river and into a birds eye view of the same woods with plumes of smoke coming up here and there. One plume is putting out extra smoke, and then with a small explosion, a fire erupts.

Vocal alarms and the help from surrounding camps keep the blaze in control. The burning area is mostly around one camp of blackened, wet, and weary moonshiners turned fire fighters.

Scene 8

Jacob, Sister, and Lady ride up in Sister's rig. They are all covered with soot and scratches with minor blood showing. They get out and trudge up to Junior. Jake says,

"Lend a hand here little brother," handing Jr two stone jugs

"Well look at you. Ya'll been out fighting fires or causing one?"

Pepper speaks as she passes inside, "Helpin' prevent one, thankee'."

A fire truck siren is heard at a short distance.

Pa says, "They won't find nothing left of Jackson's still 'cept a few burned up trees and some scrub. We got the rest."

Ma asks, "What happened?"

"Not sure, Elmo was too busy throwing water and cussing when we got there to help."

Sister says, "I think he was feeding them brown bears sour-mash again."

Ma says, "You'd think he'd learn by now. They 'most destroyed the place last time."

Pepper says, "Oh, he out did that this time,"

Junior asks, "What did you do with the still and works?"

"We put it in his truck. He said he'd be right behind us."

Pepper complains, "I think I burned my hands a little." She holds them up to show.

Sister says, "Jackson lost some of his beard. I threw a rag over his face."

Pa cocks his head and says, "There's a truck comin' Sister, you and Pepper get inside and wash up, I'll be 'round by the pump."

The all depart in different directions.

Scene 9

Maybelle and Mister are arranging fruit and vegetables at the gift shop stand. The racks and tables have a lot of tomatoes and corn but are otherwise sparsely filled. The two suits have returned and peruse with amusement. The short one says,

"As gift shops go, this is unusual. " He puts a squash in an arm basket.

The tall one is looking at a fishing rod when Sister enters wiping her face.

"They don't get no finer." she says

"Good for Blue Gill?"

"Sunfish, Blue Gill, Perch, 'most anything up to about 10 pounds,"

"10 ?"

"It's a lightweight rod, yeh, 7, 8, pound easy, 'bout a good sized Catfish, or there about."

Short stuff says, "Catfish? I Love Catfish."

Sister looks and says, "Figures. They bottom feeders too." Maybelle enters and says,

"Well lookee here, 'back from the past and better than ever.' Whachoo boys doin? Shoppin' or shop liftin'?"

"Ms Crocker, this shop is new isn't it? I mean the gift shop?"

"Well, technically it's not a shop, just a roadside stand. Mister's idea. His idea so his to run."

The taller one asks Ma, "And Mister is Sister's husband ?"

The shorter asks, "Do you consider produce to be gifts?"

Mister nods enthusiastically and Maybelle says,

"Looks like he does. He don't talk much, do you Mister?

She ruffles his hair as she passes and talks, "Like I said, His idea, his to run as he wishes. All he has to do is make money."

Sister adds, "He stocks what he wants, sells what he wants."

A car honks at the drive thru window and Mister attends. He has the purchase at the window and passes it through. He takes money and enters the sale on a pad. Maybelle looks at a screen on the counter and says,

"Came through okay, I guess you're up and running Mister."

They both give a thumbs up. Maybelle addresses the suits,

"He sells a lot of tomatoes and corn. He also takes in trade produce. It helps if people pre-order on the net. He can have 'em ready to go."

Mister fills another brown bag with tomatoes and weighs it.

The short agent says, " They look good, how much a pound?"

"Depends on whether I like your looks. For you, its more"

"You shouldn't talk that way to a paying customer Ms Crocker. I could be here shopping."

"The last time you was here you tried to arrest my husband, just how do you think I should treat you?"

The tall agent joins in, "And we'll be back for that pleasure when the warrants arrive. For now, we just want to ask a couple of questions, okay?"

"Yer time, shoot."

"Do you know Mr-"

Before he can finish she answers, "Nope."

Short agent responds, "You didn't let him finish who he was asking about."

Ma says, "Oh really? I'm sorry please go ahead."

This time Shorty asks, "Do you know-"

"Nope." Shorty turns to Sister,

"Do you-"

"No, sorry, No."

The tall agent takes out a picture and asks,

"Can either of you identify this man ?"

Ma and Sister look at the photo and compare comments,

Ma says, "Looks sorta familiar. "

Sister says, "Not bad looking for a geezer."

"Bet he's hung like a horse."

"Looks like Uncle Bud."

"Bud's ears are bigger."

"Yeah, and this nose has been broken, this way." She pushes her nose left.

"Uncle Bud's goes off to the right."

Both look up and say, "Nope."

The agent says, "Okay then, this happens to be the last known photograph of Elmo Jackson, local moonshiner and your neighbor for quite a few years."

Sister says, "Oh yeah, Is that what ol' Elmo looks like these days? Lemee see that again."

Ma Crocker says, "Oh No, this looks more like Elmo's cousin."

"We suspect Mr. Jackson caused a brush fire and we would like to ask him some questions. Have either of you-"

In unison they say, "Nope."

Scene 10

Another car approaches the drive through. Mister looks out and reaches to a screen on the counter. He reads and begins to fill a small box with tomatoes and a couple of small brown bags.

Shorty is not a satisfied customer. He says to Ma Crocker,

"I would love to buy some of these tomatoes if you would give me a price."

Maybelle looks him over and says, "For you, $50.00 a pound."

Sister breaks the tension, "Maybelle, that's no way to treat my husband's paying customers. You there, what's your name anyway?"

The shorter agent answers, "Rick."

Maybelle snorts, "That would be short for Richard."

"Ricardo, Miss smarty pants. What's Maybelle short for,"

The tall agent shakes his as he says, "I told her not to tease him."

Sister says, "She's the oldest, she cain't hep it. What's yer name ?"

"Gordon, nice to meet ya." They shake hands,

"You're Maybelle's Sister?"

"Yep, 'cept that my name too, Sister."

"That's fun." He shows the picture, "So have you-"

"Nope."

"I'll just leave this with you." He places the photo and says,

"The other, uh, the other adult female is named Baby?"

Sister says, "Yep, so far so good."

"And Jacob and his brothers are all Crockers?"

"Yep. 'cept that me and Maybelle married Crocker men."

"So you're all Crockers ?"

"This part of Carolina you'd better be a Crocker."

"How about Ms Baby? Is she a Crocker too?"

"Probably, soon. Junior Crocker has been after her a while."

"And the kids ?"

"Yes there are kids, you've seen 'em. Oh, and, listen to that. Ding Ding Ding. That sound is the end of me answering any more questions about my family."

"But I was only-"

"Nope."

"okay, gotcha, just one more-"

"Nope."

"Is Ms. Baby-"

"Nope."

"Married ?"

"What ?"

Gordon repeats, "Married, is she married?"

"Why ?"

"Well, because I'm interested."

"You're crazy."

"Maybe, ya see-"

"Nope." Sister walks toward Maybelle who speaks,

"You're city, not country. We don't belong in your world, Mr. Gordon, and you don't belong in ours. So why don't you take Ricky boy here, and blow on down the road"

Another car drives through to pick up from Mister. He passes them a bag and collects some vegetables. He enters the vegetable payment on his pad and places them on the gift stand.

Maybelle looks and exclaims,

"Oohh Mister, we got some carrots for tonight. We get any fruit yet ?" Mister holds up a pineapple.

Jacob and Junior enter from guest house. They each carry a case of bottles, they stop, look, and quickly make their exit.

They duck out just ahead of Cosmo and Gizmo coming in with the poaching box.

Cosmo and Gizmo speak alternately,

"-hey, there ain't nobody minding the bait shop-"

"-so we figured we would drop this rig here-"

"–yer fish are in here too-"

"-can we drop it here-"

"-that ok wit'chall?"

Jake and Junior re-enter disguised with fake beards and glasses.

"Delivery !"

They dispose of their cases on the fruit rack, and are making a close inspection of the pineapple. Agent Gordon is distracted by them others.

"Thanks," Jake and Jr exit taking them others and the poaching rig to the bait shop.

Gordon says to Maybelle, "Good thing we're not Fish and Wildlife."

Maybelle says, "We try to be good neighbors. Sometimes we even succeed."

Rick arrives bearing a sack, "I got a couple dollars worth. You want-"

"Nope." says Gordon and they leave.

Scene 11

Maybelle is waving the agents goodbye when Jake and Junior return. The fake beards and mustaches are falling to pieces. Maybelle turns to see them, snorts, and says,

"And who would two fellers be?"

Jake says, "Just delivery boys Mam, Where would you like your order?"

Junior picks up one of the cases and Mister walks over to take a bottle and bag it for an order he is filling. Maybelle roughs his hair as he passes,

"I think you can put it down over there, close where Mister can get to it."

Jacob looks after the agents, "They never knew we were here."

Sister returns with a box of fish, "Them Others were busy today. They gave us about a dozen good fish."

Baby enters holding a bunch of turnips by the greens.

"This country boy just paid me for bait in turnips. Are we set for dinner?"

Maybelle speaks loudly, "We just got just got some turnips in trade."

Sister speaks, "Anybody not busy could start dinner. . . ."

They all look at Junior who puts down his case, takes up the greens, the carrots, and the fish. He hands back half of the turnips and says,

"May as well put 'em on now, Throw th' 'xtras on the stand Baby, Mister will sell 'em."

Sister says, "We'll move 'em soon enough."

Baby responds, "Should be good, that boy can cook up a storm."

Maybelle says, "That tall agent, Gordon, he was asking about ya'."

"Asking what about me, pray tell ."

"Yer marital status, if I got the point straight."

Baby says in code. "N.A.C.I.H."

Maybelle asks, "And that means ?"

"Not A Chance In Hell."

Jacob says, "That's our girl."

Jacob uncorks a bottle and toasts, "Know Thyself." and takes a slash. He passes the bottle to Baby who toasts, "To the Devil we Know." and drinks.

Maybelle corks the bottle and pockets it. The main door slams open and we see Elmo Jackson wearing half a red beard. The other side of his face is dark and sooty. He is wild eyed.

"Was they the Staties? What did they say? Am I in trouble ?"

Maybelle holds up a picture. Elmo squeals, "EEEeeeee ! Hey that's me."

Ma says, "You with a nice groomed beard. Not like that brush fire you got going."

Jacob asks, "Where'd you get photographed looking like this Elmo ?"

"Seems like it was the 'Pioneer Days' reenactment. I played a settler who provided refreshments."

Sister says, "Imagine that."

"I guess I should shave. But first, Jake, I need yer help."

Jake responds, "Sho El-mo, What can I do fo' yo."

"I got about five gallons of shine that needs to be bottled, 'cept my operation is kind of on hold, could you-"

Maybelle smiles quietly at Jake as he says,

"Yep, let us take this out back, see what we can work out."

Scene 10

Baby is leaning over the counter of the Bait shop doing her daily receipts. Salty boy opens the door ringing a bell and announces,

"Paw Paw says come on now, or you get what the littlest pig got."

Baby is not about to miss, "You done called me twice." She gathers her papers and follows.

The Dinner Bell is filled with family who all serve themselves from a buffet filled with country blessings. Two tables are set, a larger one for adults and a smaller one for kids. As folks arrive they take a plate and serve themselves.

Maybelle and Jacob are sitting center with Sister and Mister to the left. Baby and Junior sit to their left. Pepper, Salty, and Spice boy Percy have their own table.

Maybelle stands to toast, "Turnips and carrots, catfish, cornbread, and watermelon all came to us through fair trade today. Eat to feed your sense of humor. Enjoy life."

"Here, Here, Enjoy life! ", they all toast. Jake speaks,

"I've always liked that toast. Not my favorite, but I've always liked it."

Junior says, "What's yer favorite then Padre ?"

Jake stands, "To Ourselves!" they all hoist, "To Ourselves!" and drink.

Maybelle says, "Junior, our genius cook, provides again." She toasts, "Junior, I thank you."

Junior nods and says, "Thanks, I'll cook for ya'll, just to be around Baby,"

Baby says, "He's smarter than I thought."

Jacob says, "Let's have an accounting, eh? Ladies first. Maybelle?"

"Nothing special, only two residents. They all paid up. Them Staties was here twice. We sold 'em some tomatoes for too much money"

Jake interrupts, "You made more than most. I hear'd you made several warrants disappear."

"Not entirely, I think they made it to the cookie safe."

"Good. Percy go get them papers she saved. Baby, how'd you do?"

"Right on schedule Jake. A little over a hundred."

"Sister? How's the gift shop business?"

"The online orders are still growing, we had ten today. They're almost all doin' drive through pick ups. Mister took in a little over three hundred a good bit of produce and some baked goods. Which was to be a surprise-"

"Surprise!" Junior emerges with a pie bearing candles.

Baby shouts, "Whose got a birthday ?"

Pepper and Salty both stand holding up their hands.

"Blow 'em out for your wish to come true."

The kids blow and they all applaud the ritual. Percy returns with papers.

Jacob speaks again, "I got a fire sale deal on Elmo's finest. Gave him a hundred dollars for five gallons of shine. We'll make it back in the first gallon."

Baby says, "I've been thinking of puttin' a drive through at the bait shop. That way we'd have one on both ends. Like a drive through circle."

Maybelle, says, "There you go, ya'll makin' me proud again. Were you thinkin' of pre-orders?"

"That's good to start with," says Salty and everyone looks at him. "I mean we could offer an on line menu and then add bait to it."

Ma is intrigued, "What would you sell on line?"

Percy says, "Picnic stuff, like for going fishing, burritos, cold fried chicken, drinks, ya know hand food for being on a boat."

Jake says, "When I was running a bait shop we talked them into about half of what they bought."

Pepper says, "I'm thinkin' we could be doing better."

Buster asks, "What's better than fishin' and a good picnic lunch ?"

Pepper says, "I was thinking beer and ammunition. They drink the beer and use the cans for targets."

Sister says, "That's my girl, Beer, Bait, and Ammo at a drive through window."

Jake says, "Make it so. Now, I need a laugh, let's see them warrants."

Maybelle holds up a glass for another toast, "To the family."

We see the wide shot of everyone raising a glass. The kids laugh as they pass the warrants and photos for all to see.

(end of pilot)

2

Earth Tales

Christmas Music to My Ears

Let's Blow Some Shit Up

Free Lance Writer

Fred The Cop

Christmas Music to My Ears

written by

T K Wallace

Silver Bells
lyrics written by
Jay Livingston and Ray Evans
(to be sung softly)

City sidewalks, busy sidewalks,

Today I did something I have never done before. I worked at a Christmas tree stand on the corner of 181st and Ft Washington. The stand rests against a long church fence and just beside a bus stop. The snowfall lasted all day and I had a great time. It was my honor to serve the neighborhood.

Years ago, shortly after moving into my apartment on Colonel Magaw place, I met the Stone family from Vermont. They were part of an evergreen syndicate which operated a dozen Christmas tree stands in New York City and more in other northeastern cities. I was interested to learn how they made the majority of their annual income in five weeks. The local office of the enterprise was a quick shack which could take two people if they got rid of the heater.

About 5 years ago the elder family members retired from selling on the street and began to send younger single couples to do the 24/7 occupation, and all sales. Being a garrulous Midwesterner I speak to my neighbors and local friends every day. So I made friends with the Stone family employees. When colder weather sets in I usually brought them hot coffee. Or I would make a chicken stew to warm them and help them feel welcome in NYC during their short stay.

Children laughing, People passing,

This year a new couple arrived for their first foray in the big city. Todd and Eyelan were dropped in the hood for the duration. I treated them as I did previous others. We became fast friends and I speak with them every other day or so while going and coming from my normal routine. I work in show business as a freelance Director, Production Manager, and Technical Director for live events.

I also write. I write about anything that amuses and engages me enough to find worth recording. I've written news, columns, reviews, gift cards, and even menus. I wrote a few one act plays for class work and grades. Today I write short stories, poetry, song lyrics, and even a cable series or two. I am professionally published, and I have hopes for more.

Silver bells, Silver bells.

Todd and Eyelan are good hard working northern Vermont people. Todd's background is organic farming. He is a muscular 5 foot 9 inch alpha male with a bushy red beard. He has a good sense of humor and he appears to be in love with Eyelan.

Eyelan is built like a willow with long flexible strong limbs. She is quite beautiful and genuinely likes people. Her smile illuminates her face. Her curious nature has led her to try many things. And her eyes twinkle when she teases Todd.

They seem to be good for one another and certainly work well together. They are planning a trip to Peru after the tree selling season is over. The unknown fascinates them and feeds their desire to shape their own future.

Spending the entire day with them was a result of being asked to help. That Saturday was to be very busy and they anticipated needing someone to process the trees for the customers after purchase. The trees need to be freshly cut and watered in order to stay fresh for a few weeks. They also need to be prepared in some way for New Yorkers to get them to their address and into their apartments.

It's Christmas time in the city

The tree stand has a device known as a Bailer. We feed the tree through a metal cylinder which surrounds it with a plastic mesh net. It also holds the tree while the bottom of the tree trunk is cut to take in more water, and to fit into a tree stand. I was asked to bail and cut as Todd and Eyelan sold. Their enthusiasm made it fun for me.

But, as in much of anything, we make things fun because we want fun to happen. People out to buy a Christmas Tree in the city are usually in a good mood. They come in all types and usually come in groups. Families are the most common and the children are filled with excitement. Their home will be transformed for a few short weeks. Their normal apartment environment will accommodate a holiday tree. The fun of lighting, gilding, and decorating all add to the excitement of Christmas.

Hear the snow crunch, See the kids bunch,

Many children refer to the tree as, Mr. Tree, when they visit the stand. Most of them want to keep the trunk piece which has been cut off. Eyelan teaches them to tell the age of the tree by counting the rings. Todd usually has them smell the wood and get the sap on their fingers. I cut many tree trunks and trimmed a lot of branches.

Some people came as couples. From young to old they want to enjoy this custom together. Their love is naked upon them and a wonderful thing to feel as I observe. Roommates arrive in clumps. They usually share the cost while being most concerned about the size of the tree and how much space it will take. Some bring tape measures.

This is Santa's big scene

One couple bought three large trees. I became most curious for they spoke some Slavic language I could not understand. And they seemed to know more about the sizing and trimming trees than most New Yorkers.

We had many people stop and ask pricing, only to leave and return with a significant other for the purchase. A few people brought laundry carts to haul their tree. Most shouldered the tree in two, or three person style. And, because it was snowing, we had a few trees leave on children's snow sleds.

Our location is just beside a bus stop for the M4. The 181st st stop was close where the route terminates at Fort Tryon Park. This state park is the home of the Cloisters museum and has some good safe sledding. We had a few trees leave on the bus. One tree was bought by a bus driver and left with us until the last run of his shift. That tree rode with its own seat, wearing a seat belt.

I only saw one person come alone. She was an older Spanish lady who bought a medium sized tree. She had no way of carrying the tree, so Todd took it home for her.

In the air there's a feeling of Christmas

Some people bought tree stands. Some had stands already. Some had stands but they were buried so deep in a storage somewhere they bought another.

Some people bought wreaths, which Eyelan had woven, and some bought branches to make their own. Some people bought small living trees wishing to plant them after the holidays.

I didn't see much haggling over the prices as I usually enjoy. The art of the Hondle is a common street game in New York City. Striking a deal through bargaining gives us a measure of our fellow man or woman. Fun is where you find it, right? I do think I detected a few cases of abnormal pricing where the sales people wished to give a discount. Maybe that's how they haggle in Vermont.

In between sales we talked and got to know one another better. Mid day Todd bought a cheese pizza from George's Pizza shop. But, just as he returned we got really busy again. When it slowed down we ate together, and that pie tasted so good. Eyelan went for hot cocoa at one point and it was welcome.

It continued to snow all afternoon and around dusk the air became colder. One neighbor, Brian, arrived around then with a French press pot full of hot Costa Rican coffee. He claimed that he had ground the brown golden coffee beans only moments earlier. I began to appreciate some of what I had done for tree sellers over the years.

Part of the spirit of Christmas is generosity, whether you are buying or selling doesn't matter. As in most of life, It's participating that counts.

Soon it will be Christmas day

Let's Blow Some Shit Up

written by

T K Wallace

I once belonged to a club for exploding things. Actually, I was a founding member. Both were a natural out growth of being able to burn our own trash.

My family lived in the foothills of the Ozark mountains in 'Southern Missourah'. Our town, Belle, did not have a trash dump and didn't want one. We were allowed to burn our trash, as long we used a large steel barrel and kept a safe watch over the process. It also meant that the burning barrel be stationed a good distance from anything else. Ours was at the rear of the property line and well away from others.

This, 'safe watch over the process', meant just what it says. The burning barrel was set on concrete blocks placed in a circle around the perimeter not only to elevate it for air flow, but to also keep the flames above the grass line. As a normal precaution there was always a bucket of water close by.

So, part of my weekly chores was to haul the trash away from the house and torch it. This chore took some knowledge and intelligence of proper incineration. You could not have too much wet trash such as food leftovers. The burnable trash could not be all on one side, etc. etc.

Just as a proper fire within a home fireplace, or at a cookout, or any campsite, the burning items needed to be stacked or arranged in such a way that oxygen be allowed to feed the flame. This also requires some creativity while monitoring the safe duration of the chore.

Common sense also considered the weather patterns. Rainy days were out. And one never wanted too much wind either. We never wanted wind that blew toward the house, the barn, your neighbor's house or barn, or toward a propane tank.

Most of the homes in our community were fueled by a

large bulbous propane tank which was positioned closer to the house than the burning barrel. Propane fed our house furnaces in colder months and our stoves and ovens year round. The tanks were usually submarine shaped with a locked and covered fill port at the center of the top.

I never saw a propane tank blow but I was constantly aware of the possibility. Among we trash burning boys and girls, the speculation of this event was probably larger than life. Would it explode where it sat? Would it shoot away like rocket to hit some hapless object or person making both explode?

Because we grew up in a rural environment everyone knew of Dynamite used for extracting tree stumps and TNT used for blasting roadways. My first experience with dynamite came at the age of 8 when my father and some cousins created a swimming pool for the local golf club. Not that they let me anywhere near the explosives, but I was allowed to observe an expert.

We had all seen war movies where flame throwers were used on things and people. And of course, explosions of any kind were desirable special effects. Some of us knew these effects were manmade for the film industry, and could probably be fabricated in your own garage or workshop. The concept of 'creative destruction' was promoted especially around the 4th of July.

This mid summer holiday welcomed loud and flaming explosions. We had small time stuff for little kids. 'Crackers' were small impact balls that exploded, or 'cracked' as they were thrown against a hard surface. Smaller kids also had 'Sparklers'. These were a hardened flammable substance coated onto a thick wire. When ignited it sent out sparks as it burned. These were especially cool at night because you could draw or write with them in the air.

'Firecrackers' were the common medium and easiest to acquire. They came shaped like miniature sticks of dynamite with a fuse coming out of the top. They came in packs of ten, twenty, or fifty. Firecrackers also came in large rolls of hundreds. Wasteful idiots would unstring the roll and set fire to one end and watch as they blew up sending the string flying and often throwing lit fuses toward excited observers. This also resulted in unused firecrackers remaining after the rest of the string blew. When the excitement was over we would scavenge and collect these extras.

There were fire ball rockets to be hand held like roman candles. We had small sized rockets to be shot from bottles or tubes which simply flew away and exploded at the end of flight. And we had medium sized rockets which required a fixed tube to fire from. These would shoot up into the sky and then explode in fire balls and sometimes in patterns. Anything bigger was for adults.

There were other explosives that were supposedly off limits to kids, but since when does that prevent anything? Tiny Crackers made a small snapping explosion which would blow up a paper cup but not a milk carton. Medium sized firecrackers, 'Black Cats', were good for larger explosions and could destroy thin glass objects, but not thicker glass like soda bottles.

Larger yet were Cherry bombs, Silver salutes, and the dreaded M-80. Cherry bombs were about the size and shape of the fruit. They would crack a heavy glass bottle into large pieces. Silver salutes seemed to go out just before they exploded, these would shatter a soda bottle, or extend the sides of a paint can. M-80's would blow holes in tin cans and split common bricks and cinder blocks.

Fireworks are made from flash powder mixed with other combustible metals for loud visual entertainment. 'Blowing Stuff Up.' was a small power allowed into the hands of children. And, like any power from electricity to religion, properly supervised, fireworks were quite entertaining on special occasions worldwide. Improperly supervised, Fireworks could be incredibly destructive and even deadly.

We all heard of stupid people who played fast and loose with minor explosives. They had scorched their hands and blown off fingers. Or they had blown up cars, boats, and houses. We were not stupid and practiced great caution in our experiments. That was the word we used while rationalizing playing with explosives; Experimenting.

One such occasion resulted in burning up half the grass in my back yard. It was late August in a dry summer. I was burning trash which had a fair amount of leftover food which did not burn so well. So I added a small amount of gasoline to the fire barrel. The accelerant built the fire very nicely. I poked the burning trash with a fire stick and got it going even better.

Two kids I knew to be violence prone rode into the far end of our alley on bikes. Greg and Terry were wearing kerchief masks which told me they were up to no good. As they got closer they both raised a hand which held something I could not see but I knew had to be bad, so I moved out of the way. They rode by hard on both sides of the barrel, threw something small into the flames, and kept on riding.

The barrel exploded the contents upward throwing burning trash all over the dry yard. I grabbed the water bucket and ran toward the propane throwing water at the burning grass closest to the tank. I ran for the faucet beside the garage. There was a garden hose attached which I grabbed and ran back uncoiling it behind me.

When I approached the first patch of burning grass I pressed the tongue of the nozzle and only a trickle came out. I said some profanities to ease the burden of my soul and threw down the hose. At this point, my mother came out the back door and turned the hose water handle. I watched the hose stiffen with water, picked it up and sprayed down the rest of the yard putting out the fire closest to the barrel.

My Mother refilled the water bucket and gave the grass by the propane tank another dose. I was relieved to see that the grass fire had not come too close to the tank, but dismayed to see all the burned grass which had edged toward the house. I looked toward my mother, She looked at me and said,

"Good job, you saved most of the yard. But I'm pretty sure your Father will not be pleased."

I walked to the burning barrel which was still burning low inside. I started to spray out the fire in the barrel and saw something I didn't want to see. Lying on the ground beside the barrel was an M-80. The fuse was not lit but I soaked it with water anyway. One of those assholes had missed the barrel entirely. I picked it up and as I looked at it, my Mother approached and took it from me.

"You know you're not supposed to be playing with these."

"It's not mine. Didn't you see them? They rode by and threw them in."

"Who rode by?"

"You didn't see them?"

"See who? I heard the explosion…." She put the M80 in her pocket.

"It's not mine."

"What's not yours? I believe you. You would never be so foolish with fireworks. We taught you not to take chances, You never have, so I believe you."

"Thank God one of them missed. You didn't see them?"

"No, but you did. You know who did this?"

"Maybe, can't be sure, they were wearing masks."

She sighed and turned toward the house.

My Father was not as lenient. Between the belting I got from him, and the razor strapping I got from my Grandfather, I couldn't sit down for two days.

By the end of summer I had blown both Greg and Terry's trash barrels.

♦   ♦   ♦   ♦   ♦   ♦   ♦

When I was almost 13 my family moved to a suburb of St Louis. Pacific, Missouri, was in Franklin county, past the western edge of St Louis county and therefore considered to be a rural area, which meant we could burn our trash.

My parents bought a split level ranch house with a good amount of uphill land right on old US rt. 66. The hillside behind us was rocky climbing and had a couple caves. If you climbed all the way over the top you came out on a cliff overlooking Interstate 44.

Our house was situated halfway between the Junior High school I was to attend, and the High School my older sister, Lorain, was to attend. Our mother got a job as assistant to the principal at the junior high. This was bad, because every time I was sent to the office, I had to wait in front of my mother.

But, it was good too, because she knew my curriculum, she made sure I studied hard, and made sure I received excellent grades. Through my visits to the office, I learned that a precocious child with good grades could get away with far more than a precocious child with bad grades. Like one of my neighbors, Johnny Grace.

Johnny's father worked in the local railroad yards as a mechanic and carpenter further out west. His mother worked the production line at the Chrysler plant closer to the city. This meant that Johnny had a lot of unsupervised free time.

My other neighbors were the Price family. Father Ollie was a successful car salesman. Mother Jessie was the assistant post master of the town of Pacific. They had a girl, Ellen, some years older than me, and two boys, Frank and Scott. Frank was one year older and Scott was my age.

Because I had moved there from Belle, Frank and Scot considered me to be a country bumpkin. That was until they discovered my hoard of fireworks and my passion for minor explosives. They did most of their 'experimenting' in the caves up the hill where no one would see the smoke or hear their explosions. Frank, Scott, and I formed a club. We called ourselves 'The Mad Bombers', because, 'What the Hell?', it was 1966, and we were teenagers.

Frank and Scott's parents had a full two car garage which contained a small machine shop. The shop was well outfitted for home use. There was a work bench with a vise, a drill press, a wood lathe, and a device that could thread pipe. Their dad, Ollie, had also collected many hand tools.

Scott and Johnny Grace had access to derailing blasting

caps. Johnny's dad used them to blow used train cars off the tracks so the cars could be dismantled. The caps were compression explosives on a long sticky band. The rail yard workers stuck this band to the track and the rolled the car over the caps. The caps blew the car up and sideways clearing the tracks by ten feet.

We didn't know what we wanted to use them for, but we knew any use would be extremely dangerous. The first plan involved strapping one to an arrow head. The location was an important part of the plan. Our chosen place was a dry river bed about five miles from Pacific, there was a railroad bridge crossing the dry river bed. We rode our bikes with Johnny carrying the caps in a back pack, Scott with the bow and quiver slung . I rode with the two fishing poles for our cover story.

When we arrived we rode around a while to make sure that there was no one around before we parked our bikes. As Johnny lashed a cap to an arrowhead, we discussed which direction the arrow should fly. We didn't know how much damage the cap would cause, we only knew it was enough to blow an empty train car off the tracks.

First. the arrow and cap absolutely could not hit the bridge. Second we wanted to be able to see when it hit, to 'observe the experiment'. Third it had to hit a hard surface, with enough impact to blow the explosives. And lastly, we didn't want any witnesses.

As we talked a train rumbled across the bridge. Scott suggested that we fire the arrow up and over the bridge landing on the other side. Johnny thought the shot should be very high to increase the impact. I was the only one with bow hunting experience, so I was elected archer.

I inspected the cap attached to the arrow and decided that the shot would not fly straight, the weight of the cap would alter its course. So I moved further away from the bridge. There was a breeze coming under the bridge so I moved again to shoot into the wind and insure that the arrow flew diagonally across the bridge onto the river bedrock.

I took my stance, raised the bow upward, drew the string as far back as it would come, and released. The arrow flew beautifully upward in a high forward curve. We felt the breeze increase and watched as the arrows' flight straightened. As it reached the apex, the arrow was almost directly over the bridge. The angle of its descent alarmed us. Johnny gasped, " Holy Shit it's gonna hit the bridge."

Scott pointed and moaned, ' "No No No, it's coming for us". I saw the arrow pushed by the breeze. As it fell and it was curving toward us. Scott yelled, "**Under The Bridge**!" We ran and jumped over our bikes. Scot and I cleared and Johnny caught a pedal. We all went down as Scott and I ducked and covered.

The arrow hit very close to where we had been standing with a tremendous explosion. A fountain of dirt and many pieces of river rock flew outward in all directions, some of which bounced off the bottom of the bridge and back down on us. We were covered with a cloud of debris. But none of us were seriously hurt.

The hole caused by the explosion shaped a large jagged bowl. It was about two feet across, a foot deep, and almost exactly where we had been standing. The large cloud of dust drifted up and away from us.

Jimmy screamed, "Why did you shoot at us?"

"I didn't, the wind took it."

Scott said, "We should go."

And ride we did as fast as we could. Scott led us through back roads to a fishing camp beside the Merrimac River. We took off our clothes, rinsed them, and went wading to clean ourselves. There was a sandbar in the middle of the river where we spread our clothes to dry. We took up our fishing poles and assumed positions as innocents. A good thing too, for not long after we heard sirens in the distance. Johnny tossed the rest of the blasting rig in the river.

Much later in the day we arrived home with the knowledge that we had performed an incredibly dangerous act, and we had caught four catfish. We also arrived with the unspoken knowledge that we had been very lucky and we would probably never try a stunt like that again.

We were never questioned by an adult or suspected in any way. Frank and his friend Stanley knew what we had acquired, but had not been invited to join our fishing party and therefore knew nothing. All they knew was that we no longer had the explosives we had once possessed.

A small article concerning a mysterious explosion was published in the newspaper the following week. It was printed beside a public service request for removing the door of any refrigerator which had been junked.

♦   ♦   ♦   ♦   ♦   ♦   ♦

Frank and Stanley had been working on a 'Bazooka' to shoot tennis balls. This was a fairly large piece of iron plumbing pipe which was open on one end and had a cap on the other. There was a hole drilled through the top of the pipe close to the rear. This is where the fire cracker was dropped.

The first time we tried it Stanly held the pipe on his shoulder like a bazooka with no handle. A tennis ball had been pushed inside the front. Frank lit the fire cracker and dropped it in the hole. When it blew inside the pipe, the ball was pushed out the front and flew about five feet.

Limited success had been achieved but Stanley was not pleased at having an explosion resting on his shoulder so close to his ear. This first try was inside Bomber's Cave, so it was back to Ollie's shop. On the hike back Frank, Scott, and I discussed how get better results. Stanley only spoke of how to mount the pipe, so it was not held by anyone.

We built a cradle for the Bazooka Pipe as we now called it, to rest upon while firing. And we drilled a bigger hole to take at least three firecrackers. Then we had to haul both items back up the hill and into the cave before the second test.

Bomber's Cave was a sluice cut through rock by water at some point in the past. It was about fifty feet long and twenty feet wide. The ceiling dripped in places and varied in height. It topped out at about ten feet. The rear was damp and of course darker than the entrance. We took the cradle to the rear built up a level surface to rest it on.

The ball was front loaded. The three firecrackers were bound together with string and held over the loading hole before they were lit. As the fuses sparked, they were dropped into the hole. The bang was muffled by the pipe as it jumped on the cradle. The ball shot out but did not reach the cave's entrance, it landed a few feet inside.

The cave had a good bit of smoke and we had food for thought. As we started to leave, Frank picked up the pipe and then dropped it from the heat. We waited for the smoke to clear and the pipe to cool. We needed greater yield. Frank told us to 'wait' and ran down the hill.

When Frank ran back he was holding an aerosol can. Scott laughed as Frank tossed him a can of their sister's hair spray. Stanley and I bound another set of three firecrackers and Frank retrieved the ball. Scott remounted the pipe on the cradle. When we were all set, I blocked the firing hole with a finger while Scott filled the pipe with hair spray. Stanley pushed the ball inside the pipe as I uncovered the firecracker hole.

Scott held the firecrackers over the hole as Frank lit the fuses. When they were dropped into the hole, two things happened. First, a flame shot up out of the hole and secondly the pipe jumped as the ball was fired through the entrance of the cave. Smoke was everywhere so we fled.

The tennis ball was easy to find because it was still smoking from where the fuzzy part of the back side had been burned down to the rubber. We were all very pleased and began to discuss other possibilities.

We could not try it again because the ball no longer fit tightly in the hole and because we didn't want to have to buy Ellen more hair spray. We went about our chores and homework considering further improvements.

◆　◆　◆　◆　◆　◆　◆

The following weekend we all arrived at the cave with different additions. Frank brought the Bazooka Pipe and a section of rope to tie it to the cradle. Stanley brought three tennis balls and a can of Extra Hold hair spray. Scott brought a small bag which had a Cherry Bomb, a Silver Salute, and a couple of M 80s. I brought a twenty pack of Black Cats and a small tin of Gun Powder.

The first test was a replication of the initial hair spray test, with the same results, a cavern full of smoke, a hot pipe, and a burnt tennis ball.

The next test changed only two items. The firecrackers were replaced with a Silver Salute, and we added a new tennis ball that had been partially soaked in gasoline.

When the shit hit the fan we watched a flaming orb fly as far as we could see before the smoke in the cave took over. Luckily it landed across town in a quarry but some people saw the flight.

♦　♦　♦　♦　♦　♦　♦

Our final experiment involved three changes. The tennis ball had holes drilled in the back side where we tightly implanted firecrackers. This side was stuffed into the pipe toward the accelerant. We augmented the hair spray accelerant with half of my gun powder. Inside the Bazooka the Silver Salute had been up graded to an M80.

None of us wanted to be anywhere near this combination when it went off, so we discussed the best way to set it off by remote. Stanley was the only cigarette smoker among us, but it was Frank who had the idea. Stanley would start a cigarette and insert the fuse of the M80 near the middle. As the cigarette burned low enough it would ignite the fuse.

Time was not normal that afternoon. The time it took for that cigarette to burn down stretched into what felt like hours. Stanley wanted to go check on the set up but Frank stopped him. Seconds later we were glad.

A deafening roar came from the cave and the ball sizzled through the air in front of us. Smoke and some flame belched from the mouth of the cave as other explosions came from within.

We watched the ball fly away with fuses burning. It was high over Pacific when the firecrackers began to blow. It was multi-brilliant, the plan all worked. We had launched an exploding object. The tennis ball had been blown apart in mid air. Unfortunately, this attracted some attention.

We should have left immediately, but we wanted to see the inside of the cave. Scott and I had left the extra fireworks and gunpowder in the cave, along with an extra large can of hair spray. All of which caused the secondary explosions.

It took about a half an hour before the smoke cleared enough for us to go inside. We found a wreck where the Bazooka had rested. The pipe was split at the back and the cradle was still smoldering. The walls of the cave were blackened and the ceiling was cracked in many more places.

There was more water dripping through some of the ceiling cracks. We looked at one another and then ran for the entrance. We got out just as the ceiling collapsed behind us.

We walked down the hill covered in soot and dust, shaking our heads in wonder and barely able to talk. But we did smile a lot.

As we emerged from the tree line at the top of my father's property, we saw a police car and a fire truck waiting. A deputy and a couple of fireman were chatting and looking at us. The deputy motioned us forward, two of the firemen opened the truck and back door of the police car. We all went along quietly.

As we were all under 16, and therefore minors, we were

not charged with anything. We were asked many questions but we only admitted to use of common fireworks. Our parents were spoken to separately and we were allowed to leave in their custody.

Frank and Scott and I were not allowed to see each other outside of school for a month. This did us no harm. We had plenty of time to plan our next experiment.

The Mad Bombers all got A's in our science and chemistry classes when we replicated the formula for Nitroglycerine. Nitro was an unstable explosive substance. But, when mixed with diatomaceous earth it formed a gel which could be ignited with a blasting cap and was then rolled in multiple layers of wax paper which created an explosive known as Dynamite.

Under the supervision of our teachers, the only stick was exploded.

From then on we rolled our own sticks of Dynamite.

We had a private unspoken motto.

Let's Blow Some Shit Up.

Free Lance Writer

Scene One

written by

T K Wallace

Cast:

T K Wallace	Writer
Jasmine May	Agent
Loper	A homeless guy
Celia	Customer / Lover
Pee Wee Herman	Customer / Comedian
Charlie Cucci	Illustrator Colorist
Tito Perez	Hawker Salesman
Literate Man	Customer / Lawyer
Miriam Perez	Tito's Mama / Sales person

Scene One

A middle aged man sits beside the park writing on his lap top. He works from a park bench which he has adorned with several bound stories and scripts.

His attire suggests a preference for loose comfortable clothing. His ball cap reads, FLW. A sign stuck to the bench reads 'Tales for Sale'.

The documents around him are bound in clear fronted binders which display a title page. Titles such as A Dangerous Island, The Ladies of Gaisler Road, New York Stories #1 and #2 are within reach. A back pack containing more copies of each is under the bench.

He thinks as he writes and writes as he thinks. Occasionally he rises and walks around. He talks to himself and drinks some water. He watches people but mostly stares past them lost in thought long after they have left his field of vision.

A young lady wishes to disturb his train of thought.

Jazz

"Sir?"

TK

"Yep?"

Jazz

"Are these your works? Are you Mr. Wallace?"

TK

"The One and Only, I hope,"

Jazz

"You hope?"

TK

"Yep, I'm wearing his skin. If I'm not me, I don't know who I am."

Jazz

"Ah yes, well, uh, very good, ah funny." She pauses, picks up a copy and reads
"New York Stories # 1"

TK

"That's a good one. Three short stories. 'A Baseball Story', 'Guerilla Croquet', and 'Gambling On Me'. All New York stories."

Jazz

"How much are you asking?"

TK

"Just 15 dollars. And it comes with a $5.00 rebate."

Jazz

"A rebate on short stories?"

TK

"Sure, why not? If you enjoy reading them and want to read more, just give that copy back to me and I'll sell you the next story for only $10.00."

Jazz

"Well, Okay, What if I like it ?"

TK

"If that's the case, you'll probably want an autographed copy, for only $5.00 ."

Jazz

"So now that's $20.00. You want $5.00 for signing your work?"

TK

"Young Lady, Let me point out that you are buying an original printing of an un-proofed manuscript, prior to mass publication, signed by the author. If that's not worth $20.00, then you wouldn't know literary value if it sat on you."

She looks skeptical by lifting one eye brow but opens her bag and pulls out a money fold. She peels off three $5 dollar bills and hands them over.

TK

"Thankee miss. I hope you enjoy your reading time and my imagination."

She walks a little ways away and sits on another park bench, opens the cover and begins.

The author returns to his work. On the small lap top screen we see:

"Lance has been imprisoned for 35 years by his own lack of imagination and self confidence.

He has tried to escape many times only to find his efforts thwarted and dragged back to confinement.

Once he was out and about for almost six months. But one day he was seen and then seized.

His personal courage and a slowly developing sense of self worth have helped him stay afloat.

Today starts the rest of his story. The story of how a man can break the bonds that bind him."

He is known to other locals. He knows most by Name, or by a Nickname. A shambling man lopes along, stopping short and announces.

Loper

"Hey You Writer. I see you!"

TK

"Hey there Loper Man. I see You too."

The shambling man lopes along with a wave of thanks. Celia is standing behind and watching.

Celia

"He just wanted to be seen, that was nice of you."

TK

"Nice don't cost nothin'. If he can see me, I can see him."

Celia

"I have a thing for you."

TK

"Hallelujah, Celia I feel the same way too. I was just waiting on you-"

Celia

"Hold it right there Stud. We've bounced that ball before."
She pulls out a manuscript. He looks at it, and looks at her.

TK

"I like the metaphor. I thought we shot and scored."

Celia
"Tru Dat. About dis ting here,"
She pauses, and looks at the book and then holds it out to him,
"Sign It."
His breath comes back slowly and he takes the manuscript and opens the cover.

TK

"Got a pen?"
She hands him one and a five dollar bill. He ball caps the bill and signs the title page.
As he hands the book back she hands him another twenty.

Celia

"I'd like a copy of # 2, signed if you please."

He whoops as he caps the bill and does a little dance. He extracts the backpack to get a copy of New York Stories # 2. He signs it and bows as it is given. Celia bows in acceptance and pockets the book.

Celia

"Give me a ring if you want to drop by, TK, " and she departs.

The author smiles and waves and then gazes on in a thought or a memory that takes a few seconds to wear out. Then he returns to his bench, picks up the cap and extracts the bills. The cap goes on his head and the money goes in the pocket.

A thin young man wearing a gray suit, white shirt, and a red bowtie appears.

Pee Wee

"Mr Author man? What's new from you ?"

TK

"Don't know Mr Herman. Which was your latest one ?"

PW

"The Ladies of Gaisler Road"

TK

"Ah, that one. You want more sex or less?"

PW

"Hardly get much more, unless you got a sequel."

TK

"Working on it. Here take a copy of The Piers, brand new. It's a rock and roll beach tale. I think you'll like it, and I hope, you'll tell your show Biz friends."

PW

"I'm not a producer director for nothing. Or maybe I am, Ha, Tune in next week."

He takes out a wallet and says, "Signed, please," and hands over a twenty.

TK

"No problem." He signs "In fact, it's my pleasure." He begins to read as he walks.

PW

"Mmm Yes, a Shelby . . . ."

The author smiles thinking about the opening pages of 'The Piers'. An Island night, a hot car, a girl, lots of music, food, and good times from sunset to sunrise. The writer attacks the story pn screen again and pushes away all sight and sound. He is off and writing with fervor, enthusiasm, and concentration. So much so that he hears a familiar phrase repeated again and again with greater intensity.

Charly Cucci / CC

"Yo Mister! Yo Mister?"
The writer blinks and sees a late teen straddling a bike and looking through a manuscript.

TK

"What, Jesus kid, what?"

CC

"Mister you have any graphic novels of your stuff?"

TK

"What ? No, no, sorry kid, I wasn't hearing very well. I was somewhere else, entirely."

CC

"Yeah, I could tell. I see you're a writer."

TK

"Correcto. You a reader?"

CC

"I mostly like comics. Do you have any graphic novels of your stuff?"

TK

"Nope."

CC

"Good, Do you want one?"

TK

"You an artist?"

CC

"Naw, I'm a colorist. My brother's the artist."

TK

"Yeah?"

CC

"Yeah, we free lance at Marvel and DC."

TK

"Good reps. Got any work to share ?"

CC

"Sure. " He pulls out a graphic novel and hands it over, "Trade?"

TK

"Sure. Let me see what to show an artist, or an artist's little brother."He picks a copy
"Hablo Espanole?"

CC

"Si,"

TK

"You might like this one. It's a Shipwrecked Pirate story. Una Isla Peligrosa!"

CC

"SI ?" He reads the cover. "A Dangerous Island. Johnny Depp?"

TK

"No, shipwrecked pirates."

CC

"Cool,"

TK

"Tell you what amigo. I'll look at yours and you read mine. Come back with your brother and we'll talk business, okay?"

CC

"Si, Si, Jefe. Buenos tarde."

He peddles away manuscript in hand. TK sits and starts skimming the pages of drawings, he nods up and down. The young lady walks back to him and holds the manuscript which she has coiled into a tube.

Jazz

"Mr Wallace?"

TK

"Yep?"

Jazz

"I like the Baseball Story. Is it true?"

TK

"True enough. Let's see. . . The only fiction is the scene between myself and the security team from Upper Deck."

Jazz

"Too bad, I liked that scene."

TK

"Then it's true too!"

Jazz

"Oh? Just a little 'literary license'?"

TK

"I prefer, 'creative prevarication'"

Jazz

"Whatever,"

TK

"The scene covers a logical step in the sequence of events and makes the whole thing more real."

Jazz

"Got it, C.Y.A."

TK

"That takes me back. Catholic Youth Association?"

Jazz

"Cover Your Ass."

TK

"That too, 'literarily speaking'. You a writer?"

Jazz

"Nope."

TK

"Publisher?"

Jazz

"Nope. I'm an agent."

TK

"Too bad."

Jazz

"Do you have an agent?"

TK

"Not so far. Why do you think I'm out here hawking my own stuff."

Jazz

"To cut out the middle man."

TK

"True enough."

Jazz

"Abso-Poso true. I've been watching you when you're here. You pick up a few hundred a day."

TK

"Do I?"

Jazz

"You do, and more on weekends."

TK

"You live in the neighborhood?"

Jazz

"Right up there." She points at the Dakota. "Fourth floor facing this way."

He thinks and paces as he thinks again.

TK

"I'll tell you what. You go finish the other two stories and the next time we meet, either you'll try to get my attention, or you'll avoid me."

Jazz

"I don't need to. I finished the other two as you were chatting with the lovely female buyer, goofing with Paul Rubins, who is obviously a fan, and bartering with the comic book kid."

TK

"Oh Yeah?"

Jazz

"So, yeah. I want to see some more of your work."

TK

"Here 'tis. "He gestures to the bench manuscripts. "At $15.00 each."

Jazz

"I am offering to represent you-"

TK

"And I am counter offering you offer. Excuse me, what is your name?"

Jazz

"Jasmine May."

TK

"Jasmine. A lovely name evoking the sense memories of a luscious aroma. May I call you Jazz?

Jazz

"Many do."

TK

"Okay Jazz. It's like this. You want another story book? You've got to pay for it. I've never met an agent yet that respects anything they got for free."

Jazz

"Okay Mr. Hard Case. Let's see what I can do for you. She hands him $25.00.

"I'll have # 1 signed, and # 2 signed as well."

TK takes her copy and signs. He pulls out a copy of # 2 and signs it.

TK

"Via con Dios."

Jazz

"You'll hear from me."

TK

"I hope so."

The Author watches her walk away. She looks over her shoulder and smiles at him before crossing Central Park West.

His phone chirps and he looks at the readout.

"Celia wants some supper. Hello? Yes mam, You know I am. Can I bring anything? Layers then."

He steps to the lap top, looks at the screen, saves the product, and begins to whistle as he shuts it down. He nods and whistles as he gathers the copies of books into the back pack.

He departs and leaves the sign behind. Stuck to the bench it reads, 'Tales for Sale'.

- - - - - - - - - -

Scene Two

We see our writer straddling the bench sideways. He is lost in thought as we hear a hawker entering our realm of consciousness. The young hawker, Tito, is brandishing a copy of, New York Stories # 1.

Tito

"Each and every New York Tale is the work of a local literary genius."

TK smiles at these words,

TK

"I actually wrote that?"

Tito

"Are you literate? Can you read and then think about what you've read?"

Several people stop and look at the kid. They smile and wait for the closer.

"Then today is your lucky day. You have a ground floor opportunity to help support the work of an emerging giant in the world of fiction for only $ 15.00."

The crowd begins to disperse. One man asks.

Literate Man / LM

"May I read some first?"

Tito

"Please do, the 1st in this series is A Baseball Story. It's about an autographed baseball passed through three generations." Tito hands him a copy.

The man stands aside and reads with a person reading over each shoulder.

Tito pulls another copy out of the back pack at TK's feet, checks the title and lays it on the bench. He puts his hand back in and draws out another as he starts the pitch again.

"Yes my friends contained between these covers are a few tales of New York, New York; so nice we had to name it twice. We have a Baseball story, we have a story of 'Guerilla Croquet', played Manhattan style, and we have the story of a young couple on vacation outwitting a very rich and very greedy man."

The reading man closes and rolls the manuscript. He gestures to Tito,

LM

"You said $ 15.00?"

Tito

"Yes Sir."

LM

"This a copy of #1, is there a # 2? " Tito reaches to the bench.

Tito

"Right here. Had one ready for ya." He hands it to the literate man.

LM

"How much for both?"

Tito

"Duh, you can read, but you can't add?"

LM

"Okay, okay, it's called 'bargaining' kid."
TK rescues his hawker by giving him some cash.

TK

"Take a break Tito, Why don't you grab some shade and
I'll finish here."

Tito

"Tanks Teak. What you want? Snapple?"

TK

"Gator Aid, any color. Excuse me sir, that will be $30.00.
If you want them signed, and that would be $40."
The literary man un rolls the manuscript and asks.

LM

"You actually want me to pay you $ 10.00 for signing your
name twice?"

TK

"Yes Sir, Absolutely. Tell me, what do you do for a living?"

LM

"I'm a lawyer."

TK

"Good, an honorable profession. My appreciation."

LM

"Thanks."

TK

"What is your specialty in law?"

LM

"Real Estate."

TK

"I write stories for a living. If people want a signed copy it becomes a collector's edition. Mind you, I offer it to them now, ahead of the mass market."

LM

"Okay, and ?"

TK

"The last time you signed a lease agreement, did you make more than $10.00?"

LM

"Well, yeah, I made, ... never mind that."

TK

"Then either pay up or get the fuck out of the way. You're blocking good business."

LM

"Okay, don't jump all salty. I liked the Baseball story, and, here's the $30. I'll be in touch"

TK

"I'll be around." The lawyer departs.

Tito

"Yo Teak, I got you blue and a cup of ice."

TK

"Tito Manrito, U da Bes." Tito smiles and opens the blue goo over ice.

TK

"I'll be right back."

The author straddles the park bench, squints off into nowhere, and begins to write.

"Lance decided when he turned Sixty that he would write out some interesting and important times.

Too many times had a friend or a listener asked, "Have you recorded any of these stories?

He admitted that he had not and that he had been asked that question many times before.

He had thought the question too big to answer, for the volume of tales seemed too big to number.

But if he wanted to finish the huge task, he had to start somewhere, and where better to start than at the beginning."

♦ ♦ ♦ ♦ ♦ ♦ ♦

TK, or Teak, as Tito has named him, looks up and stares at his hawker from the bench.

Tito

"Yo! Teak, you in there or what? I been trying to get to you . . .'

TK

"Really Tito? I was only writing for a few minutes and –"

Tito

"Dude, you were, wherever you go, Writer Land, or wherever, for over two hours."
The hawker hands him a wad of cash.

TK

"Really? Wow. And you sold some stories?"

Tito

"Yep, here's $90, for 6 at $15 each, 2 New York Tales # 1, 2 New York Tales # 2, a Dangerous Island and a Beginnings."

TK

"Well, alright, way to go 'Manrito'! The deal is 10%, throw in the Lawyer, here, take ."

Tito

"Fifteen? Thanks Teak, change ?"

TK

"Naw, get on and finish your homework. Tell your Mama, Howdy."

Tito

"As good as done. I'm gone John. Same time tom?"

TK

"I'm under the gun son; got meetings. Maybe 2 o'clock or there about?"

Tito

"Suits. Layers Teak."

TK

"Layers Tito," TK watches Tito skip away as he pockets the fifteen. "Good kid-"

Woman's Voice

"And a pretty good salesman." He turns to see Miriam.

TK

"Hey Miriam, I just sent Tito on home to you and his homework."

Miriam

"Thanks, I was watching. How did he do today ?"

TK

"Great, he did $30 before and $90 while I was, uh, concentrating, uh, writing."

Miriam

"According to him you were day dreaming and talking to yourself."

TK

"Yeah, I guess He's probably right. I never see that side of the process."

Miriam

"He's beginning to understand that part. He called me."

TK

"Why? Did I scare him? It used to scare my ex-wife."

Miriam

"No, he wanted my advice. He called to tell me that a customer wanted an autographed copy. But he didn't want to disturb you."

TK

"Smart kid, I don't respond well to some body busting into my train of thought."

Miriam

"I think the thought of that scared him. He did it once and you chewed him out."

TK

"Yeah I did. Sorry, I apologized, I thought he understood."

Miriam

"I'd say he does. So, he sold 8 ?"

TK

"Yep and didn't disturb me once, I gave him fifteen. Does he report his money?"

Miriam

"Every time. He's proud that he has a job, and he brings it all home and gives me what he has earned. I put it in the House Jar so he knows it's going to good use."

TK

"I've shopped in that aisle. Glad to know it's going to good use for your family."

Miriam

"It is, and I thank you."

TK

"Sorry I can't do more than 10%."

Miriam

"I'm not, and neither is he. I explained to him that the Good Lord only asked for 10% and that you were probably a good god fearing Christian man."

TK

"A Catholic, I'm afraid. Never could abide a man or an institution who asked for more than God."

Miriam

"I told Tito that any person who asked for more than 10 % was too ambitious, greedy, or just plain stupid."

TK

"Ha ! Probably all three. Miriam, you just gave me an idea or another story."

Miriam

"Really ? Well, Write On." She holds up a hand for a high five. He slaps and she waddles away.

The newest title page reads, **'Don't You Dare Ask For More Than God'.**

He smiles and lets his imagination wander near and far.

"Lance chooses a set of the oldest memories he can recall, and attempts to write them out.

He realizes that he has limited himself to description rather than the impressions he retains.

He rethinks and continues in a train of thought mode. Feelings and impressions from before he could walk or talk.

The first was a sense memory of a large soft hand gripping and releasing it's fingers.

The next was a sight and movement memory of learning to walk, and negotiating a step upon an uneven surface in order not to stumble again."

Scene Three

TK emerges from the subway steps on CPW juggling his two back packs. He spots Tito on the park bench. Tito appears to be sleeping with a ball cap down over his eyes.

Crossing the street, TK sees the cap more clearly. It reads 10% .

He stops in thought and almost gets hit by a cab. He moves quickly. Tito looks up and stands to grab TK to steady him and his backpacks.

TK

"Thanks Tito. What's with the cap? You saying I don't pay you enough?"

Tito

"What? No! No. Negatorie dude. 10%'s fair. We're square."

TK

"So wha's up?"

Tito

"Mi Mum's idea. She thought I would sell more if people knew what I got."

Tito takes off the hat and looks at it. TK rumbles and muses as he unloads.

TK

"She's probably right."

Tito

"She stitched it herself. No foul?"

TK

"No Foul and no harm. I'm not greedy or stupid. 10% is a fair wage."

Tito

"Cool let's get to it. Anything new today?"

TK

"Spent the night improving some old stuff."

Tito

"I read some yesterday."

TK

"Yeah?"

Tito

"Yeah. I read 'Gambling On Darn Ol Trump'."

TK

"What'd ya think?"

Tito

"I liked it. I liked the action and the descriptions. But, the dialog was the best."

TK

"How old are you?"

Tito

"17, almost."

TK

"You graduate this spring right? Have you applied to any colleges yet?"

Tito

"Naw, Me Mum says there ain't no money for dat."

TK

"Money is a bugga-boo for small minds. If you want a thing to happen, you can make it happen one way or another."

Tito

"What's a 'bugga-boo'?"

TK

"A place or thing that prevents forward progress. That stop light is traffic control. A sign saying 'street closed' is a 'bugga-boo' or a 'stop gap'. But there's always another way around."

Tito

"Guess so, if you say so. You ever write a story about writing stories?"

TK

"Naw, but I'm working on one about selling stories on the street corner."

Tito

"Now that's cool. I'd be in that one right?"

TK

"Roight. Now get to work selling."

Tito

"Ladies and Gentlemen, what we have here today is an unbelievable bargain. Fresh from the mind and fingers of the author are an even dozen works of art."

TK

"Hey, I didn't write that."

Tito

"I know, i did." TK looks at Tito and smiles

"For only $15.00, you will get a tale that will surprise and enlighten."

TK is happy to resume his craft while someone else does the selling.

(end)

Fred the Cop

written by

T K Wallace

He stood there behind his mirrored shades surveying the crowd. We thought he was scanning the crowd for anything that could cause disruption or violence. That's why he was there. Little did we know, he was remembering rice fields and armed guerilla types sneaking around, under, and through American troops. Little did we know the demons he carried along with his current command.

Fred had retired from the US Army after 23 years. He spent his final 8 years as an officer overseas. As casualties of war he had earned a purple star, a promotion to Captain, an interesting facial scar, and a divorce. When the US Army had no further use for him, Fred had no further use for the Army. He was retired into public life in the American south.

Fred was a Savannah city a cop when we first met, guess it was 1970 or so. I was helping produce a series of high school bands at the YMCA. The Board of Education wanted to unify the schools with experiments in sports, local politics, and music. We budgeted the money for safety guards in the public interest. That's where Fred came along. He was a cop who liked kids and would work a couple extra shifts per month at his regular SPD rate, plus all normal benefits.

When we interviewed Fred he was forthcoming about his concern of how local police were hard on youth of every color. He was pretty much what we were looking for, an authority figure who would eliminate any threat or disturbance with a minimum of legal involvement. I remember he elaborated,

"If we have an instance of drunken behavior, the drunk will be relieved of their car keys until a sober family member comes forward to drive everyone home."

Violence never ensued while Fred was around. The

stubborn army captain had become a teen tolerant, user friendly Cop.

There was a zero tolerance policy on drugs of any kind. This rule was firm, Fred could confiscate and evict the users. And if he saw sales, he was allowed to arrest, at gun point. We had some minor instances like smoking pot among ten cigarette smokers close to an exhaust. Fred busted a couple and they didn't bother any more, they finally figured it was easier and safer to go outside and smoke.

♦ ♦ ♦ ♦ ♦ ♦ ♦

The music was minor league, one step away from garage band level. It was a YMCA dance. The bands were loud, there was lots of room to dance, and lots of time between dancing. The room was overheated by teenage girls and boys with music and time on their hands. Off the dance floor they engaged in other activities. The room was so full of pheromones that I walked the floor between acts, just to breath, and smile.

It was after a planning meeting that Fred asked me what I thought of smoking pot in the privacy of your own home. I was surprised to being asked this by a cop so I said I didn't care, and asked what he thought. He said that he thought it was okay. He said that if he had some pot he would share it with me. I just nodded and then he asked me to buy some for him. My alarm bells went off, and I told him I could not be entrapped in such a juvenile way.

♦ ♦ ♦ ♦ ♦ ♦ ♦

It was about that time I noticed Fred was driving a different car. It was a Ford Mustang, like an early year, maybe late 60's. He said he was going to restore it and turn it. He did a fine job on the restoration. He told me that he was overseas when the car was designed in '63, then developed and released in '64. He said he always wanted a mustang. According to him, he sold the car at double his original cost.

I looked at one, who didn't, but when I looked inside it was too small. One friend said, "Sure it's a chick magnet, it's a girl size car." It was sports car low, nice lines, a big engine, and really looked best with the top down and full of girls.

The cars bothered me the most. He was divorced and claimed to be strapped for cash, yet there were the cars. He had three Mustangs in 12 months. And he drove a few more cars during that time. His said his new sideline of buying and selling, or turning, cars was profitable. He went to public auctions all over the state to buy cars that looked good. He also bought inconspicuous cars, for undercover work and resold them to the Savannah police department.

◆　◆　◆　◆　◆　◆　◆

Later that spring my boss, Toni, asked me to a meeting at a local pub because we had some issues to discuss. A detective came to the meeting and informed Toni of Fred's side line. He claimed Fred was into semi legal car trading. He was being monitored with the intent of catching him in a stolen car. They asked us to observe and report every car we saw him drive. I was amazed at the gaul and then thoughtful.

Toni asked my advice for maybe the second time in two years, "What should we do?" I asked her and she told him we would watch. I suggested we watch from Freddie's place out on Tybee Island. Toni and I had a spontaneous affair we called, Going out of Town, and we certainly tried to celebrate our freedom that night.

After a steamy night of beach life, moonlight swimming, and some investigation, we hit the Breakfast Club a little after dawn. Toni had work and I had the day off. She grabbed coffee to go and I took a booth. Bruce, a BC co-owner, came by and raised his eyebrows at me. I had been a regular customer since the early days when they opened.

I nodded affirmatively invoking my standard order. This simple act meant that a goat cheese omelet with spinach, green onions, and grits, a pecan waffle with syrup, toast with some jam, and a hot cup of coffee would soon appear in front of me.

Bruce's brother, Jody, did the BC proud by cooking the superior omelet and even adorned it with a spinach leaf on top. Bruce noticed and smiled as he served me.

I watched out of front window as I ate. I saw Freddie drive by in two different Mustangs. The second car he was driving got stopped. Fred got out and flashed his badge. He spoke with the officer for Tybee Island Police and gestured to the BC. The officer took a look at his license, nodded, and allowed him to leave. Fred swung the Mustang into a parking space beside the BC. He got out, waved at the cop and came in for coffee.

He spied me, came over to say hello, and asked me what I was doing there so early. I told him that I was 'Out of Town' with Toni for the evening. He smiled, said he approved, and offered congratulations. I tried to remember if anyone had asked me **not** to inform Fred he was being watched. But he rubbed it in.

"You and Toni like going 'Out of Town,' every now and then?"

I replied, "I like watching tension build in any catalytic situation."

He glanced at me expectantly.

"Like being asked by SPD to observe and report every car you drive."

Freddie slowly looked at me over the brim of his coffee cup. As his head rose, the coffee cup was placed on the table. He suggested that I, "mind my own business". He dropped some money on the table, left the restaurant, and drove away. We worked together a few times after that, but it was years before we had a close relationship.

♦ ♦ ♦ ♦ ♦ ♦ ♦

May 30, 1971 was the day I graduated high school. I was still 17 so had some time before my draft number for Vietnam was established. So, I went for a walkabout. I hitched to San Francisco and back. I hitchhiked up and down the east coast, to Connecticut and back. I got to see a couple of parts of the world I had always wanted to see. It did me no harm to travel.

I was in back Savannah when my draft number came up; number 37. So I enrolled in nursing school. Hopefully, if I got drafted I would have a skill that would land me in a hospital group l instead of the infantry. I immediately dove into medical training by working as an orderly on ER and OR duty within the local hospitals.

I heard that Fred had been awarded a city contract as the

main security provider for concerts and live music events. His company, AJAX Security, and his dozen or so employees also worked for the city providing stadium security for local football games.

◆ ◆ ◆ ◆ ◆ ◆ ◆

My draft number was never called. Out of the 365 days in the year, even with the expectation which came along with the number 37, the draft ended that year at number 29. With a sigh of relief I decided to travel for another year. I worked as an orderly, a cook, a ward nurse, and many other odd jobs along the way.

When I returned to Savannah the first thing I wanted to do was finish the RN degree I started in what seemed like a lifetime ago. Returning to finish was a breeze. I had learned the craft of practical nursing and finished the rest with honors. I already had an offer of an ER job at a local hospital.

Also, I fell in love with a nubile manx named Carol Jean Cox. CeeJay was a semi pro artist in both drawing and painting who had four kids. We met over her child's ER event and love happened. I moved them into my life by changing residences. We co-rented an eight room bungalow on Central Ave in Isle of Hope. This was the original trolley path to Isle of Hope during horse cart days.

We had a vegetable barn beside the house. The barn was small and had racks inside. The entire property was overhung with trees. We had Black Walnut trees covering the drive entrance and front yard. We had Pecan trees covering the back and side yards. This involved a lot of leaf raking and nut picking. And as you may imagine, I hung kid swings in several places.

This happy domestic time was the next time I saw Fred.

He had resigned from SPD just before he dodged the car sting. But, the fact that he had beaten SPD did not sit well. So, they were watching Fred with scrutiny, and beginning to investigate AJAX security in every nook and cranny.

He appeared on Isle of Hope during the full moon party. The island had a tradition of throwing a public party every full moon. The community had a nice leisure area within a generous space of massive Oak trees bearing Spanish moss. The park was outfitted for kids and adults. We had swing sets with slides, and swimming a pool close by. We had several large red brick cooking pits, and plenty of room with picnic tables. Sometimes, more often than not, there was even live music.

It was also the time of organic hallucinogens. Psilocybin mushrooms grew with gusto in the marsh lands. The 'shrooms had a round top with brown at the center peek and again out on the edge. The underside was fluted and colored in purple. They grew like crazy from organic compost when the weather was between 65 and 90 degrees, high humidity, and sparse direct sunlight.

Several coastal states never made mushrooms illegal. We could pick them wild and process them down for drinking or even freezing. The recipe was two pounds of mushrooms for one gallon of electric tea. It took one small cup to go on a short trip. Two big cups would send you flying. The juice comes on, and bang, you're trippin'. Then it was over and gone quick and clean, there was no after effect.

We called it Old Dixie because it made people get silly

and laugh a lot, as we tend to do during pleasant times down south. Ol' Dixie was an island treat at a cook out with precious people and a great sunset close to the water.

Freddie showed up looking kind of frantic. I think that's the right word, frantic, upset with a lot of negative energy, yeah, a bit frantic. He needed my attention and wanted to see me alone. I made my excuses to the others and complied with his request by walking him toward the pool while he spoke.

Fred's legal status was about to be regarded as, 'wanted'. He had learned the warrant request was pending but delayed due to no judge being available to sign it over the weekend. He came to me for help. He said he needed a place to be invisible for a couple of days while some things 'blew over'. He asked if he could use the barn. I was a little astounded and had to ask about AJAX.

"Gone. IRS took it. They said it was part of a treasury department investigation." So I asked about the used car business.

"Gone. Somebody left a kilo of pot in one of the cars. So they closed down the whole car lot. Locked it shut with a police seal. I think it was planted by the cops."

"Why do you think that?"

"Because it wasn't mine, I'm not that careless, and because what they showed my manager was still compressed. You can't sell it unless it's loose, you know that."

"So, are you guilty?" He put out a cigarette and swiped my cup of Old Dixie, downed it, and handed me the cup.

"Yeah, probably am guilty, of some of it. Never thought I was doing any harm though."

"How long you need the barn?"

"Not long maybe two or three days, or like through Monday at the latest."

I told him I couldn't tolerate any trouble because of CeeJay and the kids. He said nobody would know where he was. He arrived on foot, driving no car, with no one following. He extended his arms and twirled in a circle.

"Actually I feel pretty good, despite all the doom and gloom in my life."

"Yeah? That's good." We joined in song as we walked back toward the crowd. I sang, "Forget your troubles . . ." he joined in.

"Come on get happy, We're gonna chase all the blues away." I led him to CeeJay. She was working the drinks table with red and blue cups spread about.

"Well, here's Fred the Cop. How's it hanging Freddie, have some Ol' Dixie." She hands him a Red cup. He downs it. She hands him another as she winks at me.

I asked, "Freddie wants to use our barn for a few days, okay with you?"

"Fine by me, No contraband though, right Freddie? We got kids to protect."

"You'll hardly know I'm there. It's a quiet time for now, no cars, no flash, just me."

"Well, if rumors are true, you'll be more than enough. A few days then; another Ol' Dixie?"

◆ ◆ ◆ ◆ ◆ ◆ ◆

Fred was true to his word. We saw him down by the water on Isle of Hope marina as we left with the sitter and put the kids to bed. He was gone when we came back for a dance and a night cap.

We did almost see him again late Sunday night, someone knocked on the back door. When I got to the back door there was no one there. There was a faint moving light in the veggie barn. As I stepped into the yard the barn light went out. Another larger light focused on me from the yard and a voice commanded me to stop. Instead of complying I yelled,

"Who the fuck is making all the noise out here? I'm calling the cops." It seemed they were all scrambling, some came into view.

"Shh ... Shh ... We are the cops you idiot, Quiet !" The flashlight turned and said, "The search is moving on from here. My apologies for our men disturbing you," and then they left.

As I went back inside I took another look at the barn, and closed the door. In the middle of the door was a note curled up and extending through the viewing port. The note read ...

"I need to get out of town and need a driver. It's worth a grand a week. If you can help meet me tonight at Le Chateau."

I read and thought, read again and shrugged, then went to wake up CeeJay so she could give me a ride. While I packed a knap sack and filled a canteen, she cleared kid care with the eldest, Kelly, and then drove me to the rendezvous. After kissing CeeJay I grabbed my kit and hopped out of the car in the side lot. I waved my beloved away, and then looked inside The Waffle House.

Freddie sat at the counter beside the cash register. He was slowly scanning the windows so I waited until he scanned mine to push forward and be seen through the glass. He rose, took his go-cup, and exited to the back parking lot. I followed at a discrete distance and watched him go through a line of hedges.

When I emerged I found myself in a gas station parking area. Freddie was checking under the hood of a relatively new Cadillac. As I approached, he turned and said, "Good clean care babe." and let down the hood. I smelled light perfume and looked into the car. Freddie opened the passenger door for me to get in back and the took his seat. She remained behind the wheel. She sensed me starring and asked if I had a question.

"Do I know you? You look so familiar. Uh, is this car legal?"

"You do know me, I should look familiar, and yes it happens to be my very own car, and legal. Hi, Gabriella Alvarado, SPD?"

She extended a hand for shaking and started the car. We headed toward the bridge with all the other traffic crossing into Carolina. As we crested the bridge I took a look while the other two took a breath and slowly exhaled. I watched and smiled at them and said,

"Well, Georgia is behind, there's a load off you two. Now if you don't mind, what's up?"

They laughed, "We're just happy to be gone from there. Thanks for the help, I am relocating; Ohio."

"Then I take it we are meeting additional transportation." I sat forward. "How ong trip are we talking?"

She said, "About a week. Maybe two at the most."

"I'm paying meals and expenses, a thousand in cash, and a flight home."

I confirmed, "One K for each week plus all expenses,

every week from now til you're set. Then the flight home, deal?"

We joined hands and became as close as you can in a car. We rode with common purpose. I wondered out loud.

"How far is it to the trucks?"

"Not far, first truck stop."

"Is the truck as comfy as this car?"

Only Fred answered, "You Wish."

"How far is to this place in Ohio?"

"Two to Three days."

"Who drives what?"

"Uh, let's see, you and me, trucks?"

"Do we rotate?"

"You think I'm paying you to drive a Cadillac?"

"Is the truck as comfy as this car?"

Only Gabriella answered, "You Wish."

♦   ♦   ♦   ♦   ♦   ♦   ♦

As we stood beside the 26 foot box trucks, I noticed that each truck had a different state license. When we, 'mounted up', I found that my truck had CB radio, a marine band handheld VHF radio, and keys in the ignition. There were AAA maps marked with routes to Ohio. Nice preparation, probably her effort.

I drove one truck, Freddie drove the other, and Gabriella followed at some distance. The truck was new, the communications all worked, and we escaped. The first night we headed northwest as far as Charlotte and then tucked in for the day. The next night we went through North Carolina and Kentucky and stopped. We slept all day and that night we quietly passed through farm country all the way to Lima, Ohio.

Fred and Gabby had rented a house among some buildings on a farm lot. It was the kind of place no one remembers or even realized was there, the perfect hideout. We unloaded the trucks that night until we found they had brought too much stuff. The new house wasn't big enough. We could return one truck but still needed the other one.

So, he donated the extra furniture to the Ohio state home where Freddie had interviewed for the job. The job was managing a half way house. 'The Center' was a halfway house for indigents, drunks, castoffs, and runaways. The home was partially occupied and separated by sex. The state needed somebody to manage the budget and to run the place.

Plus they needed an authority figure to keep the pandemonium and chaos at a controlled level rather than running amok as with the previous manager.

Fred had arranged a meeting to further entertain the offer. He started the meeting with his prospective employers with a walk through of the facility. He pointed out things they did not want to see or think about. Freddie said he would accept a three year contract to turn the place around, IF, and a big IF, if three more positions were funded. The powers that be agreed.

The first day at work he had a staff meeting for the same purpose of walking the staff through the place, forcing them to look at conditions. Then he led them to the truck and had them remove the contents. He asked them to 'fill in' some empty spaces at the Center, and to create some new spaces for the guests.

At the end of that day, my work in Ohio was done. We

returned the second truck and I was allowed to drive them home in the Caddy. Driving the behemoth was a treat from Gabbs because I had driven a truck for the last eight hundred miles. As we rode, Fred asked if I wanted to stay. He said that he needed someone he could trust to give the job of night supervision at the home.

I laughed out loud at the idea of babysitting that bunch of social misfits Fred called guests. I asked who was doing the overnight job now. I was told it was, Burty the care taker. He lived at the Center as a permanent resident due to his status as a war hero.

Pvt. Andrew James Cuthburt was the most decorated war hero from Ohio in WW2. He drew a pension as well as pay for the job of caretaker, both of which he drank away every month. He was a down and out drunk who lived on leftovers and all kinds of cheap booze.

The fourth night I was there, Fred and I spoke with Burty about his drinking habit. We offered him some grass instead. He smoked with us and said the grass made him confused. He said he wanted something with more of kick to it; 'Squeezin's'. This was the liquid you got from filtering the liquid from Sterno. He said it made him see things.

We had to shrug and walk away. We left Burty to his own devices, but it was obvious that he, as well as the state home where he lived, needed to be supervised. On the ride home we talked about the operation, but Fred never again intimated that I should work there. It was a good thing too, because what I really wanted was to get home to CeeJay and the kids.

So, when we got to the house I broke out the canteen I had dragged halfway into mid America. As an aperitif, we had a cup of Ol' Dixie each while cooking spaghetti for dinner. Gabriella was the cook and dug out some dried Dixie mushrooms to cook with the noodles and sauce. About the time we came down from one, we started getting off on the other. The second trip lasted through eating dinner and cleaning up. Freddie preceded desert with another cup of Dixie. We toasted marshmallows and talked into the night as we watched sparks fly into the dark sky. It was time to go home.

♦　♦　♦　♦　♦　♦　♦

I awoke with the sun shining and bird song around me. The cook pit had gone down to embers barely glowing. There was a blanket covering me. Gabriella's singing was filling my ears while a cup of coffee filled my other senses. She was prepared to drive me to the airport in Dayton. The drive was about an hour away. My flight was in about four hours. Fred was at work but had left a card with his regards, his thanks, full payment with a fifty percent bonus, and another three hundred for plane tickets.

I packed my effects but could not find the canteen anywhere. Angel said she would send it when it turned up. As we drove south we spotted a long low barn along St Mary's lake. The roadside signs advertised it to be a button mushroom farm.

We couldn't resist. The place was dimly lit, the ceilings were low and the staff all dressed as elves and trolls. They wore robes, jerkins, and tights. There were also a few Dwarves. They offered two and four pound boxes of Double A Button mushrooms. They used ash tree compost to grow 'Waffle

Shrooms' suitable for cooking, frying, and sautéing. They were deliciously edible and totally legal.

I bought a four pound box which was large enough to require a carrying handle. My 'Shrooms were inspected at the Dayton Regional Airport but I was allowed to keep them. The box was inspected again at the Cincinnati / Northern Kentucky airport for the flight to Atlanta. This time they were commandeered by the chief pilot and required to ride in the cockpit where I had no access to the dangerous mushrooms during the flight.

In Atlanta I found a good gift shop for kids. The shop was selling small stuffed black bears, each with a collar leash that read Atlanta Zoo. I bought one for each of the four kids, thus adding another parcel for the flight to Savannah.

I found myself detained down to my underwear and rescheduled for a later flight so a security team could ask me questions, inspect my mushrooms, and probe my bears.

Once I got home the bear puns didn't stop for weeks. It was unbearable. I could barely….. never mind.

◆ ◆ ◆ ◆ ◆ ◆ ◆

I saw Freddie for the last time when he appeared out of nowhere with my empty canteen. It was early, almost 6 am on a Monday. I heard a tap tap tappng on our bedroom window. He later apologized for using the bedroom window, but explained that no one had answered the front or rear doors.

He claimed that he was cleaning out the refrigerator and found the half full canteen. Gabriella was working the weekend and he had the time off too, so he took a straight slash. 36 hours later he found himself in the marsh wandering the old Isle of Hope trolley tracks in search of our house. I welcomed him and presented to the kids as Uncle Freddy, whose eyes always pin wheeled that way.

The kids couldn't have cared less and after breakfast went outside to play. CeeJay and I exchanged glances at Fred and waited for him to start. Once he did start we could hardly get in a question. He wandered about in his rambling monologue.

"I have made a decision. I want Gabby to marry me. I had to think about it before I asked, so I went for a road trip to clear my head, or at least re-focus my efforts on more basic necessities, which one does when hitching hundreds of miles and tripping for two days and nights. I mean long days and nights, but fun and funny. 20 rides, too many people, faces, smiles requests to, 'do me a favor'…. and the miles rolled by, and I am here!"

"Yes," I replied, "Here you are, back in Savannah, back in the land of being wanted. Fred, what are you doing here?"

"I needed to talk to someone and I trust you two. You have always been kind and understanding, even when you weren't given enough details to make adequate plans, standing up for me in your own home … … … I thank you."

CeeJay got involved, "You said you have decided to marry Gabby. Have you asked her?"

"No not yet, I'm too much of a flake, I know that. I can't see any reason she would want to marry me. I'm afraid she'll say no."

"First things first. Did you let her know where you were going?"

"Yes, yes, I did, I left her a note for when she got back, she gets back Sunday night."

"That would be, got back, as in last night. She got home from work last night."

"Last night?"

"Yep, last night, It's morning now but-"

"Wo, that entire trip was two nights?"

CJ said, "Look Fred, . . . no, never mind. First, call her so she won't worry. No, wait, I still have the number, I'll start the call. I'll be right back." and she left.

I thoughtfully looked at Fred and waited for him to speak.

"Today is Monday? Wo, dude, that was a good trip. It started in Ohio on Saturday."

"And you needed to talk to me. I am flattered, but why didn't you call?"

"I can't be with you on the phone. I need to feel your presence and . . . . . wisdom."

"Too early for that, for me not for you, you are way into tripping wisdom right now. Tell me Freddie, when was your last cup of Dixie ?"

"I finished the last two cups in Macon, that was right before the night,…yesterday?"

"Last night, okay you should be down soon. Are you tired? Can you sleep?"

"Okay." He said, then sank back against the sofa and began to snore.

CeeJay came in with the phone.

"Gabby?" I asked, "She okay?"

"She's better now. He looks like he's out, you wanna talk?", and hands me the phone.

"Gabriella? Hi babe, Fred's here, but he's passed out. He's been on the road for two days." I listened and then responded.

"Yeah he looks good, Gabby listen, he said he wanted

some advice and had to talk to CeeJay and I. But he was still trippin' pretty hard from that last batch of Dixie."

After that I just listened.

"You're right, of course...yes, of course you're right. But listen, the reason he is so twisted up is that he, well, he wants to marry you. . . . . . And he's afraid to ask."

I listened again.

"Yes, he is, all of that, yes all of that and more . . . listen, I'll have him call, okay, . . . bye."

I handed CeeJay the phone and looked at Freddie. "I have to go to work. Are you okay with him here? When he wakes up, if he's still tripping, call me and bring him down to the ER. I'll have a doctor look after him."

I didn't get a call all morning so I called home. No one answered. I called again.

No one answered. I called again in the afternoon, and CeeJay answered. She said that Fred had left as soon as he woke up. She was in the yard playing with the two youngest kids when she saw him leave.

I spent the rest of my shift expecting to be called to the phone or to the desk. I signed out and began to leave only to be intercepted by a note under the car's wiper.

Comrade,

This is the best word for you. You fit the description better than anyone I have ever known. You have been there for me more times than I can count, including now.

I have once again raided the Ol' Dixie freezer locker in the barn to fill my own supplies and get my ass back home to marry

Gabby. That's right, I asked and she said Yes. So I'm off and going home.

For now I owe you a canteen of pure Dixie sipping elixir. Tell CeeJay nobody brews it better than her. Also, I am borrowing a gallon of pure frozen extract, so I guess I'll need a car to get me home. I'm pretty sure I have an 83 Cobra stashed in an auto shop close to here.

Gabriella sends her love and I leave mine to You, CeeJay, and the kids.

Happy trails.

Fred

Fred was a character I once knew. He was an Army Captain, A Cop, and an aging entrepreneur.

He was also a thief, but it was only Ol' Dixie.

(end)

3

Earth Tales

Magnolia's

I Was In a Coma Once

A Baseball Story

Just An Idea

Rao's

Magnolia's

written by

T K Wallace

The first gay couple I knew well were named Stanley and Shanon. It was 1972 and I was living downtown in Savannah's historic district. Stanley worked in a Mod retail home furnishing store called The Seven Seas. Shanon worked for an antique dealer, Arthur Smythe, re-arranging furniture for sale.

Stan and Shan had relocated from San Fran's Haight Ashbury district to Savannah for Stan to be closer to his elderly Grands. I had just returned from a three month cross country trip to the west coast and back hitchhiking both ways. I lived in some hostels, slept in the park, and sang on the street for money feeling incredibly hip.

The Hip scene in Savannah had yet to emerge into modern times. The three of us were revolutionaries surrounded by apathy. Mod was about as close as it came to progress at that time. The Seven Seas sold rock posters, black lights, and rolling papers without tobacco. The day I walked in that door opened many doors afterward.

Stan was behind the counter, being cool and looking very thoughtful. He was dressed in a band uniform, ala Sgt Peppers, without the hat. He looked me over and asked where I had found the bell bottoms I was wearing. They were wide bells with striped cut ins to expand the bell at the bottom, and I was proud of them.

"I brought them at Sid's."

"Sid's in the Haight?" Our eyes connected

"Yep."

"When were you there?"

"Just got back. I was there for the summer." He put out his smoke.

"My boyfriend and I returned this past spring." My eye brows arched.

"And you returned here, why?"

"To care for my elders, and to live in relative luxury again."

"How long were you in the Haight?"

"5 years, I miss it a little, not much. We were very poor out there."

"Yeah, me too. I crashed wherever, but it was fun most of the time."

"What do you do here?"

"Waiting to be drafted."

"Bummer, wanna be gay? It'll get you out. They won't want you."

"Don't think so, nothing against, just not my bag, ya know? No offense."

"None taken, be true to yourself." He extends a hand, "Stan."

"Chris." We shook and then advanced into a grip and then fingering.

"Nice to meetcha, boyo, what brings you in today?"

"I heard you sell papers."

"Yep, ten kinds. You got any grass?"

"Some Mex, I used my last wrapper this morning, Wanna share?"

He threw me a pack of Bamboo. "Looks like we're closed for lunch."

"Cool. Got a bathroom I can use?"

"Through there," He pointed and dialed a phone "I'll call in the reserves."

I ducked into a small bathroom and found a tray beside

the stool. On the tray were the remnants from a previous effort. I dumped them and started over. When I left with my mission accomplished, I cleaned up after myself and tucked the tray away. Stan introduced me to the owner, Mrs Dixon, and we excused ourselves.

As we walked Stan said. "Let's do the alleys."

And that we did, as we did what we did. When we picked up Shan, Stan asked "Ms Wilkes?" Stan handed Shan the rest of the joint.

"Fine by me. I'll be along." He tarried a bit.

"Back door okay with you?"

"Whose back door?"

"Ms Wilke's silly boy. The back door to the kitchen is off the alleyway."

"Got it. Know it. Love it"

Ms Wilke's take out is a great meal at half the price. Southern cooking at it's finest is always accompanied by biscuits, a slice of sheet cake, and a cold iced tea. For three hippies with the munchies, it was ambrosia, simply the best.

As we walked back from lunch, Shan asked me if I had a job.

"Not yet, looking, know of anything?"

"Yeah, my boss is going to need someone to replace me. Stan and I are starting a new place over on Drayton. The boss doesn't know yet."

"Is he gonna be pissed?"

"Maybe, a little, but I think I can diffuse it by having you and Stan along when I tell him. Then I'll slide you in for a look. And, we'll see, ok?"

And that was how it went. A. Smythe was surprised and

felt a bit abused over the short notice. Shanon came out and spoke to me directly.

"Chris, What is you legit name, Christopher?

"That's my second name." I stood, looked down at him, and smiled.

Stan said, "OK, Chris then, just four letters."

Shan followed, "Good, now, this is a nice man who has been kind to me. I wish him well and want to do right by him. So, if you have a problem with his sexual preferences you should decline this meeting. No harm, just do not work for him."

"Doesn't matter to me. Hey, it doesn't mean you're not nice people. Is he Bi, or homo?"

Stan fielded this one. "We think he's Bi, been seen both ways. Go meet him. See how it feels."

Shan led me to the boss, who stood, but I spoke before he did.

"Good afternoon, Mister Smythe," I advanced and took his hand. "I hope you don't think me too forward in looking for a job. I'm a college student waiting out the draft."

He looked me up and down.

"Young master, Christopher. My, you are a big one, how tall?"

"6' 6" sir, two meters."

"And how old?"

"Just 18 sir."

"Your major?"

"Nursing, at Savannah State."

"How long?"

"Two semesters, four to go."

"So, you'll be in school for another . ."

"A year or so sir. Unless they draft me first."

"What is you lottery number?"

"37, out of 365."

He paused, "They say it's slowing down."

"That's why I'm enrolled in nursing school, maybe I'll be a medic, or in a MASH unit. Anyway, I'd like to replace your furniture mover."

"Smart kid, He'll do Shanon." They shake hands and then embrace.

"Mr Smythe, may I ask, do you want me to work within the shop, or do you have other locations?"

"Yes Chris, we have a warehouse as well, do you have a license?"

"Several. I am also a licensed practical nurse, I hold a 2nd class FCC for radio work, hunting and fishing, state of Georgia. But I imagine you mean driving; Yes."

Mr. Smythe looked at me and smiled.

"Could you do 25 - 30 hours a week? That's what Shan has been doing."

"Possibly. What is the hourly wage?"

"May we start you at $10 an hour?"

"Did I mention, I also bring carpentry and electrical skills to the job?"

"Well then let's say a dollar an hour for each of them. $12.00?"

"And 50 cents for luck?"

Shan said, "$12.50 an hour? That's more than he ever paid me."

"You were never worth it. He does carpentry and electricity too."

"Say Chris, would you help us build out our store?"

"Say yes now, there's not much to do,-"

Mr. Smythe asked, "What's the address?"

"Charlton Lane and Drayton, downstairs."

"I know he place, there's a lot to do."

"Hey you, butt out. You are now my former boss."

Smythe drawls, "Speaking of which, when are you easily replaced?"

Shan turns to me and asks, "When can you start?"

"Tomorrow?"

Shan shines, "Good, a week from tomorrow is my last day, I'll teach him everything I can."

Arthur raises his hand and Stan offers a high five, "Chrisy baby, good show. Welcome. Love ya, mean it." We slap palms.

Shan looks at us all and says, "Well, that settles that, looks like I'm finishing the day,"

"We'll have Champagne, Stanley do come back around 5 and imbibe."

Stan kisses his cheek. "Will do Arthur, Come with me young Chris."

As we walked I shook my head. I muttered in wonder. Stan looked at me.

"Want to see the place? Do you have your own tools?"

"Yes and no, not with me. What is there to do?"

"Mostly shelves and racks. We have a display case but the lights don't work. Hope you can fix that."

He opened the door of the store and I saw a long rectangular space with a side room at the back.

"What kind of shop is it gonna be?"

"A head shop." I laughed out loud. He quickly shut the door.

"You two are going to open a head shop in Savannah? In '72? You been smoking too much Stan. Or you been tripping?"

"I know, but Shan wants to try it. Thinks it'll be good for the community."

"Stan, you're a native?"

"Yes."

"How about Shan?"

"He's from Charleston."

"Okay. Then you know what to expect from the locals."

"I know, it's crazy right? We're giving it a try. How much work do you think needs to be done? Shan says he's a carpenter, but I've yet to see him lift a tool, other than mine."

"OK, shelves and racks, what covers the walls?"

"Tapestries, sarongs, and posters. Some mobiles with some lava lamps up front. We're thinking maybe a black light room back there with day glo posters and a couple of water beds."

I pondered and guess-timated, "Looks like about three weeks work, if I work nights around A. Smythe. Is he open on the weekends?"

"Half day Saturday, No Sundays. Could you do those days here?"

"Yeah, let's see, can you afford what I see? Maybe $1,000 in labor, maybe half that in materials."

"Our budget is $1,000 total. We put in $500 each."

"Can you see taking in a third partner? I'll wave $500 and take 33%."

"I feel okay about it, gotta talk to Shan, but he'll go for it."

"What's the shop name, Do we have a sign?"

"We thought, 'Magnolia's'."

"Like the big tree with the large white flower?"

"Nope, for our favorite restaurant on the Haight."

"Yeah, the late night place, burgers, pastry, cakes, pies, ice cream right"

"You know it, I worked there for a while. My friends Magnolia and Rubin own the place."

"Native Americans right? Indian, don't know the tribe."

"Shosone. Took the last name of Thunder Pussy. Just so they could be the only one in the bay area."

"Sounds like a better name for a head shop. Thunder Pussy!"

"Wo, Christopher, you know Savannah's not ready for none of that."

♦ ♦ ♦ ♦ ♦ ♦ ♦

Nursing classes continued and soon I settled in to a steady rythym of work. I had classes during the morning, Smythe for a few hours in the afternoon, the Magnolia build out in the early evening, and then nursing homework before bed time.

At the end of the first month I was exhausted, and asked for a day of rest. Shan had been attempting some simple carpentry at the shop. Stan held his job at 'The Seven Seas' for the extra income to buy stock for the store. Magnolia's was well underway, the boy's were beginning to decorate, and I took Sunday off.

I was renting a studio space in a renovated park side home. My window looked into Forsythe Park and I shared a bath on the floor. The studio had a small ships' galley kitchen. It was all one piece, in stainless steel which would fit into any 8 foot by 10 foot space with adequate plumbing.

Mid afternoon on my day off I was studying a cross reference table of temperature, pulse, and respiration. I had passed out over the book while evaluating my own temp, pulse, & respiration. I was face down in the tables when I heard the door bell ring, once, twice.

When I finally got to the door A. Smyth was there.

"Good afternoon, oh, did I wake you?"

"Yes sir, yes sir you did. One minute I was studying, T. P. & R. tables and the next minute the bell was ringing."

"I am glad to see you putting your day off to good use. How are your grades?"

"Could be better, trying to improve,"

"Magnolia's is almost done?"

"Yeah, I let the boys start decorating, it's almost done, they need to open."

"That they do, here's $250, get 'em open as fast as you can."

"I'll have to steal the hours from you."

"Take 'em to the finish line straw boss."

I took the money and closed the door. The phone rang and it was Stanley.

"I know it's your day off, but, are you busy? Shan just shorted something and the lights and power are all off. Could you drop by for a few?"

"Be right over. Give me a few, take a break and don't touch anything."

I dressed quickly and hurried through the short cuts to the store. The front door was closed and all the lights were out. I let myself in and the bell above the door announced my arrival.

Stan and Shan emerged from the water bed room half dressed. They had refrained from touching anything electrical, but not from touching each other. The air was thick with pot smoke.

"So what happened?"

"I'm not sure, I was trying to wire an outlet over there and we saw sparks and then everything went out."

"If you saw sparks the electrical circuit was live. You didn't turn off the breaker. You're lucky Shan, you could have been electrocuted."

Stan stopped and crossed himself, "Madre Dios."

I looked at the outlet and examined the charred wires. Then I went to the breaker panel and kicked a breaker off. I twisted the correct wires together and then kicked the breaker back on. The lights came on and we cheered.

"Thanks Christy boy. Sorry to disturb you."

"You didn't, Arthur did, I was studying, face down in a book, dull stuff."

Shan asked, "Arthur came to see you at home?"

"Yeh, looked fancy too, like he had just come from church."

"That old queen loves pageantry."

Stan asked, "What did he want?"

"He asked how it was going here."

Shan swore, "Damn snoopy slitch, he could look in the front window and tell."

"I think he had already done that."

Stan said, "Why do you say so?"

"Because he gave me $250 to get you open."

Shan asked, "He did?" I put the money on the counter.

"Yeah, here, you want it? We need the cash."

Stan scooped up the money, "Want it? Need it, every which way."

"I figure he knows that, he asked me to get you open as soon as we can."

Stan waves the money, "I can have the license issued tomorrow."

"What does it say?"

Shan says, "Gifts and Novelties. Not intended for actual use."

"Perfect. How about that Indian Hookah there?"

"Ornamental, just like the tapestries, gifts and novelties"

"Love It, how many tourist gift shops does Savannah have these days?"

Stan says, "A couple dozen licensed. None with this inventory."

Shan exclaims, "I'll never let Arthur know, that I know..."

"He knows where it went, to finish opening."

Stan compliments "My faith in you is justified." He stands on tip toe to kiss me on the cheek.

I blush and change the subject. "What's the outlet for?"

"Lava lamps."

"Let me finish that for you. But before I do, we need to have a discussion about the shop and smoking. We need to keep it clean around here and maybe at home too."

"You think so?"

"I know so, we're not even open yet and some of the heads at school are estimating how much product we're going to move."

Shan says, "Product, that's funny."

Stan admits, "Yeah, the gay bars are talking too."

Shan says, "People wish us success, but most of them think it's a front."

I explain the rule plainly. "Well, the joke's on them, not a speck, not a seed, not a stem on the premises. Ok?

Shan says, "Mickey, my favorite bartender at the Blue Parrot says the cops are asking questions."

"Which cops?"

"Dunno, how many are there?"

I laugh, "One is enough. One arrest and we're done. The shop closes and someone goes to jail."

Stan says, "Well, that settles it. We run a clean machine."

We all agreed on the policy and from that day forward held true.

♦   ♦   ♦   ♦   ♦   ♦   ♦

We opened Magnolia's the next weekend to a whopping $28.00 worth of business. We had no money for advertising so it was basically word of mouth.

Stan's idea of marketing was to be seen doing crazy things like riding his bicycle around, handing out flyers for the store with a Magnolia strapped to his head. Shan began a painting project where each brick on the store front was painted a different color of the rainbow. Be that as it may, many drivers slowed just to look at Shan's butt as he climbed a ladder while wearing short shorts. The rainbow was adopted at Magnolias as a symbol of freedom from oppression.

Within a month or so we were visited by SPD, the DEA, and the FBI. They began with direct questions and asking permission to look the place over. We always complied, even when they started sending in agents in costume.

Oddly enough, some of these were our best customers. They would come in wearing brand new Hippie clothes and bad wigs sometimes with the tags still attached. The cops in drag would buy up the place. They bought water beds and tapestries and black lights and posters and scales and incense and pipes and papers and comic books.

They would usually pose as being from out of town and slyly suggest that maybe I could help them find some 'Stuff' to use with all the gear.

Whoever was on duty at the counter would simply point to our license and state that we were a gift and novelty shop. The smoking apparatus were decorative or ornamental and not for actual use. None of them ever returned but it didn't stop the powers that be from sending new ones. It was a crazy time at first, then it got boring.

We took hand made items on consignment, like candles and leather goods, and did a profit sharing thing. We made some of our own items like sand candles, and kid's toys, and roach clips. There was a bamboo research farm out past the army base that would allow people to take any bamboo that had already fallen over. So I showed the boys how to make bongs from bamboo and some bee's wax.

These bongs were selling pretty well until Shan created a sign advertising US Government Approved Bongs. Our supply was cut off so we got rid of the sign. We had to send in secondary bamboo gatherers.

Our acceptance among the liberal locals was amazing. They all thought it was about time for the Seventies to replace the Fifties in Savannah. Suspicion among the populace extended through society. The local newspaper and some magazines did stories and articles on the pro's and con's of us having the balls to be in business.

I had one customer who would come in on Saturday

afternoon. Michelle was a school teacher from Baxley Ga. and was quite amused at our presence. She said she had wanted 'some cool people' to hang out with. She would hang around past closing. She didn't smoke but always had homemade brownies in her car.

The first time she offered me a brownie I was hungry and didn't stop to think they might be laced. I ate two, she ate one and said I couldn't have any more. It took about a half hour, but I got off like a rocket, locked the front door and did my best to entertain her on a waterbed. We created a joke about 'Sea Trials' for her to stay past closing and do a durability test on our water beds. Nice girl, she loved to get high and make love.

So that was the way it went for a year or so. Business kept increasing Stan and Shan did weekdays, I did evenings and weekends. My draft dilemma ended as the war effort wound down. They stopped drafting civilians that year at lottery number 29.

I stayed in nursing school for the duration and got my R.N. certification. A Smythe was happy because he brought in a craftsman who specialized in vintage repairs. Buddy, or Bud, was also gay and moved in with Arthur, so I got the boot.

Stan and Shan got tired of having to be so cautious at work and at home. There were also a series of vicious beatings of gay men. They were being, 'rolled' while trying to pick up young boys down by the water front. Stan & Shan had done okay with the shop and wanted to move back to SF and try a shop there. They really wanted to get out of town, so I went looking for a partner.

My first partner was a high school friend who came from a proper native family, whom I will not name. I hesitate from identifying the family because I respect their own rules of propriety. My pal, Howie, and I pooled resources and began to share the hours of operation. He concealed his involvement from his family for as long as possible, almost a month. He lasted another month after his investment was discovered.

I found two willing but unlikely investors who were not interested in shop tending. They were both local pot farmer / dealers, Bob and Doug, who had more grass than brains. I knew I could not trust either of them for very long. After all, one of the reason's it's called dope, is because it makes you stupid.

So, I sold out to both of them. One took Howie's share and the other took mine. I agreed to continue shop tending for a few weeks. One day when I came in and found evidence that someone had broken into the shop from a back window. They had slashed the water beds and the place was a soggy mess.

Whoever it was had spray painted swastika images over many posters. I called the partners to ask if I should report the B&E to the police. We called the police who took 4 hours to arrive. SPD sent a patrol car with one veteran officer and one rookie, but no investigator.

They took a verbal report and left. I hired a couple of kids from the neighborhood to help me clean the place and board up the back window. We replaced all the defaced posters and opened for business that afternoon.

A DEA agent named Rollins came round early that evening to say he had heard of our misfortune. I knew he was busting my balls because of the way he kept smiling. He asked me where my 'panty waist partners' had gone off to. Said he hadn't seen them for a week or so. This confirmed something for me, we were still being watched. We had become lazy as the community had accepted us.

The agent asked if I could identify one of my regular customers and showed me a photograph of one my new partners, Bobby. I said yeah I knew him but didn't know his name. Rollins wanted to know what he usually bought, I just shrugged and gestured to the display case full of pipes and papers. He shrugged in return and left.

I thought long and hard about the turn of events and started feeling paranoid about the time the sun went down. I closed early that day and went over to A. Smythe's place to have a chat. He knew Stan & Shan had left for the west coast but not about my new partners. When I told him who they were, he called a friend and asked some questions.

It turned out that the person he spoke with was an undercover narcotics officer posing as the school teacher with whom I had been making love. Arthur told me that she had cleared the way for us, by reporting that we were too smart to deal out of the shop. She had heard of Bob and Doug through the grapevine of information the feds shared with the locals.

Arthur was of the opinion that since I had already sold to them, I should get away from the business as fast as possible. He felt bad times were on the way. So, I made preparations to do so. The next day I went to Chandler hospital and applied for a job. I got some shifts for that weekend.

I gave Bob and Doug two days notice of vacating the job at Magnolia's. They were pissed and stiffed me on the pay, and told me to get lost. This meant that one of them would have to tend shop until they found more help. One of them had a girl friend they put behind the counter.

Several days later I heard that someone had put a few bullets into the sign we had hung over the sidewalk on Drayton. I went around to look. The pretty sign that Shan and Stan had created was in poor shape, several petals had been blown away. I was sad for days gone by.

Agent Rollins approached me one day as I left Chandler. I was surprised and said so. He said he had heard about the sell out. He wanted to know what my plans were and I told him I wasn't sure. The draft thing was over, nursing school was over, and the shop was over

He nodded and said he was glad I knew that the shop was over. He advised me not to do any further business there, even for papers. I stopped and looked at his firm jawed DEA countenance. I met his eyes and nodded, extended my hand and took his to shake.

With his free hand he pulled something out of the breast of his overcoat. I stopped the shake and squeezed his hand only to watch his hand extract a business card. It was one of his and had a number hand written on the back. He gave it to me and turned to leave. Before he got into his car he said,

"There's this school teacher in Baxley who would like to hear from you. That's her number, she said to give her a call." I did so and went to the country for a long weekend.

A week later Magnolia's was raided and three kilo's of pot were found in a brown paper bag. The girl behind the counter swore the police who raided the place had brought the bag with them. Bob and Doug were both busted while driving a pick up truck with another two kilos inside a brown bag in the back.

Magnolia's closed and the rainbow of bricks was whitewashed.

I went through some interesting changes while waiting there. But, it was a good time, for the time it lasted.

end

I Was In a Coma Once

written by

T K Wallace

It happened in Atlanta. Atlanta has always been a costly place for me. Me and others I have met. Cost me a couple of fingers one time. But that's another story.

I had just completed an acting job doing summer theater at my alma mater in Savannah. Must have been the summer of 82, I had to get out of the city swelter and accepted a gig with the theater department at Armstrong State College. I stage managed "Ladies of the Alamo" and acted a supporting role in, "Boeing Boeing".

Anyway, after the end of the summer stock I stopped through Atlanta to audition for the Alliance Theater Company and the Atlanta Children's Theater's upcoming season. My friend Patty Kakes allowed me to hang out with her for a couple of days. I borrowed her roommates bicycle to make it to the theater for my audition, only I never made it back.

Patty lived in an older Victorian rental in Chandler Park close to Little Five Points. I rode the bike from her place across N Highland Ave toward Piedmont Park. As I was crossing Ponce De Leon I was struck by a car. The bike jerked forward as the front wheel was knocked loose. The bike forks went down and so did I, into the pavement.

Some days later I was informed that I had suffered a concussion with a hair line crack in my skull over my right eye. Other injuries consisted of my nose being ripped partially away on the lower right side, my upper lip was split and needed to be sewn back together in the middle where the cleft used to be. My teeth had survived but the bottom set scooped out a portion inside my lower lip, and I had three rather nasty gashes, one on my right chin, one beside, and one above my right eye. My right shoulder and arm were also banged up pretty good.

The accident had been witnessed by a gang of construction workers on North Highland. They saw a late model sedan making a left turn as I was coming through the intersection, we both heard a horn blow, and they saw my crunch into the street. The cops arranged for medical transport and did the report of a hit and run. The driver never stopped, just kept going. Nobody got the plates.

ICU

For me, being in a coma was like lying on the bottom of a pool of water at night. It was dark and cool, it was very safe and quiet. I don't remember any dreams or any thoughts at all. But I could tell I was alone. Every now and then I could see the surface, way up there where it was bright.

After a while I floated up closer to the surface toward the brightness. As I got closer I could feel the heat increasing and began to feel uncomfortable. So I went back down where it was safe and cool. Why would there be pain?

Little by little I began to think, just a little at a time, you know, little by little and bit by bit around very large spaces of nothingness. I began to question where I was and what was with the dark cool safe space and the bright hot painful space. Some more time went by and I floated upward again to find the same thing, only this time there were sounds.

I went back down to rest, and to think a bit more. After some more time had passed I realized that I was definitely alone wherever I was. This dark cool safe place was quiet and I was all alone. That bright hot place up there had other things like sounds and maybe those sounds were other people. I thought about this for some more time as I slept.

The next time I went up, I did so intentionally, and I woke up. I had been out four days. Everything was painful, hot, and way too bright. It was so bright I couldn't see at first. I couldn't focus my eyes. I hurt too much and I needed to pass out again. But, I did not go back down, I simply slept a while.

The next time I woke up my friend Patty Kakes was there waiting. I could focus a little better but only one eye worked. My left eye was still out of focus and my right eye was bandaged. I then realized that I had been wearing my contact lenses on my way to the audition, and that I normally wore eye glasses. Patty had my glasses and was sitting on my left.

"You gave us quite a scare."

"Wha hapen?"

"Hit and run, some asshole whacked you and took off."

"I hurt. How bad, I hurt..."

"Cracked your noggin', You been out four days."

I raised my left hand to my face and felt the bandages around my head.

"How bad is it?" I was struggling to keep up, but I wanted to know.

"Well you have a concussion..." and then I faded out.

When I woke again it was darker and Patty was still there. She said,

"Hey there, you gonna stay with me this time? There's some food here if you can eat."

"Don' know. I 'member gettin' hit .... the wheel flying off."

"Let me call a nurse." She did and the process of my recovery began.

Fortunately I had a note from Patty in my backpack

stating times and places to meet when I got to Atlanta. Someone at the hospital tracked her down and informed her of my situation.

She had arrived while I was still in surgery and took a look at the first repair over the right eye. It had been stitched up in a crude manner. She asked to speak with attending physician and informed him that I was an actor and that I would probably like to have a plastic surgeon do the rest my face.

Somewhere, is a black and white photograph of me holding a cold bottle of Heineken against the stitches that covered most of the right side of my face. I was in Piedmont hospital for another couple of days and then released to mend on my own. It cost me all my savings and I still owed a few thousand.

Old Home

Patty had contacted my parents who were in my home town of Belle for the final weeks of summer. They flew me to St Louis, picked me up, and drove me home a hundred miles for further convalescence.

Life in Belle was pretty simple especially when you looked like I did, which was scary, like Halloween scary. Most people avoided talking to me because I looked like it would cause me great deal of pain just to speak. Anyone who wanted to know details asked my parents what had happened, and were given the story of the accident.

The healing process which my concussion took was kind of like watching a snow globe when shaken. During coma all the brain matter flies around waiting to settle. It was a real effort just to operate on a normal basis. It was slow going at first, even simple things like speaking. As the snowflakes settled, my brain had to reconnect the dots for more advanced functions to reappear, like walking a straight line, whistling, not trying to hit the correct note, just the act of whistling. Counting inside my head came along the more I practiced. I could do it on paper before I could free form the math in my mind.

One day in early September my mother asked me how long I intended to stay and heal. I said I did not know. She assured me that I could stay as long as I needed to, but that she and my father wanted to return to their winter home in Florida. They were planning to meet my maternal grandmother, Hannah Davis Martin, for her Florida vacation.

A few days later my father asked me to drive him into St Louis for an appointment of some kind. We chatted about any number of things while I drove him into the center of St Louis, downtown near the old train station.

During the waiting time I drove around to some of my old haunts without stopping to say hello. I had lunch at a Steak and Shake and picked my father up about 2pm. We drove back to Belle arriving just before dinner. Dinner conversation was a question and answer session about how I felt, where I had gone during my father's meeting, if I had been missing any knowledge concerning directions to and from the city.

I was proud to report that there were no gaps or indecision concerning the day. My parents were concerned but obviously anxious to get on with their plans. My mother told me later that my father had lunch with a former associate as a reason to test my cognitive skills. He wanted to examine me more closely by watching my decision making process, watching how I did what I did, how I expressed myself, and other ways.

The next day my father announced that they would be leaving for Florida in a week. They gave me the choice of going with them or staying in Belle for as long as I wanted. I decided to stay where I was for a few more days. I borrowed $500 to get started on when I returned to New York. He gave me cash and my mother snuck in another $250.

My paternal grandmother, Marie Theresa Wallace, still lived in Belle at that time and assured my parents that she would look after me. And she did. I ate at her table more than a few days. Marie was a great believer in taking naps every mid-day. She was also a believer in taking a healthy snort of Old Grand Dad a few hours after dinner. She could snore the paint off a barn.

A little more than a week later, I asked her to drive me over to Rolla, so I could take a Greyhound bus back to New York. She agreed and did so the next morning. We left early so I could meet the noon bus going east. I did this on purpose so I could wave her off before the bus got there. She fussed over me a bit before she left me to wait for the bus.

After she left I picked up my backpack and walked out to interstate 44 to hitchhike back to NYC. I was too cheap, stubborn, and beat up to waste the bus fare. And I felt I needed a challenge like cross country hitch hiking to help bring me up a notch on the mental activity level. Most of all I needed to think.

I had survived critical possibly life threatening wounds. I had survived and was carefully healed by loving parents who did not really understand me or my ways. I had been allowed a slow lovingly patient healing process and I was happy to be alive.

The Road

The first ride I got was with a mother and son driving to the St Louis airport. They dropped me on Interstate70 where I got a ride all the way to Indianapolis with some hippies going to a rock festival on the Bull Island river peninsula. I figured 'what the hell' and went along. When we got there the place was packed and we could not get within a half mile of the stage.

I was about to leave when I heard an announcement from the stage requesting anyone with medical training to come volunteer at the Over Dose tent right down front by the stage. I had taken Life Saving and Red Cross CPR classes as a life guard, so I volunteered just to get closer to the show.

It was a crazy, lunatic ridden three days of treating doped up people, both audience and performers. There was a very strong batch of windowpane acid going around sending lots of people to the OD tent tripping their butts off. Their pupils were so dilated you could not see color in the iris.

To further complicate things, there were a bunch of junkies from Kansas City selling crushed up laundry bleach as cocaine. We had doctors who treated these unfortunate souls while we ran triage for the incoming.

I was tending entry of the front tent when these two biker babes came screaming up demanding someone to come help Big Leo. I ran with them calling out for someone to follow with a stretcher.

Big Leo was on his back trying to suck in air, and not

being very successful. He was blue in the face and wide eyed as his chest heaved violently. 'Shit', was my first thought, 'I have to try CPR and maybe do a mouth to mouth on this guy?'

I cleared his tracheotomy and found nothing. I noticed some vomit on his shirt and chest so I pumped his chest a couple of times and started mouth to mouth. He coughed and after the third or fourth pump he 'fountained' covering me with puke. I got him rolled onto his knees so he could get the rest out.

Big Leo stabilized pretty quickly. His color came back and he could talk, or at least bellow. I went down to the river and cleaned and soaked and cleaned and soaked. By the time I got back to the OD tent I was having a hard time understanding reality.

Somewhat later in the day Big Leo came to see me with the two babes. Turns out they were from a Hell's Angels club in Kansas City. He wanted to thank me by offering me the babes for the night. The babes wanted to thank me for saving Big Leo's life. I declined claiming I was married. But, I asked him for a favor.

I asked Leo to find those KC junkies and take their bleach away. He said he would see what he could do. One of the guilty junkies left the festival in an ambulance, another was found dead in the river.

I wonder to this day, if I did the world a favor that day. Okay, I had probably saved a life. But had I caused a death? No, I had not dealt that blow. But had I dealt the cards of that hand? Probably, I didn't investigate so I'll never know.

The festival wound down on Sunday evening and I got a ride back to Indianapolis. I spent that night getting short rides to a truck stop outside Evanston, Illinois. There I caught a great ride with a trucker going all the way to Philadelphia. This guy was a speed freak and just wanted to talk. He talked at me most of the ride without ever waiting for a reply.

By mid afternoon I was standing in a parking lot of a Howard Johnsons just off the Jersey turnpike. I went in for some clams. The waitress who was serving my station saw my backpack and put a placemat in front of me. It was decorated with a block game of the turnpike for kids to play while waiting for their food.

About every fifth or sixth block read, "Remember, it is illegal to hitch hike the NJ turnpike. Both Motorists and Pedestrians will be fined." I picked up my rig and left without ordering.

I got a ride from the parking lot of the HoJo with a drunken pilot headed for Newark airport. He needed someone to drive for him. After opening a couple more bottles of beer on the door handle he passed out and slept for the next 50 miles or so.

When we got to the airport I woke him up and asked him where to park. He gave me directions to pilot's parking and then asked who I was. I laughed and told him I was just a hitch hiker he had picked up close to Philly. He thanked me and offered me $40 for getting him to work.

I regarded the offer as a good sign, took the money, and hopped on a bus into Manhattan. The Forty bucks covered food on the road, and a bus ride into the city. I had traveled through to the other end of my journey with a profit of $15.00.

In the singular comfort of my commuter bus seat I drifted through the past few days of being on the road. It had taken me four days and five nights on the road to get from my home town, Belle, Missouri, to Manhattan. But, it had taken me two months to get back to New York from Savannah.

Back in the City

I went directly to the sublet I still shared in Hell's Kitchen and let myself in. My friends Mark and Elizabeth and their dog Beau were there and startled to see me.

They had been able to follow when I left Savannah and then lost the track. I had contacted them from my parents place about a month later. And then, selfishly enough, I made no further efforts.

So, they made me tell the entire tale, just as I have told it to you.

Coma was a weird thing, and now a part of my past. But, from the bicycle accident, through the long healing reconnection period, out onto the road to test myself, the rock concert incidents, and my safe return to the city, I was thankful.

Out of luck and the ability to heal, it made me hit a reset switch in my life.

A Baseball Story

written by

T K   Wallace

Game Time was the obsession of my day dream. I can hear the crowd in the stadium. All of the players on the field and all the fans in the stands are there with me at the game. The pitch comes in fast as a breaking curve ball. The batter swings and another souvenir is launched into the crowd. The foul ball is coming toward me. Do I dive for the prize, or stand there and watch?

My occupation is helping produce live corporate events for some of the worlds' biggest companies. If my clients want to announce a new product, hold an information based meeting, or just offer an exclusive party, they come to me and mine and we make it happen.

I am also a baseball fan. From listening on the radio, or watching television, then on cable, or now across the net, and most especially in the stands, I'm a fan, and so was my old man.

When I was young my father gave me two autographed balls. One had the signature of "Stan the Man", Stan Musial. The other had the signatures of the entire team of the 1963 World Series winning St. Louis Cardinals. I leave them and many other sports treasures I have added in his custody. He has more time and a better temperament for collecting.

So, when I did an event for the Upper Deck trading card company, it gave me the opportunity to ask one of the guests of honor, Mr. Reggie Jackson, for an autograph. He was accompanied by Joe Montana, Wayne Gretsky, and Lou al Cinder, aka Kareem Abdul Jabbar.

Upper Deck was doing their east coast launch of offerings to collectors, distributors, and investment analysts. Their overall plan was to decrease the numbers of issue, up the quality, and of course, bump the price per item.

The location of the corporate facility I was managing was in midtown Manhattan, close to Rockefeller Center. The building held 50 stories of the fortune 100, and needless to say many well to do sports fans. Because the event was, "By Invitation Only", many corporate sports buffs were not invited. My office and stage phones rang off the hook that week. I had to refuse them admission citing proper client privacy ethics.

One request I could not refuse came from the head of security for the building. He asked if I could obtain an autograph on a baseball. Almost all corporate security people in the city are ex NYPD. I knew which side to butter that bread. So even though I had told the CFO of MCI that I could not help him, I told my chief of security, Tom, that I would try. I asked him to send me the ball and he brought it himself.

He delivered the ball in a brown paper bag and I left it in the coat check with Melinda. At that moment Misters Jackson, Montana, Gretsky, and Jabbar arrived at street level with the security entourage of Upper Deck. They were mobbed by the crowd. Tom and building security helped to keep the collectors at bay while we escorted the sports stars backstage and secured them in the green room. I then returned to the theater and opened the house for the show.

On my return backstage I detoured through the coat check and picked up the paper bag. When I arrived, I announced to the Upper Deck execs that the show was about to begin, and that they should take their seats in the auditorium. They all left and it gave me the moment.

Reggie was speaking with his manager and a reporter

about a press conference he had with Michael Jordon in Chicago. He was commenting about Jordon's recent aspirations in baseball and wondering aloud about scheduling problems involving the upcoming spring training.

"He's a big guy. He's really tall and his shoulders are as wide as mine." Jackson saw me and asked, "How tall are You?

"I'm two meters", I answered. "6 foot 6."

"I thought so. What suit coat size do you wear?"

"I wear at 52 tall, extra long."

"Try this on." He said as he started to remove his coat.

"What ?" I managed.

"Try this on." He handed me his coat. "I'm a 52 short but I thought we were about the same size across the shoulders."

As I took off my coat I said, "Well, okay but Jordon has at least five or six inches on me." I pulled on his coat and buttoned it. "It fits across the chest, but...." We all laughed because the sleeves were up to my elbows.

"Yep he's probably a 52 XXX Long and Tall. Thanks." He stuck out a hand. "Reggie" As I handed him back his coat, I took his hand.

"Ted. I run the place."

"Nice place, thanks for getting us through the crowd. We didn't get stopped once." I nodded as I picked up my jacket which I had put down over the ball bag.

He asked, "What you got there?"

"uh, Mr Jackson . . ?" I said as I lifted the bag.

"Will I sign this?" He asked.

"Yes Sir, you see I have a friend . . ."

"A friend? This is for a friend . . ." He said in disbelief.

"Yes sir. It's actually for the chief of security. He helped us out just now in the lobby. He asked me to get it autographed."

I stammered as I began to remove the ball from the bag. It was double wrapped in two plastic bags and already had some other signatures.

He took the ball from me and said to his agent. "This is a Reacher."

"That's an old ball. Old American League?" was the reply.

"Right. Look at the stitching. They used alternating red and blue threads. And look at this. That looks real. I know, I have one." He turned the ball so we could see the small space between the curving stitches.

The signature read, 'Babe Ruth'.

"Wow," was all I could manage.

"Where did you get this?"

"Just as I said, from the chief of security."

"Do you know what I could get for this ball if I took it out onstage?"

"You wouldn't do that, would you?"

"Nope." He took out a pen and turned the ball around to the other small space between the stitches. He signed the ball in the opposite spot the Babe had used.

"Thanks." I said.

"Thank You." He said but continued to look at the ball. "Here's Phil Neekro, Warren Spawn, Micky, Ted Williams. What a bunch of bums."

"Jesus, I had no idea." I held up the bags from the wrapping.

"This friend of yours, Is he ex-NYPD ?"

"Yep, retired and doing corporate time these days."

"That makes it my pleasure. The boys in pinstripes can never do enough for the boys in Blue." He tossed me the ball, "Tell him if he wants to retire in style, Upper Deck will auction this ball for him."

"I don't think he -. . . . Thanks again." was all I had time to say, as we walked toward the stage and the event began. I returned the ball into the bags and took it to my office by the back steps.

Work, is after all 'Work' and we all had a job to do that day. And as I like my job I forgot about the ball until later while I closed the four stars into a limousine for a private get away.

I went back into the theatre to supervise the breakdown of the event. The Upper Deck people were handing out free packs of player cards to the audience as show gifts. I like free stuff so I asked for a handful of the packs for my crew. Even though these were being given away to the audience the young man giving them out looked me over and said that he would have to ask permission.

Onstage banners and big cards were being taken down and into the green room to be wrapped and taken back to the Upper Deck offices. The stage manager I had hired for the show came over and said,

"One of the execs told me that he liked the show and the way the place was run. Said they would be back." We slapped five, high and low. And, as was our custom we bumped fists three times saying,

"Da Dum Dum Dum, Another one bites the dust."

An Upper Deck exec and security person with a badge asked to see me off stage. We used a dressing room and I asked "What's up?" The security lady took out a box of players cards and put them on the counter.

"We would like to know what went on with you and Mr. Jackson in the green room just before the show."

"How do you mean?"

"The reporter who left said you were exchanging coats with him. It is against the policies of Upper Deck for anyone to obtain personal materials belonging to the players."

"Oh that, he was trying to figure out if he and Michael Jordon wore the same size."

"Why would that matter?" asked Beth the security person.

"Don't know, Something about He and I and Michael having the same chest size, but me being in between the two in height. I think he was talking about Michael's baseball career."

The security lady said, "That doesn't look like his coat you're wearing."

I could only laugh, "He certainly didn't wear mine on stage."

I extended my hand, "Ted."

She grasped firmly and shook. "Beth."

Mr Upper Deck said, "You were also seen carrying a bag into the room and then out again. What was in the bag?"

"A baseball."

"I have explained that it is against policy for employees to ask ...."

"I don't work for Upper Deck. But no worries, Reggie said he couldn't sign it due to his contract with you guys."

"Can I see the ball?"

"Nope."

"Why not?"

"Because I don't have it."

"Where is it?"

"I gave it back to the guard who asked the favor. He coaches."

"We could go around you to get that ball."

"Yeah, you could make a big fuss over a blank baseball. In fact go ahead. My chief of security spent 15 years at the 34th pct, and today he did your security guys big favors in crowd control."

Upper deck paused and thanked em for the information. I glanced at Beth and noticed she was wearing a NYPD lapel pin. I smiled at her and she smiled in return. She handed me the box of player's cards.

As they left I asked, "Are these signed?"

I waited all afternoon for Tom to call. I got the crew out, finished the paperwork for final billing on the show and was about to leave when the phone rang. I reached out and punched speaker phone.

"Hello, this is Ted". It was Tom,

"I just got off the phone with a security chief who called to thank me for helping out today."

"Good for him."

"He also asked me if I knew anything about an illegal autograph."

"What is an illegal autograph?"

"I asked him the same thing."

"What did he say?"

"He said, 'Never mind' and thanked me again before he hung up."

"He's a twitchy fellow in my opinion. Takes all types I suppose."

"Yep."

There was a pause. "So did you get it?"

"Of course, but I told yer Twitchy Boy that Reggie turned me down... ... ... Now if I could only find the damn thing."

"What?"

"Well I tried on Reggie's coat and we tossed the ball back and forth."

"You played catch with Reggie Jackson, with that ball? No Shit?"

"Well, just a little. But then during the show I put the ball away and I can't quite remember where."

There was a snapping sound that came from the phone and I could have sworn that I heard his phone hit the floor. Outside my office a flash of light and the smell of brimstone preceded a knock on my door.

"It's open." I called. Tom entered trailing small wisps.

"Leave it open."

"Tell me you didn't lose it."

"Tell me why you set me up."

"I didn't set you up."

"I'll look for it. I'm sure it's around here somewhere."

Tom almost turned purple, "You can't loose that ball !"

"I think you owe me the story behind the ball." He sat in relief.

"Okay, okay, It's an heirloom. Started by my Grandfather."

"Let's hear it."

"When he was a kid, Pop Pop used to work at Yankee stadium as a vendor, you know selling stuff out of a neck cart. You see, he was a die hard Brooklyn Dodgers fan would never pay to see a Yankee game. He always said that they would have to pay him to be there. But, he really loved the game. So he got a job selling beer in the stands. He said that he would stop selling every time he heard a ball was hit and the crowd began to roar.

Anyway, one day he was selling along the base line close to the dug out. The Babe was up to bat and he hit a high foul ball which was coming Pop Pop's way. He stripped off the neck cart and tossed it to some kids yelling, "Hold This". And he dove over some other fans for the ball.

He landed on top of the dug out with the ball in his hand, and then slid off the front. His fall was broken by several players. He said the players cheered him on and he was passed back up, and over the front of the roof.

He was also cheered by the fans as he displayed the ball. Then he looked around for his neck cart he found it completely empty. He said he saw several fans with beer cups who would not meet his eye.

When he went back to vending, he had to explain to his boss what happened with the beer, and he was fired.

Several days passed and the Babe, Mr. George Herman Ruth, showed up at my great grandparents place and asked to see Pop Pop. My great grandma didn't know the Babe from Adam, so she asked him what he wanted. The Babe was flustered and said he had some unfinished business with her son.

Great grand Marie, god rest her soul, stood her ground and told him to explain himself or go away. The Babe explained that he worked at Yankee stadium, and that there had been a mistake over Pop Pop's job. Marie called Pop Pop to come in from his chores out back.

My grandfather said that when he saw the Babe on his family doorstep, he could barely speak. The Babe asked him,

"Are you the kid who caught my foul and fell in the dug out?"

"Yes Sir, ... but all my beer got stolen ..... and I got fired."

"Yeah we heard." The Babe said, "The team's assistant manager went to your boss and used a little influence to get your job back, okay?"

"Pop Pop was happy, but not too embarrassed to pull the ball out of his pocket and ask the Babe for his autograph.

That's how the ball got started, from Pop Pop to his son to my Dad, from Dad to Me, and from Me to Tommy Jr. It's being passed from father to son.

My Dad says his Dad was a Yankee fan from that day on. They asked many other players to sign the ball over the years. He said that every time the two of them went to a game the ball went along securely zipped into a coat pocket."

Tom looked much younger as he spoke of his family.

I reached out and lifted a Yankees cap up off of my desk to reveal the ball. He blinked and picked it up.

"Sorry about not telling you about the other signatures. Didn't think it made any difference." He began to unwrap the ball.

"It did to Reggie. Look where he signed it." Tom turned the ball and as he looked he got misty eyed. In a choked voice he said,

"Thank You. My dad's gonna love this."

"Reggie was nice about it, he asked if you were an ex cop, I told him yeah and he said, "Good. The boys in pinstripes can never do enough for the boys in Blue."

The mist in his eyes and the tightness of his lips was all the response I needed. He smiled and nodded as he left my office. He walked down the hall, he tossed the ball lightly into the air and caught it with the same hand.

In my head I can hear the stadium crowd. The seats along the base line are full. We are in the stands and with the snap of a bat, everyone follows the flight of a high foul ball that comes towards us. Do we stand there and watch, or go for the ball?

I dive and yell, " MINE !"

Just An Idea

written by

T K Wallace

We open with a singer's day dream, she is singing on stage at the Apollo.

We hear and see the performance. A woman in full show costume singing into a microphone while dancing with three others. They are dressed as males but their moves leave room to wonder. The song is 'Everybody Needs Somebody'.

**"Ev-ery-body needs somebody to love
Someone to love (Someone to love)"**

Flashing into reality, we see that the event is not a concert, but a music audition. There is a sparse stage with only one other person who is playing the piano and doing backup vocals. Two suits are in the seats listening.

**"Sweetheart to miss (Sweetheart to miss)
Sugar to kiss (Sugar to kiss)"**

Outside on Harlem's 125th st, just to the side of the Apollo we see two street vendors selling CD's from a folding table. The same song is playing in the back ground. Zoe and Jackie are the selling CD's as they move with the music.

**"I Need You, You, You.
I Need You, You, You."**

Zoe starts, "Yes Sir, this song was performed and recorded by Mr Wilson Picket. One of many he made famous for Motown Records."

Jackie works as shill and steps up to say, "That takes me back some!"

"CD's are Two for $5.00, That's right, Get 'em here, Get em today, Get 'em hot, or Get 'em Not. Same price for any disks here at 'Sister's CD'. Two for Five."

A handsome and nervous young man steps up to the 'Sisters' table. He pulls on a hat as he looks behind him. Two suits in black and white move past him as he shuffles through the disks.

"What you looking for mister,' Zoe watches him as the suits pass, "You looking for music, or just looking for some way to avoid trouble?"

Jackie crowds in to take a look at this Latino. "Wha's up, Pup?"

The man looks and blinks, as if seeing them for the first time. He keeps his head down, he laughs, and says,

"If there's an elevator under this table I'll buy every disk you have."

Jackie starts, "Well that's mighty tempting, but the closest elevator going down to the subway is on the other side of the street."

Zoe slaps away a shop lifters hands,

"Get yo sticky paws outa here child," turns to Luis and adds,

"But we will sell you as many as you can carry." She indicates the man purse he shoulders. "How many you want?"

She looks away and says, "Cause here they come again."

We see the black and white suits pass more slowly this time. The Latino loses the shoulder bag adjusts his hat and picks up several CD's and sashays,

"Oh Yes, Is that song on this disk? And I'll take these as well."

He starts to hand over some cash, when one of the suits takes an arm.

"Excuse me Sir, Would you come with us please?"

"Why would I do that? I'm shopping here." indicating Zoe, "Aren't I ?"

'Yo mister, that's a paying customer you're bothering. You can at least wait until he buys something before you TAKE HIM INTO CUSTODY !" She yells this last to bring the attention of everybody else on the street.

The entire section of 125th street in front of the Apollo looks at the suits. Latino man throws some money toward Zoe and dashes across he street. He crashes down the subway stairs, and through the crowd. The suits push Jackie away and curse Zoe as they follow their prey.

The people of Harlem are not easily intimidated. They do not aid or assist in any sort of apprehension. One sole Grandmother blocks the way of the suits as they attempt to descend the subway steps. As one suit moves to push her aside a cane rises to strike him between his legs. The other suit turns on her only to be confronted by several suspicious and unhappy people around her.

Zoe and Jackie lose track of the escaping man. Zoe kicks his shoulder bag under the table and waits. When she is sure no one interested, she pushes it further under with a cane. She doesn't need the cane to walk, but she keeps it close for; well, like now. Jackie rescues the bag and sits in the van to check the contents.

The Latino man dashes out of the subway, crosses the street, and then slowly moves down into another entrance. He spies the suits surrounded by angry people and backs out again.

He quickly exits and crosses the street to 'Sisters'. He looks at Zoe and the place he dropped his shoulder bag. It is gone.

We hear Emma Franklin's blues singing, 'Piece of my Heart' coming from the big portable speaker under the table.. Mr. Latino looks at Zoe who throws him his hat in a no-look pass. He runs as the suits spot him, and start after him again. He dodges through the Apollo. One suit goes after him, but the other stops at the table to speak with Zoe,

"So, you sell music? Two for Five? What do you buy, and for how much?"

"I don' buy nothing. I can't even imagine you having anything I want."

"You didn't buy anything from that guy? He leave anything with you?"

"He had out a twenty befoe' you goons chased him away. Tanks for Dat."

The suit sneers at Zoe and takes out a money clip. He peels off a bill and drops it on the table.

"You haven't seen us, okay?"

"Actually he had out a C note? That would make me forget."

He throws down a few more bills and starts off after his partner.

The chase continues through the front doors of the Apollo, down the aisle, and out a side door. The theater occupants stand amazed and then continue. After doubling back through the alley and out onto 125th street, Luis enters a bar and strips off his jacket. A suit runs past in high chase mode barking into his radio. Luis grabs a girl and pulls her to the dance floor. '**Who's Making Love**' is coming from the juke box.

◆　◆　◆　◆　◆　◆　◆

Inside the theater we see the singer start another piece. "Rescue Me" is in full swing as the suits come tearing through like they were the only things in the room. They have radios and pictures they show people and ask for whereabouts.

"Cause I'm lonely, And I'm blue
I need you, And your love too
Come on and –

From the stage we hear the singing stop and a hearty woman's voice says,

"What the hell is going on back there? Can't a woman sing a song here?"

One suit ventures toward the stage holding up a picture of Luis,

"Yes mam, sorry Mam, Could you tell us if you have seen this man in the neighborhood.?"

"And when was I supposed to have seen this, is that a guy? I was up here trying to make a living. Or am I supposed to do that after you assholes leave?"

"Look Lady It's a simple question-"

"The name is Neary. Do you have a badge? Do you have any ID that obligates me to speak with you?"

A new voice enters the fray, it belongs to the theater manager; Mr. Sutliff.

"These persons appear to be security, but not policemen.

You're under no obligation, but I would consider it a favor, if you would take a look at the photo."

"Hey, for you My Sutliff, no problem. Now, 'soldier boy', bring that over here again and lemmee see."

The suit does so and Neary looks closely.

"I don't know who he is, but he flew thru here a few minutes ago."

"He was here? You saw him?"

"I said so didn't I? What is wrong with you people that we have to repeat ourselves for you to understand? Yes, he ran through here a little while ago."

"Where did he go?"

Neary looks at the suit while placing one hand on her hip, tapping her foot, and shakes her head. The theater manager asks,

"Are you finished young man?", and the suit departs. Mr. Sutliff resumes,

"Very good Miss Taylor, we would like to see you perform this Friday and Saturday in the VIP lounge. Could that be arranged?"

♦　♦　♦　♦　♦　♦　♦

Outside Zoe is turning the table over to Jackie. We hear 'Green Onions' by Booker T playing from the stand.

"All you have to do is say, 'you just got to work', and look at them like they're stupid. I'll be right here in the van. "

Zoe rounds the van and gets into the drivers seat. In the passenger seat is Luis's shoulder bag. She lifts it to look as Luis speaks from the back seat,

"Looks like I found a way out after all."

"Who said you could get in my ride?"

"Nobody, but I thought you may lend a hand and get me out of here."

"Boy, you have a lot of nerve. Why are they looking for you?"

"Why did you lift my bag?"

"You dropped it under my table. What am I supposed to do, ignore it?"

He laughs at himself, "Thanks rescuing my bag, now how about me?"

"We'll see about that, What's in the bag?"

"I think I saw something no one was supposed to see."

"Like what?"

"I think someone is going to destroy the Apollo."

Zoe peels out.

◆　◆　◆　◆　◆　◆　◆

In the theater seats we see Amos Sutliff and a younger version. Both are medium brown men in good suits. The older speaks,

"I think Neary will be excellent, 'after show' talent in the VIP tent. You said you had three bands?"

"Yes Sir, one for the electronica dance show, and one classic rock for the money crowd." The piano player starts to play 'It's All Right' in the background.

"And the third?"

"That one is one we talked about. It's after show hours and we don't really have a permit. It should be okay. The party is out back in the tent."

"Why not in here?"

"The band stand and the dance floor take up a lot of space. Then there's the rigging, lights, and sound systems. If we did it in here we couldn't remove anything from the show until the party was over."

"So ?'

"Holding the entire load out of the show for an after party is a bad decision. That gets real expensive, real fast. We have the tent, we should use it."

"Oh, Yes. Please do so. We certainly can't afford any additional expenses. This 'fund raiser' is far enough over budget."

"Our key funding 'Angel' would have a fit to underwrite even more."

"Watch where you put your feet, try to keep them out of your mouth."

Sutliff looks at his phone as it rings, "Speak of the devil." He answers, "Sutliff. Oh, hello Madeline... ... Yes,..... we did see security from your building."

Sutliff listens and nods. He holds the phone away from his head and rolls his eyes. "Yes, yes, we saw a man run through, I thought he was an usher. In what way was he associated with you dear?"

His assistant is trying not to listen but having no luck because Sutliff is pretending to listen but making faces away from the phone,

"Oh he wasn't with you.... Oh he was here, but left, suddenly, . . . No we didn't, no he didn't, well then, okay, bye." He hangs up and shrugs as he smiles.

"Sir, if I may, what was that about? Who were they searching for?"

"Some vagabond who had snuck in off the street and

interrupted a private party. Something about being hungry, or wanting money."

"Ah, well, goodness knows the Apollo could use all the money we can find. So, he snuck in? Or, what happened?"

"I'm not quite sure. As long as I've known that woman, I've never become accustomed to her impatience. She's seems rude, but that's just her way."

The younger says, "She's quite generous was all I was trying to say."

Amos smiles and pats him on the shoulder, "You're getting there."

♦   ♦   ♦   ♦   ♦   ♦   ♦

We return to the scene of the crime by looking up the face of the Apollo marquis and vertical signage. Behind and above looms the new Victoria tower. There is an unfinished floor at the top with several people sharing a luncheon and business meeting. They are in the potential penthouse of the Victoria Corporation. The documents on the tables are filled with numbers and figures. There are large blowups of the tower and other buildings nearby. The Hotel Theresa and the others are much smaller.

Luis, the luncheon coordinator, hovers over the fare and listens to bits and pieces of conversation. One of the large pictures has a round temple covering the roof top, as if there is a dance floor under the stars. Another has a huge craved egg on a pedestal.

A stately woman of obvious wealth addresses the group.

"I hope to welcome each and every one of you personally.

I appreciate you coming from around the globe to attend our meeting, We can write this off can't we?"

As they chuckle she looks across the crowd and picks out several nationalities with nods, winks, and smiles of welcome.

One Gentleman asks, "Madam Stout, what progress can you share?"

"My friends, construction is progressing at a normal rate for New York City. We are half way done with the exterior and moving quite well despite the neighborhood. The proper officials have been satisfied as to our permits. The construction companies have confirmed our determination by agreeing to labor salaries at double minimum wage."

Another person speaks, "Is that really necessary? It seems like a waste of money just to -"

"It is a necessary part of the larger picture. Let my assurance be enough to satisfy your curiosity."

Madeline glances at a younger woman and they exchange nods. The younger woman is dressed conservative Indian fashion, complete with a facial veil. She moves in quietly and speaks with the objector.

The servers clear the luncheon dishes and drinks. The boss; Luis, asks,

"Pardon me, do you wish coffee and desert served at this time?"

"Yes, please do so. The service is set by the windows? Good, proceed."

The dozen or so attendees move about reading the reports and looking at the blowups. The servers and Luis clear away the vestiges of lunch along with a couple of the reports. The business group gathers by the window where a large blowup of the Victoria Towers looms above the Apollo.

The spokesperson speaks again,

"Of course we are counting on the Apollo to share the 'notoriety' of many musical acts and parties. We will be housing and feeding the biggest names in show business before and after they perform at our favorite landmark."

We see Luis clearly for the first time as he assists other servers begin the coffee service. Once he is in the kitchen area, he stashes the pilfered reports in a shoulder bag with the other's coats and outerwear.

Luis re-enters to see the blowup of the towers has a different roof piece. There sits a huge piece of sculpted stone. The carving resembles a very large Faberge Egg. As he wonders what happened to the idea of a roof terrace. He overhears someone say,

"The best design I saw had almost 4000 seats." The speaker was admonished as their hostess turned the blowup toward the wall,

"Douglas, such things are not spoken of prematurely." He is not easily deterred,

"I was just saying is all." and then, "Sorry Madeline, it's your party."

She waves him away and begins a conversation with a couple of security looking suits. Douglas moves to the blowup and turns it slightly. As he does, Luis can see the other side which has the original roof top ballroom terrace. Douglas allows it to relax and Luis can see the boulder on top of the building again.

Luis blinks and thinks. His eyes shift back and forth searching for understanding of what he has seen and heard. His exit to the dressing area is observed by two suits. He takes his street clothes from the rack into a side room. From outside the door he hears a voice asking,

"Perdon Senorita, did you see the Latin gentleman who was serving?"

Another voice is heard to say that she had seen him leaving a couple of minutes ago. Within a few seconds a short knock happens on the changing room door and a hushed voice says,

"They're looking for you. You should leave now." And then silence.

We hear Archie Bell playing '**Tighten Up**,' during Luis's escape through the Victoria lobby and onto the street with the security suits in pursuit.

Returning from the flashback - We see a dashboard and hear Smokey Robinson's version of '**You Really Got A Hold on** Me', coming from the radio as the city streets go by.

Oh Oh Oh, I wanna split now,
I can't quit now, ya really got a hold on me.

Luis leans back and croons to Zoe. She looks doubtful and starts on him,.

"So, I get you out of Manhattan and you give me $100.00?"

Luis considers, "Almost, If you help me stop this, I'll give you a lot more."

"How much is a lot?"

"I'm not sure, I'm going to sell these reports in Brooklyn. You want in?"

"No way. And I don't like being kidnapped either. I'll just take the $100."

"Fair enough. We'll fight the fight without ya."

Zoe eyes him sideways as he scans the reports
The music changes to ' **It's All Right** '.

It's all right to have a good time,
Baby it's all right, yeah it's all right.

Luis shrugs and says, "I just thought that maybe, with well, with you being a music fan and all, that you might, uh well-"

"Might wanna what?"

"Turn right down here and drive onto the docks. We're in the houseboat."

♦   ♦   ♦   ♦   ♦   ♦   ♦

Well along the dock we see a lower deck with Chinese lanterns. A small gathering of people are eating, drinking, and dancing to James Brown.

My hearts delight, that's what you are,
Ya know you're outa sight.

The music gets to Zoe. She stops to overlook the scene and says,

"I was there for the Godfather's wake. I was right outside the theater night and day. Over thirty thousand people came to see James one last time."

"Did you sell many CD's?"

"I did James proud. I sold out two van loads, bout 1,000 units."

"... at 2 for 5?"

"Oh hell no, those went 2 for 10."

"You think James approved?"

"I know he did. This one time, when the Sutton family ran the theater, James was scheduled to do a show. But the Suttons only booked one show. James told them he'd never done one show, and that he always sold out both shows."

"Well before the first show started, the producers realized the mistake and asked for a second show. He said that he could do two shows, but the second show had to be full price, and paid in cash. The promoters squawked, but they came up with it, all tens and twenties. They delivered it in brown paper bags."

They stand, and listen to the music, and watch the people dance. Luis says,

'When James hit town, it drained the neighborhood of all spare cash. I don't think there was ever a time, James Brown didn't sell out the Apollo."

"Yeah, even at his wake. He sold out the Apollo out 20 times over".

The music changes to,

Please, Please, Please, Please.
Baby Please Don't Go.

♦　♦　♦　♦　♦　♦　♦

Passing the party on deck, they entered the houseboat. Inside are a group of shaded figures. Luis seemed to be expected. A pretty lady approaches, and takes his backpack.

"Ah Welcome Luis. Hello, how did you do? Luis, will your lovely friend continue forward and allow us a few minutes."

Luis backs Zoe and says,

"Now, show some respect for my choice. If I say she's okay, she's okay. Gina, Ladies and Gents, may I present Zoe Maxwell. A magician extraordinaire. She got me out of a close call in Harlem."

Zoe adds, "I know some of you, seen some you buying music from me."

3 say, "She's been around a few years,"

"Yeah, I've seen her"

"Bootleg."

Luis objects, "Don't look down on thieves, Happens to be what you hired me to do." He takes out the pilfered reports and passes them around,

"I only scanned these, but I think they're why you sent me."

As the group scans and reads, one of them whistles,

One says, "Gina, we're gonna need more than a magician."

"What do you mean?" says the hostess.

"These look like income reports on 4 years. The last two and, next two."

"Like a Before and After study.

"After what?" there is a long silence.

Zoe speaks up, "After they take the Apollo? That's what you think right?'"

Gina asks, "Luis who did you see? Do we know anyone who was there?"

Luis pulls at a cheek as he looks at Gina,

"Well, it was Madeline Stout's meeting. There were a lot of well dressed peeps, mostly investor types I guess."

"How about the Sutlilffs?"

"No, I saw the elder in an audition as I, uh, passed, by,"

Zoe coughs, and then she pokes,

"At high speed, and continued outside." they laugh and slap a high five.

Gina says, "Okay, we need to read. There's food in the galley."

Luis leads Zoe to the galley. She takes out her phone as he gathers food.

"Jackie baby? Yeah, its me, You should shut down and roll on home."

She smiles at Luis and winks at him, as he hands her a beer. Ramsey Lewis does '**Hang on Sloopy**' in the background.

♦　♦　♦　♦　♦　♦　♦

On the street, Jackie pulls out a remote and points, then she stops and arranges a few items away from the edges, then she points again, this time she hears a beep, and she presses another button. The CD's stack and straighten themselves into rows. The stacks are engulfed into the tables as the table folds, and then folds again. When all is done she has a medium sized pull cart. She walks away leading the cart toward the subway while being followed by the suits.

♦　♦　♦　♦　♦　♦　♦

In the galley we watch Zoe and Luis dance around one another while they gather food and drink. '**Papa's Got a Brand New Bag**' comes from the outer deck. As they pass in close quarters, they seem to enjoy touching one another.

Luis serves flutes of Champagne from a pony bottle. The toast and drink.

Zoe lifts lids and Luis asks, "Is that potato salad any good?"

"Yep, looks fresh too. So, these are pot luck leftovers?"

She turns to him and he moves toward her. She stops him with a spoon.

"I'm not sure, I like what I see."

Luis is interested. "Well, I like what I see.'

"You got a look in your eye."

"What kind of look, ?"

"I know that look. Uh, huh, my cousin's got three kids from that look."

She pushes him away with her plate. "Get back Jack ." And walks past him.

He picks up two glasses of Champagne and follows her onto the fore deck.

◆　◆　◆　◆　◆　◆　◆

We hear, "**You Can't Hurry Love**," coming from the boat speakers as the two burglars lounge under the stars, feed themselves, and drink.

Zoe leads, "So, you and your friends know something is up,"

Luis counters with, "Up ?"

"Yeah, Up, as in 'Plans made by others'; Up."

"Yeah, I guess, I wanna tell you more but you need to be vetted."

"Is that Vetted or Voted? What kind of political shit are you into here?" Luis has to consider, he decides, and says,

"Well, we think of ourselves as Protectors. We protect

public trusts in Harlem like parks, landmarks, playgrounds, hospitals, like that."

"Sounds like ya'll got money to do all that."

"Some do, most don't. We try to preserve history and its landmarks."

"Like the Apollo?"

"Like the Apollo."

"As a part of history, the theater stands proud. But public funding has not been enough. It's over 100 years old and needs work just to keep it from falling apart."

"I thought they still do lots of shows."

The music changes to Jackie Wilson,

Your love, lifting me higher
Than I've ever been lifted before

Luis says, "Don't let the advertising fool ya.. Not 'A Lot' more like, 'A Few', not as many as they could. If someone was to privately fund it and make it jump alive again."

"Why don't the Protectors take it over?"

A voice comes out of the shadows. The hostess Gina, speaks again.

"We actually have a plan in place. But when we brought our offer to the table, the people in charge didn't seem to care. They wouldn't even listen to the offer. That's what made us suspicious."

She extends a hand, "Hello, I'm Gina, welcome aboard, Ms Zoe."

"Uh, well then thanks," Zoe takes the hand and shakes.

"Most of us are business people. Luis is one of our people

we can ask to do such a thing as he has done." She hands him an envelope which disappears.

"Thanks, but-" Luis is impatient, "-what have you found ?"

"We think we see a pattern but there are pieces missing. We need you Zoe, would you care to join us? Work some of your natural magic for us? Will you stand as the 125th st lookout and help us save the Apollo?"

Zoe pulls back and thinks before she speaks.

"Well, first I wanna ask, what's in it for me?" She looks inside at everyone else.

Zoe speaks again, "And then I can't ask . . . . . So; OK, I'm in."

Luis is up and out of his chair spreading his arms in greeting.

"I knew you were the one. I told them, You were the one I wanted most."

Gina smiles," And it looks like you were right."

"Almost right, I am in business with my sister Jackie. She has to be a part."

"Good, we figured you would say that Zoe, let's go meet the others."

They all go back into the boat to Irma Thomas', 'Time Is On My Side'

But you'll come running back (I said you would baby)

You'll come running back, to me, me, me, yeh.

Gina turns to Zoe and takes her hand.

"Zoe, your last name is Maxwell? We do know some

things about you. I guess in this case I'm sort of the gang leader. Come in and make yourself comfortable."

Zoe is met by two others, a women and a man who extend their hands and smiles of introduction. Gina asks both,

"So what did you find?"

Zoe asks, "Weren't there more people here before?"

Stella waves a report. "We have to study these further to make the right guess."

♦ ♦ ♦ ♦ ♦ ♦ ♦

As the party inside winds down, so do Luis and Zoe as they relax. The evening moon and music take on soft look and feel, as the two of the relax a bit. Zoe watches a cloud passes before the moon. She rises to adjust the tarp cover for the chairs. She pauses to look at Luis as he mumbles in his sleep, She is curious about the grin on his face as she thumbs a number on her phone.

Jackie's phone vibrates on a night stand close to a couple in the throes of passion. Jackie stops for a moment to look at the phone readout. She is wearing a man's shirt open to the waist, and gun holster hanging from her shoulder. As she puts down the phone unanswered, her other hand raises a pair of handcuffs.

"I must warn you that anything you beg for, may be used against you."

♦ ♦ ♦ ♦ ♦ ♦ ♦

The CD table is playing, 'You're All I need To Get By'.

On the street, the two sisters confab as they set up a tent top. Jackie looks up at the sky.

And it was plain to see,
You were my destiny.
With my arms open wide,
I threw away my pride

Zoe asks, "So how long you think it's going to hold off?"

Zoe speaks patois, "We live on an island. It comes and goes fast you know, So 'Ya never know darling, ya never know'."

"Yeh,? Where are you? You're distracted, off somewhere. What's up?"

"Ah, I feel like the rasta mon. Ridin' the wind Tinking 'bout shit, girl."

"Wouldn't have to do with your passenger, Ayeh?"

"Have I ever told you that's one of the reasons I love you so?"

"No, or maybe not lately, do tell."

"Because of how intuitive you are, how much you care, and want to be involved in any worthy cause . . ."

Jackie frowns, "Oh, that reason . . hang on, what's that I hear coming?"

She makes huge sucking noises, "Uh Oh, Look Out, Here it comes !"

She makes more sucking noises, "Look Out, Z, You getting' sucked in . . ."

"Stop it, you're funny. Jackie, I need you to help me save the Apollo."

"Again? Save it again? What did we save it from last time?"

"We're not sure."

"We're not sure why we saved it? It was only like 10 years ago."

"Well that was then. I'm asking you to help me save it now. For real."

Zoe looks at her Sister, who says,

"So how did we get sucked into this rescue?"

"Luis. The runner, or escape eee, or whatever. He offered me $100 to drive him to Brooklyn, to the docks, not far."

"And?"

"And he explains that he was a spy who lifted something for other people to see. They showed me that someone wants the property. Well, actually from what they showed me, I figured they want even more."

"Whoa, that's three thoughts, there. Questions."

"Okay, ask."

"First of all. Did he pay you the $100.?"

"No, but he promised more."

"Uh huh, I'm holding my breath, we'll get to that."

The music changes to an instrumental,

'Soul Finger',

Jackie continues, "Second, who wants to do what with it?"

"The same people who turned the Victoria 5 into a condo."

"I heard that deal was struck dead. Dead in the water. We were there."

"I don't think there is any such a thing in real estate. Stalled, maybe."

"Ya, think?"

"I'm sure. Mama Roux saw it in the leaves. She said she saw the front looks the same but the rest was all built up."

"Jeez, Zee, you 'member we used to go there for the movies."

"Right, from the fire escape off the back."

"I ever tell you I used to sneak into the Apollo that way too?"

"I know you did. I did too, but never let it out, til now."

"Who was the best you saw?"

"Little Stevie Wonder. Only we wasn't so little by then."

"Was it a good show?"

"Oh Yeah. He played the new stuff and some of the old. I remember he dedicated a song to "Uncle Ray', he played, 'What'd I Say' in like 3 parts,…"

"Right, he'd stop and we'd cheer him to start again, and play some more."

"Just like Ray would do. 'cept for Stevie it was true, he'd play all night."

They pause in reflection. "Would you like the Apollo torn down?"

"HELL NO !"

"And that's how I got involved,"

Music changes to, **Tell it Like It** is by Aaron Neville,

**If you want something to play with
Go and find yourself a toy,**

"Simple as that."

"The thought of all that, the Apollo, going away, forever? Never."

"Yeah, I get it. I'm in. Wha' da we do Zoe?"

"Ride de winds Mon, an we'll see what we see. " They slap a high five.

Zoe is curious, "How did it go with the suits, they bother you anymore?"

"They followed me home, and one of them stayed the night."

"To watch?"

"Yeah, To whatever,"

"Whatever?"

"Yeah, Whatever. How do I know who is who around here?"

The music continues,

**If you are serious
Don't play with my heart, it makes me furious**

Luis enters the scene, extends a hand to Jackie,

"Hi, I'm Luis, we met yesterday. Sorry about any trouble."

"Not at all honey, Wo. look at this young thang Zoe, mmm, mmm, mmph You spent the night with this one, and you askin' me about a security guy?"

"Jacquelyn? We are just friends who slept under the stars, together."

Luis smiles and shrugs at he looks at Jackie.

"Yes, Mam," She gives respect, "but I would like to introduce to Leroy."

"Who's Leroy?"

"He's the guy following Luis."

We all see a suit on the corner in shades looking both ways covering Luis.

"Leroy is, uh, whatever,."

"Naw, you didin'"

"Well, it looked like rain, and ... whatever,...Wait, he said Luis was a thief."

Luis admits, "He's Right. Well, today, I'm not sure what I am. I'm on my way to work. The caterers from the job called and said that The Towers execs were having another event just like the first, and asked if they could have the same staff."

"But wait, do they, or don't they, know you're a spy?"

"We'll see, how would I know? Are they still tailing me, or is it you?"

Jackie waves away the suggestion as, "Whatever."

Luis walks to Zoe and takes her hand,

"I wanted to thank you."

His lips kiss the back of her hand as he pushes $100 into her palm.

The muted background music is Show Me by Joe Tex,

'Show Me a Man Who's Got A good Woman, Show Me.'

♦ ♦ ♦ ♦ ♦ ♦ ♦

At the beginning of the meet and greet we see the same boardroom suite. There are large blowups of the Victoria and of the rest of the block. The Apollo is prominent among the rest. Madeline and her handmaiden are running the show.

The business meeting has no music. After the introduction of new investors, the pitch begins. Luis directs the servers to circulate the appetizers as he scans the crowd. He makes eye contact with Madeline; she smiles and nods. Luis directs a server to accommodate her needs.

The meeting goes well, the same reports were discussed.

Once again Luis was able to remove it during clearing the luncheon. It is given to a porter who makes a dead drop to the sisters. The report waits in a brown paper bag on the front of the CD table. Stella walks by and makes the pick up.

A large slide projection displayed the estimated income. To Luis, the report looked the same. The only difference was the new 'Victoria Towers Theaters', or 'VTT' heading. Luis was trying not to look. Madeline pretended to watch the show a few slides and then asked Luis for coffee.

"On the terrace. Madam?"

"Yes Luis. Tell me what did you think of the Towers project?"

"I can't say I paid much attention. May I ask what the meeting is about?"

The veiled handmaiden stands in attention, watching and listening.

"We are projecting the risk and rewards of restoring the old film theaters. Some of us want to restore the theaters, and some of us want new ones."

"I see, and why have you asked my opinion Madam?"

"Well, I noticed the last time you were served us, you hung on every word. This time, you looked like you tried to ignore every word. Why is that?"

"We are trained to focus on our jobs. The content of the meeting is your business. Sorry. We do coffee and food, what can I get you?"

She bares her teeth and hisses at him,

"You can tell me if you hear of anyone attempting to block our progress."

Luis spots Gina's tell tale earrings being worn by the handmaiden.

"Well, perhaps I could do that, if it were in my best interest."

Madeline extends her hands, when Luis takes her hand he feels something pass from her hand to his. They shake and depart as he pockets the pass. He smiles as he makes sure the coffee pots are full and the fruit and pastries are covered to remain fresh. As he walks away, he sneaks a peek at a few $100 bills

♦   ♦   ♦   ♦   ♦   ♦   ♦

The houseboat music is softly playing '**Soulful Street**' sounding far away. Luis and Zoe sits with Jackie and Miriam on the couch.

"These reports look like the same ones as we saw before."

"That they are, except for the new heading on the top. VTT Victoria Towers Theaters. Replacing the theaters was not part of the community board's approval."

Miriam speaks, "Which they do not have to do. It looks good and sounds good, but the replacement could be as small as an entertainment room."

Gina, says, "The corporation is only obligated to commemorate the theaters. Like, you know, with a plaque."

Miriam says, "I think these are a red herring. I think these are dummied up to look like what Luis stole the other day. I think they know the reports could go public and so," waving the report, " these were prepared."

Luis says, "And asking for me to be there, was a way to get the word out."

Zoe says, "Maybe a feel up to see if she could turn you with cash."

"Like that would ever work,"

Gina asks, "Which one honey? The feel up or the Cash?"

Jis laughs, "Funny. It works, but it's not honest, such vows are usually forsaken."

Miriam asks, "What do you mean?"

"Well, like this guy in Vegas. He's in a bar at the casino and a hooker sits down close. She looks him over and says,

'Mister, for $500 dollars I'll do anything you want."

The guy says 'Oh, yeah?'

'Oh yeah. Deal?'

He pulls his wallet, takes out the money and says, "Paint my house."

They all snicker and Zoe asks, "And the lesson here is . . ?"

"Money may get things started, but rarely finishes them."

They all look at each other as the music changes to, 'Oogum Boogum',

**Ah, I say Oogum, Oogum, Boogum, Boogum, Boogum
Now baby you're casting your spell on me**

Zoe asks, "How do you get that message, out of that dumb joke?"

Luis answers, "The hooker took the cash but didn't paint the house. See? Never mind. So, Gina, don't you want me to take the cash?"

"Oh hell yes, take the cash, but feed her some names of her own people before you snitch on anybody else."

He pauses, "That was my plan. Step over here to discuss details?"

They step aside as Luis says, "I saw you there. Explain yourself."

"I know, look here, I'm involved on both sides. It's for the best, let it be."

"Nope. That doesn't explain anything, fess up, or I tell the others."

Gina pleads, "Please believe me, I'm doing what's best at every turn. But, most of these people would not understand."

Luis gets intense, "Look at me, I don't understand."

"You don't? Really? You don't understand how it would be better for us to know Madeline's plans?" She crosses her arms in disgust.

"I thought that's why you sent me in. To collect information."

"You were sent to collect the information she was sharing with investors. My mission has a little more to it. Patience darling, ride the ride to the end."

"So, the whole second meeting thing was a blind to do what?"

They rejoin the group, "To take us off the trail, maybe." Luis reflects, and Gina says, "You need to tell the group about the missing Egg."

They enter and Gina asks, "What's new off of the street? Anybody talking?"

Zoe says, "I went to a community board meeting. You know the buildings have small storefront entrances, but both spread out inside."

Jackie adds, "We used to sneak in from the fire escapes to the balcony."

"How many seats does the Apollo have?" asks, Luis.

Miriam says, "1,500 with both balconies."

"That place has two balconies and still only 1500 seats?"

Gina asks, "Are we off course? Look, the place is a National Landmark."

Zoe asks openly, "Yeah, so, what do they do? How do they take it?"

Gina says, "Only if it were heavily damaged, and then condemned beyond repair."

Miriam says, "That could work. Damaged how?"

Gina muses, "It would have to be total destruction, beyond restoring."

Luis adds, "You know, there was one thing missing from the meeting."

"Is it significant?"

"Maybe. The last time I saw a picture of the roof terrace. It had a huge craved granite stone on stilts. It looked like a huge art piece, shaped like an egg."

"And it wasn't there today?"

"Not that I saw. There were other graphics, but they weren't the same as the other meeting."

"Do you see any pattern?"

"Hmmmm, how big was the, Egg shaped thing, you saw in the picture?"

◆   ◆   ◆   ◆   ◆   ◆   ◆

The guided tour comes into the lobby of the theater being led by Barbara, the head usher. She shares trivia mixed with rumors as she moves the herd along.

"Built in 1913, the first time the Apollo was forced to close was by none other than our own Mayor La Guardia for public indecency, it was a burlesque house."

Still photo montage of Strippers and B Girls with posters.

"The dancers all protested. They say the picket line was pretty interesting."

Mr. Sutliff and Madeline Stout watched them pass.

She says, "I love that story."

"It's true."

Madeline almost sneers, "I know, that's why I love it. The place has been closed before and will be closed again. It's the natural order of things."

"Too bad we weren't around to see that." He starts a pocket recorder

His lapel mic records, "We've been here a while, Amos, but not that long."

"Been a while, yeh? But you're as beautiful as ever."

Madeline snorts, "And I'm about to make you a rich man."

"I'm already rich, as are you. Harlem has been good to us."

"I'm about to increase your wealth."

"Why do you want this property so badly?"

Medline stiffens, "I was shamed here once. I came for amateur night try outs.. They rejected me before I finished the audition." She looks far away

"My friends told me I was good enough, but later, they laughed. When they saw I was distraught, they laughed at me even harder and made fun of me."

She regains composure, "I've wanted control of the place ever since then."

Mr. Sutliff stiffens, "Madeline, I know I told you I would not stand in your way. But I must insist on knowing what you have planned."

"I thought 2 million dollars took care of your conscience'."

"Well, ah yes, well,-"

"Because if it doesn't, I have a friend who is a reporter

right around the corner at the Amsterdam News who would be very interested, if everything doesn't go as planned."

He nods and asks, "When do you expect to finish the tower?"

"A month, maybe six weeks, right around hurricane season."

"Oh? Well, damn it all, I'm supposed to be lecturing for a few weeks during the fall. The theater is usually dark then, saving our pennies for the holiday shows."

"The tower should be completed by Halloween. The ball should drop soon after. The timing couldn't be better."

"Madeline, I'm sorry, but my conscious forces me to ask, do you anticipate any collateral damage . . . . . especially to people . . . . . I have family here; daily."

"You'll have plenty of notice. Your family will have a chance to be safe."

"What about the holidays? Lots of people on the street?"

"Any one of consequence will be staying home, or out of town."

"What about others?"

"What others?"

"All the others. People who work here, people who work the street?"

"The vendors?" She laughs. "Do you think any of them, I mean any one of them, has a license to be out there selling, all the crap they sell?"

"We have quite a few that sleep out of the rain under the Marquee."

"If that's the case, you should make sure they spend the night somewhere else."

Madeline stomps her way to the orchestra seating area.

Sutliff turns away and exits the front doors. Outside he can see Zoe and Jackie's stand of two folding tables and a cover with CDs all over. Jackie swarms over him, and as he pretends to defend himself, he passes her a small recorder.

Madeline looks at the theater interior. In her imagination a huge boulder of Granite crashes through the roof and demolishes the ceiling, the stage and many seats.

She frowns and takes out a laser pointer. She points it at one wall and looks at the readout. Then she turns about and looks at the other wall and points. As she reads the screen she takes out her phone and says,

'Sydney', and then says, the phone beeps at her and she leaves a message,

"Sydney, call me about the size again, the angle still worries me. Call now."

♦   ♦   ♦   ♦   ♦   ♦   ♦

Outside Zoe is conversing with Gina, they both have on large floppy hats and sunglasses. Jackie is on the phone. Little Anthony fills the air,

'Yes, I think I'm goin' out of my head
Over you, over you'

"I'm just saying," Zoe starts, "The rear entrance will have room to swing Limos in and out. It's 126th st, and semi private compared to out here." She gestures to the daily circus of 125th street.

Jackie gets off the phone. "Eddie can help. He's got

wireless minicams for the sign posts. He'll do it for $7,500, but you have to provide the people who know what to look for."

'I want you to want me, I need you so badly
I can't think of anything but you'

"And will they be watching the 126th st. entrance?"

"He says he can put them anywhere. The cameras are motion activated with a wide shot and a close up pre installed. They conserve on power only shooting when something moves."

"For $7500 I could get 5 women to watch screens in a van for a month. Sorry Jackie, thank Eddie, and tell him we need to go a little more low tech."

"Hmmph, Ya get what Ya pay for," and she hands the phone to Zoe.

"Gina, look at the front. It's still boarded up. They say it's not happening."

"Jackie, go look at the back, It's happening, they're just playing out the time frame with the city. It's still happening babe. Look at that western tower. It must be about done. It's gonna be the tallest thing in Harlem."

Luis checks his text. "300 feet when it is done. Taller than the Theresa."

Zoe asks, "Did you actually read any of those reports you stole?"

The music changes to an instrumental by the James Gang, '**Ya Dig?**'.

Luis replies, "Why would I want to do that?"

Jackie says, "To make sure of what you are getting into here."

"What do you mean by that? We're saving the Apollo."

Zoe says, "Right, and that's good. But let's speak more realistically, we are trying to prevent it from changing hands, or being torn down?"

"What's your point? Let's get an Italian Ice." Luis buys.

"We are trying to 'Preserve the theater and thereby its history from the time during which it operated.' Right?"

He hands her a cup, "Still waiting. Your point?"

"It's a landmark, a National Landmark, and famous world wide."

"Also a State and City Historical site."

"Do you know how much funding that guarantees you get every year?"

Luis slurps at his ice, "No, how much?"

"Zero."

"Nada? Nothing?"

"Zippo. See, becoming a Landmark only means that you qualify to apply for grants and other funding. Obtaining financial support is chancy. Annual grant money for Landmark sites is, 'up for grabs', competing with 500 other places of national historical value in New York state, county, and city."

"Are you saying there is no permanent endowment support fund for the Apollo?"

"Nothing guaranteed. They live from year to year."

◆　◆　◆　◆　◆　◆　◆

We see the A team, Gina, Zoe, Jackie and Luis are lounging on the fore deck of the houseboat. They are in various stages of relaxation with Jackie Wilson's '**Lonely Teardrops'** coming out of the speakers.

Shooby Doo Wop ba baa (hey hey)
Shooby Doo Wop ba baa (hey hey)

Zoe is so relaxed she is smiling, and so pleased with herself that she asks Luis to dance. He is surprised and delighted and they enjoy one another's arms.

Just say you will, say you will (say you will)
Say you will (say you will)

Estrella emerges from the boat and watches the couple. She pitches Gina a sketch book, and steps forward to 'break in' and dance with Luis. Zoe is okay with that and pours herself another drink.

"Yo Jazz? You wants?", referring to Jackie and the pitcher of boat drinks

"I gots, Z. I gots." She is twirling the hair of Leroy the former security guy as he sits at her feet humming the song softly and smiling as he studies the sketch.

Gina is looking at another sketch of an Egg on a tower and thinking into space, ""Then they need something to make it fall. They'll need a demo team . . ."

Zoe looks at Gina and pours as she says, "To drop the rock?"

Leroy says, "Well, first they need a crane to put it into place, they could drop it then. Otherwise-"

The music changes to The Isley Brothers, 'That Lady.'

Zoe offers "An act of God?"

Jackie muses, "Terrorist attack?"

Luis says, "A lot of Explosives?"

Gina, says, "Ding Ding Ding. We have a winner."

'Who's that lady
Beautiful lady'

Gina mutters, "Shit, who do we know in that business?"

Leroy asks, "How many stories are there to go before they hoist the rock?"

Luis responds, "A few, maybe 8 or 10 stories in steel frame work."

Gina says, "We need to go undercover in every way. We need spies who want to make money while they spy. We need to recruit people that can get a job assisting with construction?"

"I can get a few relatives to come apply for a job, especially if they think its undercover work."

Zoe says, "We'll put out the word, there's a party at the end."

It was love at first sight
I just saw her tonight

♦   ♦   ♦   ♦   ♦   ♦   ♦

The song plays on as we see a dress up party on the boat where everybody has a box for Jackie. She stands amazed at the generosity of her friends and several bottles of various types are being poured.

One by one they dress Jackie in a very official uniform

from the cap on her head to the toes of black shiny government shoes.

"I can't say I like the costume so far. Who am I supposed to be?"

Zoe pulls out credentials and a badge. It has a poor picture of Jackie and the title, 'N. Y. C. Safety Officer All Area Access'

Jackie looks at the credentials, "Where did you get this picture?"

Zoe says, "From your passport."

"Honey, You couldn't do any better?""

"I looked at your driver's license, but it was worse."

Jackie nods, "DMV? Shit, they take the worst photos known to mankind."

"Even this is better than DMV."

"Tru Dat. One time, I had my picture taken by DMV for my license, it was so bad, they put a slip of paper in the envelope saying, 'You may want to have this photo re-taken.'"

"Good thing it looks like you then isn't it?"

Jackie responds, "Yeah. Hey!"

Zoe laughs "Just trippin'; made you laugh."

"I like the authority though, "Safety Officer, All Access', that's cool."

Gina says, "This will get you inside and anywhere we need you."

"Did Luis arrive with his team?"

"What team is that?"

"He searched out some people he knew in the Army and was trying to contact them. They sound like the kind of people we need."

"What do they do?"

"Well, Luis is not sure what they do now. He said

when they worked together before, it was mostly death and destruction."

"Sounds promising. When do we meet?"

♦   ♦   ♦   ♦   ♦   ♦   ♦

The bayou sound of **Mama Roux** fulfill the musical background

Ooh why, can't cha spy boy
Prepare yourself to die boy

We see a meeting on the other side of 125th st. Gina, Zoe, Luis and a pair of twins stand looking back and forth between the Victoria Tower and the Apollo.

"Gina, Zoe, these are the Cucciara brothers. David and Derek."

Hands are shaken and questions start from Gina,

"So Derek, what has Luis told you?"

"He said you wanted our opinion about droppin' a building. Eh, D.?"

David speaks, "Yeah, not much more than that."

Gina responds, "That's a good start, well, Luis, continue."

"The new Victoria Towers is going to be 300 feet tall. We think they're going to finish the East tower and then have an accident. The accident is going to be an art piece of carved granite will fall from the top of that tower."

David asks, "Hmm, yeh, accidents will happen, but will the accident just happen, like for the insurance, or will it destroy something in particular?"

Zoe says, "We think they want to completely destroy the

Apollo so they can get their hands on the real estate rights to build there."

Luis continues, "What we want to know from you, is how they could do it, and what to look for to, well, maybe how to stop them."

Better not get in the way
Got the second line fever today

Derek says, "Before we go any further, I should say that you are asking our professional opinions, and that means doing business."

Gina says, "We expected that. How much would you charge for a private discussion involving your opinions and expertise?"

"Today's 'Opinion Rate' is negotiable. Of course, 'Action Rates' are of a different nature. Let's say we start at $2,000 a day, and go from there. Ok?"

Gina answers, "Agreed and done, let's walk and talk. You guys hungry? There's a great place on 126 at the far end of the block. Fresh fish and we can sit and talk."

Singin' wham bam hangin' ham
Come on down boy and now follow me

◆ ◆ ◆ ◆ ◆ ◆ ◆

As the five of them walk the 126th st block they take a few pictures from different angles. Gina stops them halfway along the block and gestures to a flatbed truck with a large crate labeled 'Art' secured to the trailer.

"The Towers entrance will take up the entire width of the property on this side. The East tower you see going up will have that big ass piece of art on top."

David asks, "What's it made of?"

Gina answers, "Granite."

Luis says, " Hmmm, solid or hollow?"

Zoe says, "Should be solid. It 's a piece of art ."

Gina says, "I wouldn't bet on it. I've seen a lot of art in the making."

David asks, "Yo D.? How much does granite weigh?"

Derek replies, "You want exactly? How big?"

"It's pretty big, maybe,10 feet by 10 feet, by 16-18 feet tall, yeh?"

Derek takes out a tablet to help him figure, "Okay, solid would be like, uh, 170 - 180 lbs per cubic foot? 1000 cubic feet. Do the math. 85, 90 tons. It's gotta be hollow."

David says, "Yeah, well, assuming its hollow, it could be more destructive. You could definitely fuck up a building by dropping that on it."

Jackie asks, "What would it do to the Apollo?"

David answers, "Well, no matter where it landed. It would punch a big assed hole straight through the place, that's for sure., Yeh, D.?"

"Yeah, even hollow, maybe 40, 50 tons? It would punch through, 'Wham', Right into the bedrock of the island. Are there any trains under there?"

"No, they're all east and west of here. Let's go eat some fish."

◆   ◆   ◆   ◆   ◆   ◆   ◆

Sitting at Manna's and listening to soul music and food, David commented,

"Not the way we'd do it."

Derek says, "Not very efficient,"

Gina says, "What do you mean?"

"The egg, rock thingee. You'd do less than half the place that way, eh D.?"

"Yeah, we'd never leave anything half done.."

"What would you do?"

"You want anything left? Like I mean anything except rubble?"

"Well, for the sake of argument, No, nothing but rubble."

"Well, then, I'd dump the whole tower on it. WHAM! Only Barney's left."

"Barney?"

"As in 'Rubble'. Barney Rubble? Didn't you ever watch cartoons?"

"Eh, no, not really, . . . the whole tower . . . Wham. Blam!"

The Cucciara brothers broke out in soft laughter and big smiles at the thought of the whole tower going over. We watch the collapse in abject horror.

David says, "But, hollow, the inside could be made of who knows what, it could blow apart even better, without mass destruction."

We watch the revised CGI scene with the damage reduced.

◆　◆　◆　◆　◆　◆　◆

The same collapse is being considered by Madeline Stout as she meets with her agents considering the project.

They compare photos and computer projected imagery. The demolition experts consider the project to be of little consequence. To them, a job is a job, especially when it pays well.

A very fit and very tan man walks toward Madeline with hands out,

"Madeline, You look more radiant every time I see you."

"Bob, what a charming white lie." She passes him. "Charlie, Thank you to coming. Let's have a seat."

Charlie takes Bob's place at the table. The three hover around a map.

"Yes, Ms Stout. We can do what you want."

"Good." Madeline answers.

Bob asks, "What is your schedule?"

"Just after we have the art in place."

Charlie asks, "Who gets the blame?"

Madeline smiles, "It's either a terrorist act, or, it's the rigging company."

Bob smiles and says, "Gonna make a hell of a mess."

Charlie says, "Should be spectacular."

Madeline smiles, "I do appreciate your enthusiasm. There will be a trail of upcoming projects, as if no 'untoward' actions were anticipated."

Charlie contributes, "Very good. And true."

"And since we are insured against accidents, I might even make money."

Bob muses, "Well, I should hope so, What else is there? So you want the tower to fall here only?"

Madeline points, "Yes, directly on the property, and especially this rear section. There are two areas for collateral damage. One is the small parking lot here to the west. And, the school yard across 126th is expendable."

Bob wonders, "What about the school?"

Charlie responds, "Obviously the drop must be target specific. I have the perfect guy. He'll love it."

Bob adds, "There will be some explosive residue. It's unavoidable I'm afraid. How do you plan to explain it?"

Madeline inserts, "Terrorists, most likely, either Local or Foreign. We have received threats since the day we started this project. Although, I would like it to be foreign."

"In that case we'll make sure the explosives come from overseas."

"Good, good, Gentlemen, if all goes as planned, I'll let you bid on the excavation project, the debris removal should be massive."

♦ ♦ ♦ ♦ ♦ ♦ ♦

Diana and the girls are doing '**You Keep Me Hanging On**.'

'Cause you don't really love me
You just keep me hangin' on'

Gina is pacing the deck of the houseboat. She is reading and muttering to herself as she strides with purpose. Stella comes out with a small cook pot and a spoon,

"Here, taste this before I make any more. Come on, you won't hurt my feelings, taste it."

She offers a spoon. Gina stops and looks at her as if first seeing her.

"What is that?"

Stella says, "Soup, just taste."

Gina tastes and continues, "It's good, Thank you, what kind this time?"

Stella passes a spoonful to Zoe and says over her shoulder, "Chalk ."

Zoe laughs and tries a spoon, makes yummy sound, "Split Pea."

"Not that she would notice," throws out Stella, " She gets wound too tight for her own good some times. I could feed her dog food if she had ketchup."

Gina enters, "You tried that once, or was it twice. I didn't want to say, what a lousy cook you are sometimes." She kisses Stella on the head.

Stella reacts, "Keep it up. You can take over the cooking any time you want."

They both stiffen and look at each other in horror.

Gina and Estrella both say, "Or Maybe not." And they both laugh.

Gina says, "You know that cooking gene that some get? I didn't. She cooks."

Why don't you get out of my life
And let me make a new start

Stella offers, "I also rock at research. Sit down and look at the projection from the numbers Madeline provided."

"Can you give me the short version?"

"Okay, according to these numbers, the place will never be much more than a museum. Sadly, it will never regain it's former presence as a performance hall".

"How so?"

"Money! It's quite simple. There are not enough seats for the ticket price to be reasonable for tourists, much less affordable to the neighborhood."

"Not what I want to hear." Gina storms out of the boat.

Estrella yells after Gina, "Sorry, maybe you should adjust your hearing."

Zoe asks, "You're saying it should be torn down?"

"Not at all. Look here where dollars make sense. The average show costs between 25 and 30 thousand dollars a day to rent the theater and provide a crew. Then you have to pay the talent. They must be a well known act to fill 1500 seats, so they probably cost another 20 thousand, that's a commitment of 50 thousand before you sell tickets."

Zoe is amazed, "That much?"

"That's cheap by today's standards. Remember, there are 800 prime orchestra seats and 700 balcony seats. Now, what do you charge? $40 a head? That's a gross of $60k with a full house and no discounts for balcony seats. If you drop the balcony seats to $30 a head, your possible gross goes down to like 55-60k."

"So your potential profit could be as low as $5k, maxing out at 10k. Not much."

"Actually, it's a little less because there are always extra expenses."

Zoe exclaims, "Thank god for the daily tours -"

Stella agrees, "The place would have probably been torn down years ago."

"But the tours make money, right?"

"Like clockwork. But even at $15 a head, the profit is taken in daily operating costs long before the fiscal year is over."

Zoe says, "They say that more than a million people a year go on the tours."

"Positively un-true. What they say to the press is, '**The Apollo Theater draws an estimated 1.3 million visitors annually.**' These numbers can't reflect actual tourist dollars, or there would be over 3,000 visitors a day, 350 days a year."

Jackie says, "That ain't happening, that's for sure. If it was we would have a lot more customers out front."

"The numbers don't lie, I wish they did."

Harry Nilsson comes over the radio with,

You're breakin' my heart,
You're tearing it apart
So fuck you

Gina comes storming back in and announces,

"That bitch, Madeline just had a meeting with the demolition team."

"How do you know that?"

"Luis and Jackie put her niece, Gwendy, in as a server for Madeline. She said they just met. And they had computer images of the whole tower falling."

"Oh sweet Jesus." says Zoe.

Luis says, "Gwendy girl also said that she heard them say they had the perfect man for the job. Then they went outside and she could not follow."

Gina swears, "This means she has someone to blow the place. That also means that we are further behind than I thought. It's time to make things happen."

Zoe asks, "I guess we need to have our own demolition team. Yeh? Who do we know?"

Luis says, "We know the Cucci Brothers. It's time to make a deal."

You stepped on my ass
You're breakin' my glasses too
I've had enough of you

♦   ♦   ♦   ♦   ♦   ♦   ♦

Derek is lounging on the deck of the houseboat while David is having a discussion with the Luis, Gina, Stella, and Jackie.

"I couldn't' believe the cell rang and it was him." says David.

Luis says, "Really, the Colonel called? What are the chances?"

David says, "Pretty good now that you ask. Derek is one of the best."

Derek adds, "The hard thing was not correcting him on the math I had already done. The Colonel always wants to do it his way."

Luis laughs, "And we always let him think we did everything just as he said. He's too smart to argue after the fact, right? He always told us what he needed done, and we got it done."

David says, "Everybody needs support, only the prideful and stupid ones won't take any help when it's avaliable. We always got it done."

Derek chimes in, "Ya know, the crew that toured with Elvis was his posse. They always had his back. They always made sure he had what he needed. Elvis bought them all rings or whatever jewelry they wanted. Each had a lightning bolt that read TCB, for Taking Care of Business."

David adds, "Some say it meant Two Cheese Burgers."

Luis says, "So the Colonel took the job and wants you to do it for him?"

"Looks that way. D. has a meeting on site later today."

"If the colonel wants the tower blown what's to stop him no matter who he hires? You say Derek is one of best?"

Derek speaks, "I certainly hope I am. Isn't it better to know the plans of your enemy before you do anything to stop them?"

Gina throws a look at Luis. He nods and smiles.

Luis says, "We know what they want to do-"

David says, "But they don't know we know their plans. So we have the upper hand here. I'll go to the meeting and pretend it's all new and interesting."

Derek says, "Maybe ask a leading question or two. Get what they feel comfortable with you knowing. Maybe even contribute a few suggestions on how to do it better, yeh?"

"After all, they can't know we're up to speed on their plans."

"I should take an assistant with me. You wanna be a part of this Gina?"

"No, I can't, I mean I don't know who will be there, I mean somebody who might recognize me. We wouldn't want to tip our hand. Right?"

"True dat, how about you Stella, wanna be a demo expert?"

Stella just smiles, "Sure, I don't know any of them. Gina was gonna introduce me once, but-" Gina interrupts,

"But we ran out of time that day. And I didn't see any

need to letting Madeline and her people know our strengths, or our numbers."

Stella looks at Gina and echoes, "What she said."

'**Is That The Way You Look**?' begins to play in the background.

Excuse Me, Excuse Me Miss
Is That The Way You Look ?

Gina hands Stella a device. "You go in wired, okay? That way we have some proof. With that, maybe we can stop them."

Luis is thinking aloud, "What if we can't stop them? Who'll will listen that has enough juice to stop Madeline and her investors?"

Gina says, "We have to do what we can do. Derek, any questions?"

"At this point it pretty much meet and agree to the job. I'll be asking them for half the money up front, but that's normal."

David agrees, "They will be expecting that and probably have it in cash.

Zoe asks, "How much will you charge them?"

Derek scratches his chin and says, "What do you think D. 100k?"

"That's what he'll expect after Dubai ."

"Yeh, its basically the same, they have to provide the explosives. We don't handle anything in America. The hair fiber testing is getting too accurate."

Gina says, "We need to have a date when they plan to do this."

"That will be my third question out of four. Right after 'What do you want done?' and 'Where do you want it done?'"

"What's the fourth question?"

"Where's the money?" Derek smiles.

◆   ◆   ◆   ◆   ◆   ◆   ◆

Baby, maybe I'm dreaming, but I'll be bound-whoever wakes me up, I'm going to knock him down

We see Derek, the Colonel, and his assistant walking and talking, pointing and entering data on a pad. Derek checks his pad and they nod in agreement, shake hands, and a large packet is traded.

**I asked my friend and I shook my head,
But baby, is that the way you look?**

◆   ◆   ◆   ◆   ◆   ◆   ◆

We see the large packet of money hit the table.

"I wish Bass fishing was that easy. I just ask, and they give it over, no muss no fuss, just cash."

Gina asks, "When's it going down? No puns intended."

"Funny anyway. They said the art / rock gets lifted into place sometime next month, and the explosives will be here about then. Evidently the explosives package is coming from somewhere overseas."

"What else can you tell us? Who all was there? Stella who did you see?"

Stella considers, "Just the two guys and their assistant. At least that's who they said she was, their assistant."

"Did they call her by name?"

Yeah once, that's why I don't think she was who they said she was. They asked her to show the computer images."

Derek says, "And she was pretty old for a assistant."

"How old did she look?"

"Maybe 50 –ish. Well dressed, and kind of exec like, well, 'in charge', if you know what I mean."

Gina smiles, "I know what you mean. Madeline would have found it difficult to let them act without her knowledge and consent. She's a bit of a control freak."

Luis asks, "Who had the money?"

David says, "She did, the assistant."

Gina asks, "There's 50 k in that envelope, can I borrow half of it for 90 days? We're gonna need more money, we always do."

Derek continues, "They want me to show them the placements as soon as possible for the colonel's approval. The drop is a little tricky. I am told I cannot hit anything but the Apollo, Zero room for collateral damage."

"Can you do it?"

"Of course I can, I just don't like being told how to do my job. But it was the Colonel, ya know D.?"

David says, "Yeah, don't worry, this will be the last deal we do with him."

Derek agrees, "Yeah, his rep probably won't be worth shit after this one."

David says, "There is an alternative. He doesn't know I'm involved and-."

"You thinkin' the old double bluff then?"

Gina asks, "Am I missing something?"

David says, "We figured to add a little something extra to your job."

Derek says, "First we've never let him know we are twins."

Zoe says, "That could be useful."

D. says, "Also we told him that to do the whole property, we will need to load the interior of the egg with extra explosives."

Gina yells, "What? Whose side are you on?"

David waves, "Yours of course. You were the first money in. it's a matter of honor with us. Otherwise-"

Derek finishes, "Plus we're stealing most of their C4 to use on other projects."

◆　◆　◆　◆　◆　◆　◆

A few days before the lift, the Yardbirds sing, **I Ain't Got You**,

I got a mojo and don't you know?
I'm all dressed up and no place to go

All of the Protectors are there protesting the dangers of such a monstrous rock being hoisted straight up over 30 stories into its semi-final resting position. The protests didn't have any effect, but the spectacle looked good on TV.

Jackie had been a very busy girl approving twenty extra cartons of safety equipment for the workers. Electricians were installing emergency lighting. After Jackie made sure it all went to the right place, the 'new equipment' was all accounted for and secured in a storeroom at the base of the Western tower.

The music changes to a longer version of 'Expressway to Your Heart'

I've been tryin' to get to you for a long time
Because constantly you been on my mind

Conveniently enough, David was able to copy Derek's IDs. He was thereby able go wherever he wanted, moving whatever he wished.

Derek and his team began placing the charges. The wiring was run to the top of the Western tower and temporarily left without any sort of attachments, like detonators.

David and his team were able to work at the same time dressed as electricians. They stayed closer to the Western side of the tower as they installed all the boxes for emergency lighting.

The West tower explosives were replaced with fakes and ready to be deployed. As ordered, these particular goods were all stamped 'Made in Iraq'. Derek's plan was to fake 33 placements designed to buckle the tower and destroy structural supports which held all upper levels. Supposedly, the upper levels would collapse in sequence, dropping the steel and rock inside the target area.

David and his team put up 3 lines of 22 placements each, for other plans.

A fellow started to shower
You with love and affection

♦　♦　♦　♦　♦　♦　♦

And so the time came.

From Madeline's seclusion she watches the crane foremen safely guiding the massive load of 'Art' above the heads of the gathering crowd. Madeline thought the rock should be placed more quickly, so she could go to the beach for the weekend. No one could get through to her at the beach, she would be out of town and unavailable until Monday morning. The answering machine at her public relations firm would receive all inquiries. Calls would be returned Monday.

♦   ♦   ♦   ♦   ♦   ♦   ♦

Gina turned away from the rising rock to call an Officers meeting of the Protectors. Gina raised the question of safety. She passed the hat and made small talk. She told them all to line up for the reporters to say how the Victoria Towers has disturbed the landscape with this 'monstrosity hanging over people's heads'. Sound bites like ' This Symbol of Oppression' and ' The Bad old Times', and 'We had hoped for better', all rang for the press, and were well worth broadcasting.

♦   ♦   ♦   ♦   ♦   ♦   ♦

We see Madeline and her guests in a room with a view of the late night collapse. An elaborate buffet is offered for her guests,. The room has a glass ceiling so she can see the outcome of her orders.

On the grand table is a simple hand held radio. On the receiving of the radio we see Derek sitting beside a switch panel. Two rows of switches are lit green and ready. Below is one master switch. The down position is labeled 'No', and the up position is labeled, 'Blow'.

The meeting room doors burst open. A gun toting cadre pushes in shooting at the ceiling. As the panic subsides the leader orders.

"Attention! All of you are not guilty and will be released. Please keep this simple and do what we ask."

Another burst drops another section of ceiling.

"Leave with me people NOW!"

The crowd rushes to the exit. Two of the intruders grab Madeline's arms and prevent her from joining the departing guests. When all are gone the doors close once again.

One of the unwelcome persons pushes back his hood and reveals himself as a smiling Luis. He opens a bag, takes out two more radios, and places them on the table in front of another hooded figure.

Madeline starts railing at him,

"I don't know what you are doing or why you are here, but I insist you leave. You are on private property and disrupting a private gathering."

She sees Jackie among the crowd,

"Officer, do you have a gag?"

Jackie looks at her over her glasses and asks, "A gag for him or you?"

Luis says, "We are here for opposite reasons. You are here to blow up your own property in order to destroy a national landmark."

Madeline begins to speak but stops when she sees Jackie remove a scarf.

"We are here to stop you." He picks up her radio and sets it aside while leaving two new radios on the table.

Another hooded figure steps forward, Zoe unmasks and says,

"We figured out your plan Madeline. We anticipated what you might do. You are planning to blow the 'Art' tower and destroy the Apollo."

Jackie stretches the scarf and steps forward as she speaks,

"And we can't have that, can we? As safety officer I must tell you that the line of explosives planned to drop the rock have been disabled."

We see several blocks of C4 with the wires cut and bare ends exposed. We see Derek's former position now empty. The two rows of switches are dark. The master switch is at 'No'. As we watch the C4 is taken from the wall.

Another hooded voice says,

"However, we do have a choice. One radio is ready to signal the detonators that will blow the Art tower the other way, into the Eastern tower, which is also wired. They will both go down. Your crowd of investors are now being held in the East penthouse.

She pulls out a portable switch and pushes a button. We see the emergency light boxes on several floors begin to flash a green light. She says,

"Unfortunately, some of us may die, and the towers will collapse on the buildings all the way to the other end of the block."

Luis adds, "And that will be more horrible than our deaths. Hundreds more will die. But, the Apollo will survive."

"And you people are willing to die to save that broken down music hall?"

Zoe takes off her hood and says, "Yes, If we have to, if that's what it takes"

Jackie interrupts, "And hey, if somebody has to go. . . .
Get this, we could tie her to a chair and then blow the tower
from outside and she would be the first one to die, am I right?"

Zoe speaks again,

"And then we have a third option in this radio. It is
connected to the detonator that blows only the interior struts.
The towers collapse inward and destroy only this property.
You will die but, the Victoria project will go away forever, and
the Apollo will stay."

Jackie takes the radio from Zoe,

"Oh I like that option best. You two, tie her to a chair.
Let's get out of here before I blow the joint."

The two hooded figures attempt to move Madeline but
she breaks free. Madeline is beside herself with confusion
and grief for her well laid plans. She grabs the first radio and
keys it on,

"Blow the goddamn tower!"

But nothing happens as we see the empty room and the
switch box disconnected with wires hanging loose.

Luis says, "Temper, temper, we told you we can't allow
that to happen. The Apollo is more than a building. It
represents the heart and soul of the music and life of Harlem.
Put the radio down."

Madeline throws the radio through the room and turns
on Zoe,

"You can't make me kill all those people. They are all
innocent. I just can't kill-"

"No, You can't." the masked figure reveals herself, "I'm
glad you can't."

Madeline stares in shock, "Regina?"

Gina, drops her mask, "Hi Mom, we came up with a much

better idea. But the last time we approached you you wouldn't even listen."

Estrella steps forward with a set of plans and starts on Madeline,

"Now, we know you've been thinking of destroying the Apollo. This is a way for us to save the Apollo forever, and build a sister theater to accompany it."

Zoe speaks, "It's called Air Rights."

Luis speaks while Madeline and Gina look at each other,

"In exchange for preserving the Apollo exactly the way it is, partially functional and a lot of tour business, and in exchange for building a new theater in the new building overhead, the city will probably grant the Air Rights to anyone who will comply."

Madeline is agape and stammering,

"…but that would cost-."

Gina steps to her mother and asks,

"Mom, can I borrow a few million dollars? I'm good for it."

♦ ♦ ♦ ♦ ♦ ♦ ♦

We hear Ray Charles **Wha'd I Say**.

Hey mama, don't you treat me wrong
Come and love your daddy all night long
All right now, hey, hey, all right

♦ ♦ ♦ ♦ ♦ ♦ ♦

Out in front of the Apollo on 125[th]st. are star plaques imbedded in the side walk. The Apollo hall of fame includes

<u>Aretha Franklin</u>, <u>James Brown</u>, <u>Michael Jackson</u>, <u>The Supremes</u>, <u>Stevie Wonder</u>, <u>Marvin Gaye</u>, <u>Elton John</u>, <u>Little Richard</u>, <u>Hall & Oates</u>, <u>Ella Fitzgerald</u>, <u>Smokey Robinson</u>, <u>Billy Eckstine</u>, <u>The Jacksons</u>, <u>Quincy Jones</u>, <u>Chaka Khan</u>, and <u>Patti LaBelle</u>.

As we back away from the front we see the larger more welcoming façade of the Apollo with a huge building built up gracefully over the top. The lower marquee is lighted and announcing, 'Amateur Night.' An electronic streaming arrow shoots up the face to explode on the marquis of the upper theater.

When you see me in misery, come on baby see about me
Now yeah, hey, hey, all right
Well, tell me what'd I say, tell me what'd I say right now
Tell me what'd I say, tell me what'd I say right now
Tell me what'd I say, tell me what'd I say

Say it one more time (just one more time)
Say it one more time yeah (just one more time)

end

Rao's

written by

T K Wallace

I originally come from the Midwestern state of Missouri. My home Town, Belle, had about 1000 people and no specialty foods. We had one diner in town when I was a boy. The Golden Rule diner was an early morning to mid afternoon place, the menu filled with staples, standard breakfasts, standard lunches including hot plate dishes, everything very good but a limited menu tuned into the small town palate.

Since living in New York City I have tried to widen my palate internationally. But the sampling here is so large between all the nations of the world being fairly represented, that I dedicated myself to finding older long established café and restaurants within my price range, which is not that grand.

On the Italian side of the palate I have had many pleasing experiences. The old Carmines, in the fish market is magnificent at 5am. Finelli's on Prince is a frequent lunchtime visit. Carmines family style on the Upper West side is a holiday and celebration place, especially for Thanksgiving. From Ray's Famous Pizza on 11th and 6th, to the old Trattoria in the Village on Bleeker and Carmine, to Vinnie's Pizza on Amsterdam, It has been my pleasure drop by for a take out, or to sit and enjoy some simple fabulous meals.

I have heard of Rao's restaurant for many years, and finally had one too many reasons not to check it out. It was a literary reference within the works of Linda Fairstein's novels which piqued me. So, one afternoon in mid January, I map searched and found adequate directions for a visit. I knew I was likely to be rejected, but I wanted to see Rao's and see how the rejection was handled. And hey, who knows, right, I could get lucky. The most interesting deeds are occasions done in person, and then you live to tell the tale.

Parking on the far end of the block of 115th was easy at about 5pm. Crossing the street I saw the empty, well lit establishment, Rao's was open but still setting up for the evening trade. The entrance was a step down, I went through the weather door erection and then paused at the main door to see inside. A well dressed gentlemen glanced at me and continued with the place settings on the first family style table.

I let myself in the main door and said, "Good Afternoon", to the gentlemen who then stopped to look me over. He was in his sixties with graying hair peaked in the front and neatly combed back. He wore a soft brown jacket and a maroon turtleneck. He was handsome, smiled easily, and showed good dental care.

The aroma of good home cooking began to saturate my senses. The kitchen of Rao's is in the front across from the entryway. Four chefs were bustling around the large and small cookery, stirring, pouring, shifting pots and pans, all dancing to the mutual glorious harmony of Italian cooking.

"Good afternoon, May I help You?" I shifted to the host, while tasting with my mind.

"Yes Sir, I hope so. May I eat here?"

"Do You have a reservation?", asked the man with a hopeful positive smile.

"No Sir, I do not. I was hoping to beat the evening crowd. May I make a reservation?"

"Sorry, We're booked all full. " I asked,

"Well okay, how about the rest of the week ?"

"We're booked for the rest of the year."

My astute mid-western intellect kicked in and I said,

"Wow, Really?"

He smiled and turned away to continue his duties. Smiling in thanks, I said

"I have heard about the food here for years, but never got around to finding the place." Glancing around I ask,

"Do you serve food at the bar ?"

"No food at the Bar. Additional guests may drink at the bar after we open at 7pm."

At this point I should describe the dining area of Rao's. The foot print of the dining area is about 30 ft by 25 ft. There is a small bar with five six or seven stools on the right. The room has two large tables and one small table running the centerline of the dining area, there are four booths on the left, four across the back wall, and none on the right hand wall. There rested an older dimly lit juke box.

Each and every wall from the chair rail to the ceiling is adorned with drawings or photos of the honored clientele.

"I think I understand Sir. This is a family, and local friends establishment?"

"Yes, Most of our guests have standing reservations, some weekly or monthly. But yes, mostly family and regulars, Others by invitation only. So, I'm sorry, it is very hard to even get in line." He smiled.

"May I look around ? "

"Of course." I gazed around at all of the framed letters, posters, and photographs as I moved toward the Juke Box.

"I like a good Juke Box. What on the playlist?" I looked at the two pages displayed and the albums available. I saw Patsy Cline's, "Greatest Hits", opposite Willie Nelson's, "Stardust".

I laughed aloud and said.

"Isn't it great that these two are together? Uncle Willie

and lovely Patsy? Did you know He wrote one of her top songs?"

"Which one ?"

"Crazy, He wrote Crazy for Patsy Cline." I replied.

He looked at the display and asked, "Is that on this album ?"

"Yes, well, it's here on hers, not on his. I heard Willie performing with Johnny Cash. They talked about the song afterward. Willie said He changed the title from when he first wrote the original song."

"What was the original title?"

"Willie said the original title was 'Stupid'."

He thought for a second and laughed, he said, "Well some of the lyrics fit when you think about it being written by a man."

"Yes, the lyrics were changed to protect the innocent."

I glanced at a wall with a few Fairstein's book covers framed.

"I first read about Rao's in one of Linda Fairstein's novels."

He gestured toward a booth, I noted a couple of familiar book titles framed above the table.

"Ms Fairstein is one of our regulars. This is her preferred booth. Perhaps if you knew her . . ."

"No I do not know her, I have read her books. I like her work but do not know her. I would not presume to pretend otherwise." I sighed and he smiled.

"I see that your table lamps are made of Rao's Marinara bottles."

"Yes, that's right we bottle our own sauce."

"So, as I am here but cannot dine, May I buy some sauce from you before I leave?"

"Of course. Let me get that for you."

He left the main floor to go behind the bar. I turned to check out some of the art on display, I saw a Hirschfield of Lisa Minnelli, a photo graph of Barbara Walters, and noticed a vintage fight poster of Jake LaMotta, the Raging Bull of the Bronx.

As the gentleman returned from the room behind the bar with a paper bag, the entrance door opened and a young man in the dress blues of FDNY entered. My host enjoined the new comer as befit his trade. The guest was clean shaven, combed, shined, and a little nervous.

"Good afternoon Officer, may I be of help?" The young man blushed and stammered,

"I hope so Sir, I asked my Captain at the fire department if he knew anyone at Rao's I could speak to about dining here with my mother for her 50th birthday "

"I am sorry to say, as I was telling this gentleman, that we are booked for the rest of the year."

"Wow Really?"

I smiled.

"Are you Mr Pelligrino?"

"No I am not. I am Joey."

The fireman laughed, "My boss, he said that if I met Mr Pelligrino I was to call him Mr Pelligrino. And that he would probably say, 'Call me Frankie', but I had to start formally."

"Yes um," Joey waited, "What is your name Sir?"

"Oh sorry, Anthony, Sir," and extended his hand, "Anthony Giardono."

I murmur, "Pizan. He can have my place in line."

Joey glances at me and smiles. "Do you have a card Anthony ?"

"Yes Sir, right here." He withdrew his wallet and retrieved a card.

"If there is any chance, even with short notice, or even without any notice, My mother, and I, would appreciate it a lot."

"As I said, we are all booked in advance. However, if a chance does occur, and if you write your private number on the back, anything comes available the owner may give you a call."

The young fireman looked both disappointed and relieved, and replied.

"Sure, of course," He took back the card and wrote as Joe said,

"If perhaps Mr. Pellegrino does call, I am sure we would all like to see you attend in full dress uniform, most especially Mama Giardono."

"Of course. Yes sir, absolutely." He stammered as he backed out the door and up onto the sidewalk.

Joey turned to the bar and picked up the bag and handed it to me.

"Well done." I said.

"I'm sorry to disappoint you, here take this. This is on me." I took the bag and looked inside to see a bottle of sauce and a bag of Penne pasta labeled Rao's Homemade.

"Thank you very much. I am honored." and took that as my cue to leave.

I got outside and walked to my ride, seeing the young firemen standing by his ride talking on the phone. As I started off, he hung up and smiled at me.

I stopped beside him and said, "Wasn't that awesome?"

He smiled and said, "Totally iced. My Captain said that

when I met him I had to address him as Mr Pellegrino, and that he would say, Call Me Frankie, but that wasn't him."

I smiled at the nervous ramble. "No that was Joey. What a delightful gentleman. He gave me a bag of pasta and sauce for the disappointment of turning me down."

"How cool is that?" He asked

"Not as cool as you will be when you get the call."

"Ya' think so?"

"Yes, I do. I'm sure you Mother will love it."

"Cool, I hope so, thanks." As I began to drive away I called,

"Good Luck, And don't forget to wear your uniform." I saw thumbs up in the rear view mirror.

While driving away I fondly remembered my first Pizza being cut into servings on a cookie sheet. Each piece was square with a piece of hamburger on top. My mother made it from a Chef Boyardee box mix and then adorned each square with hamburger and some white stringy cheese. It was delicious. Imagine my surprise when I found out most of the Pizza world was round and cut into triangles.

I smiled and looked at the bag of custom cut homemade pasta and marinara on the passenger seat. Then I thought of the wonderful aromas coming from Rao's kitchen. I am far from my home and many years have past. But, it seems I will be dining on Italian home cuisine tonight.

tkw

About the Author

T K Wallace is the author of another short story collection, **Water Songs**, as well as several screenplays, serial comedies, and stage plays. He currently resides in Thunderbolt, Georgia.

For more about T K and his work, visit 'tedkwallace.com'.